MURDER BY PERSUASION

ANNEGALE NESTER

DEDICATION

To Mr. N,
the love of my life,
for the good times.

ACKNOWLEDGMENTS

First and foremost, Jesus Christ, for without Him, I could do nothing.

My late husband Randy, a.k.a. Mr. N, who encouraged me, and did all the things a good husband would do. But most of all, loved me. I love and miss you, Mr. N.

My children and extended family members who all helped to piece this novel together, encouraged me along the way and did not let me give up. I love you all.

My many friends and members of the Christian writer group who read pieces of drafts, critiqued, offered advice and also encouraged me. Too many to list, but you know who you are.

My proofers, Rosanne and Elyse, who made sure all my "t's" were crossed and my "i's" were dotted.

My youngest daughter, Joanie, for the fantastic cover design. Luv ya bunches.

Thanks, and blessings to all of you, and my readers.

Draw near to God and He will draw near to you.

JAMES 4:8A

MURDER BY PERSUASION

CHAPTER ONE

"I'LL KILL YOU! I'll kill you!" Alistair Hawkins awoke to the sound of a man's voice in his Manhattan condo. As he stared at the pillow in a stranglehold of his own two hands, he realized it was his voice he heard. The nightmare was back. Beads of sweat dropped onto the pillow as he slowly let up on his grip; the grandfather clock, in the living room, was chiming. It was midnight.

———

A LATE NIGHT modeling shoot in Central Park made Anna Marlet's arrival in East Hampton later than she wished. She stood alone as the old stately clock in the cemetery echoed the sound of midnight. With her flashlight shining on the barren mound of dirt that covered her best friend's grave, she continued to feel something was wrong, definitely wrong.

"You wouldn't commit suicide, Jill. You just wouldn't," Anna cried aloud, tears watering the single yellow rose she held. Kneeling, she placed the rose near the headstone that read, *Jillian Marie Evans,*

Beloved Daughter. Anna's tears flowed now as she read the dates. Jill was only twenty-three.

Drying her tears, she looked around. A shadow flittered over a headstone across from Jill's grave. Anna shuddered. Perhaps the late hour had her imagining things. She probably shouldn't have stopped here before getting to her parent's place, but she *had* to visit Jill.

The white oaks that lined the row of graves seemed to give a sense of peace and serenity. So why was she so edgy? It was bad enough that she didn't believe that Jill committed suicide; now she was imagining someone just might be after her. The chill in her heart matched that of the late autumn breeze surrounding her.

Anna, again, noticed movement across the path. Clouds parted to let the moon peek down; she saw the figure of a man standing near a headstone a few feet away. It was not her imagination after all. Maybe he was just a late visitor too. She needed to get her nerves in check and get out of here. As she rose to leave, he bowed his head and rested his hand on the top of the headstone. *Was it his wife? Was he lonely? Did he wish to be with her?* These questions led Anna back to questions of her own. What would she do without her best friend? Could she prove that Jill was murdered? Those two questions had haunted Anna ever since she had discovered Jill's body two weeks earlier.

What to do? Where to turn? Certainly not to the police. They termed it suicide—case closed. But if Detective Hawkins was still with the homicide division of the NYPD, he'd know what to do.

———

SATURDAY BLENDED EFFORTLESSLY into Sunday as Anna pulled into the driveway of her parents' home… the home she had grown up in. Still in possession of the house key, she let herself in and tip-toed to her old room. Kicking off her heels, she sat on the bed. Not bothering to undress, Anna lay down and pulled a comforter over her tired body.

———

STRETCHING, Anna looked at the clock. Had she really slept till noon? Apparently, her mother thought she needed to sleep and hadn't bothered to wake her for church. She would have refused to go anyway. Her emotions were still too raw for the stares and insincere words of comfort from people she and Jill had known. The funeral last week had been difficult enough. Instead of comfort, most people seemed to find fault; even Anna's mother kept saying, "I knew it. I just knew something like this would happen one day. Both of you becoming models and, of all places, in the city!" Anna had cried even more. Better to stay here and try to relax. She padded to the kitchen and poured herself a cup of coffee.

Back in the living room she plopped on the sofa. Drawing her feet under her, she sipped at the hot brew and looked around the room. It hadn't changed much since she and Jill had moved to Manhattan. The windows still sported the floral summer curtains. Her mother would have their housekeeper, Bella, changing them soon. The pearl-gray walls looked a little faded but were still attractive. Her father's roll top desk was still against the wall between the dining entrance and staircase. The piano was moved, she noticed, nearer the bay windows. The bookshelves that framed the windows had a new inclusion—a bust of Beethoven.

Thunk!

The morning paper hit the porch. After retrieving it, Anna searched for the comics when her eyes fell on an ad.

Hawk Detective Agency,
in the heart of Groveland Hills.
Alistair "Hawk" Hawkins,
twenty years with the NYPD.
Five of them as a homicide detective,
now in private practice.

The ad went on to give the agency's address, telephone number, and hours. He was exactly the person Anna needed and Groveland Hills was only seventeen miles north of Manhattan.

Anna had hoped coming to her childhood home and visiting Jill at the cemetery would give her a little more closure. Nothing about Jill's death rang true to her, and that thought still had her concerned. The police had closed the investigation and her parents thought she was obsessed with her doubts about Jill's suicide. But she had known Jill too well.

Friends since kindergarten, living a block apart from one another, the girls had been inseparable. They thought, acted, and sometimes dressed alike. Each was the sister that the other one didn't have. Both wanted to be models when they grew up, even though coming from influential families they didn't need to work. Anna recalled the many times she and Jill would play dress up and walk an imaginary runway.

Hearing a car pull into the driveway, Anna realized her parents were home from their usual after church lunch at the country club. She wondered if Jill's parents had joined them, and if they were doing any better. She rose to greet her parents as they entered the house.

"Mom, Dad… did Aunt Beth and Uncle Ralph join you for lunch?"

Anna's father nodded.

"How are they doing?"

"As well as can be expected when one loses a child," Anna's mother chose to answer.

"Yes, Margaret," Dad said, "but they did say how good it was to get out for church and lunch."

"Oh Bill, didn't you see how Beth looked? Her eyes were still puffy and red. I bet she hasn't stopped crying yet. Think how you'd feel if it were Anna."

"Mom. Dad. Please."

"Sorry, dear," Mom apologized. "Did you eat?"

"Just some coffee. I'm not really hungry."

While Anna's father made himself comfortable in his favorite chair and settled in with the newspaper, Anna remembered.

"I found an ad in the paper for Detective Hawkins. You remember? He used to work NYPD homicide? Well, he's opened his own agency in Groveland Hills. I'm going to see him first thing tomorrow morning."

"Anna... a detective isn't going to prove anything different. It's over," her Dad said, "drop it!"

"Dad, really..."

"I'm tired of these conversations, Anna. I can see you've made up your mind. Do as you wish, but I still think you're wasting your time and your money."

CHAPTER TWO

FINDING the Hawk Detective Agency was not a problem, but looking at the old Greystone Manor was. Anna stared at the entrance door, wondering if it might fall off its hinges the moment she entered. With black paint cracked and peeling, the old wooden door did nothing to bolster Anna's resolve. The gray brick building seemed to be standing without fault, but the wood shutters and window frames did not. They sported the same black, cracked, and peeling paint. The eave above the second story windows looked rotted, and there were pieces missing.

Well, it's now or never, Anna thought, as she cautiously slipped through the door. The foyer had a twin door, with the same black paint. It had almost as much cracking and peeling as the one she had just stepped through. The walls were a dismal gray and bare of any pictures. As she opened the second door, Anna heard the tinkle of a bell. How quaint.

As she entered what appeared to be a reception room, she noticed three closed doors and an opened archway that looked as though it might lead to a hallway. She expected a suite of offices, yet the reception room was virtually bare. No sign of a receptionist; only a file cabinet with open drawers, and a pile of papers stacked neatly atop an old, scarred wooden desk. A beat-up chair, its stuffed seat torn, was behind the desk. A ladder-back chair stood next to it. Hanging askew at the open archway was a dull green curtain. The floor was gray tiles, a few of them missing. Anna began to have second thoughts about her visit. Maybe it wasn't the best idea after all. She turned to leave; reaching for the doorknob, she heard a man's voice.

"May I help you?"

Anna turned to face the voice. It was the Hawk—Alistair Hawkins himself. He was taller and more muscular than she remembered from newspaper photos of him in the last few years. He sported a clean-shaven face and a prominent nose. There was a hint of a smile complimented with elongated dimples. Detective Hawkins' hair was dark brown, parted in the middle and over his ears. All in all, he was well worth looking at.

"Yes," Anna managed to whisper. He motioned her to follow into what she supposed was his office. Did she dare go into this inner sanctum with him? Butterflies were warring with her tangled nerves; even her own ideas were beginning to sound bizarre to her. How would the Hawk react?

———

WHEN SHE STEPPED into the room, Anna was immediately struck by the contrast between the crudeness of the reception room and the luxuriant décor of his office. The walls were celery green and the windows were adorned with thick, slated blinds. An oriental area rug of various shades of green and ecru graced beautiful wood floors. A gold-plated coat tree, between two windows, held a light gray Fedora, an equally light gray scarf and a charcoal gray suit jacket at the ready.

Detective Hawkins, legs astride, stood by the window as Anna chose one of the leather chairs that was in front of a polished mahogany desk. Every item on the desk was arranged as though a decorator had just finished their job. The leather desk set bespoke of someone who enjoyed the finer things in life, right down to the gold pen lying atop a few sheets of paper. As she glanced around, Anna's gaze registered philodendron and Boston fern arrangements; an oversized sofa set against a wall; on the opposite wall built-in bookshelves and a door. Did it open to a closet or another room? On the credenza behind the desk were candles of various sizes, all of them lit. Soft-hued paintings warmed the room while wall to ceiling windows provided daylight.

Detective Hawkins turned, and Anna noticed the pants belonging to the jacket seemed to fit him like the proverbial glove, while a gorgeous hunter green silk shirt caused his piercing brown eyes to sparkle. *Yes, definitely worth looking at*, she thought.

"Excuse me, but… do we have an appointment?" he asked.

"No," Anna quickly replied, "but I desperately need your help."

Detective Hawkins crossed to his desk in two quick strides. "Desperately?"

"My best friend… her name is… was… Jill Evans, is dead and I believe she was murdered," Anna's voice quivered. "The police have ruled it suicide, cut and dried, but I don't believe it. I can't believe it. Maybe it was made to look like suicide," Anna concluded as tears began to fall. Detective Hawkins produced a box of tissues. As he sat down, he spoke.

"Let's say I might be interested in knowing more about a closed case, but first—would you mind telling me who *you* are?"

"Oh, yes. Of course," she sniffled. "It's Anna Marlet and I live in Manhattan. I grew up on Long Island and my parents are still there. I'm a fashion model with Stella's Modeling Agency in the city," stated Anna somewhat nervously.

"Miss… Mrs.? Marlet," he continued.

"I'm single."

"Okay, *Miss* Marlet, just what is it that makes you think your friend may have been murdered?"

"She had an online account, listed on FriendsPage; since I was the only other person to have her password, the family asked me to close out the account and clear her computer. But before I did, I checked to see if anything needed attending to or if there were friends to notify, such as her online lover."

"Wait," interrupted Hawkins. "An online lover?"

"That's what I'm trying to tell you," Anna said, "I think he may have killed her. I found all the emails between the two and I've printed them all out, starting from the day he first sent Jill a friend request. It's all here," Anna said, handing a large, thick manila envelope to the detective. "I want to hire you to find this Ted and bring him to justice," she added, more confidently than she actually felt.

"My fees are not cheap, Miss Marlet."

"I assure you, Detective Hawkins, I am not without funds. I'm the sole heir of William and Margaret Marlet of East Hampton. I model only because that was always my dream as a little girl."

"East Hampton? There's something in today's paper about a murder in East Hampton over the weekend."

Her body stiffened as Hawk picked up the paper, turned a few pages, then handed it to her.

Anna scanned the article, looked at the picture. "Oh," she gasped, "I saw this man when I was visiting Jill's grave! I recognize the clothes, his hat! It says that the police caught him coming out of the north entrance of the cemetery. I was there! I saw him! *And* he saw me! He walked right past me! What if he's Ted? He could have killed me! What if he thinks *I* called the police?"

"Take it easy, Miss Marlet. That's too many what-ifs. The newspaper also says that the suspect was hoping to elude the police by going through the cemetery—but he's locked up now with no bail. As far as him being Ted, hmm." Hawk paused. "So, did you email Ted that Miss Evans was dead?"

"Yes, and ever since then, I've had this feeling that someone is after me."

"That is an intriguing thought; you have me interested. I believe you've just hired yourself a detective, Miss Marlet."

―――――

AFTER SEVERAL HOURS of poring over emails and instant messages between Jill Evans and someone calling himself Ted Ashby, it appeared a real love affair had blossomed. Alistair was beginning to understand why Miss Marlet might have reason to think as she did. Yet, as much as the man called Ted professed his love, he made it very clear that he and Jill Evans needed to give it time: at least a year before they would meet face to face.

Hawk began to review the Evans' report, a file sent from Officer Kincaid, of his old precinct, when the phone rang.

"Detective Hawkins here."

"Hawk. Kincaid. That report I sent you on the Evan's case. I mentioned to Donovan that you had asked for it. He told me to tell you to leave it alone. He said it's a suicide, and the case is closed. So, remember—you didn't get it from me." Click. The line went dead.

So, thought Hawk, *Donovan wanted it left alone*. But Donovan wasn't his supervisor anymore; and, he had a client. He was going to work this as an ongoing case, closed or not, Donovan or no Donovan. But he also had to consider the chances of proving an outcome other than suicide.

Concentrating on the report, he recalled that it was rather succinct. An autopsy showed an overdose of well over the prescribed five hundred milligrams of chloral hydrate—a sedative. Hawk recalled that Miss Marlet mentioned Miss Evans took sleeping pills. A copy of the suicide note stated that because Jill couldn't have the love of her life there was no reason to go on. The note also included a list indicating to whom her belongings would go. Examining the list again, Alistair found it curious that a stuffed purple teddy bear was to be given to Ted—the man whom she couldn't have. The report concluded that no foul play was indicated.

His eyes tired, Alistair leaned back in his office chair, while partial words of a William Gladstone poem walked through his memory.

"When the world is all at odds
And the mind is all at sea,
Then cease the useless tedium
And brew a cup of tea."

Yes, he thought... *a cup of tea.* He opened the doors of the credenza and brought out an electric kettle, cup, and tea bags. He might need more than one cup, for his mind was certainly "at sea." He padded to the office kitchen, using the door between the bookshelves.

As he filled the kettle, he glanced about at the rundown condition of the room—no cabinets to store the kettle, let alone anything else. The counter-top was broken and tiles were missing in the floor; the walls were a drab gray. He had bought the building at a reduced cost in exchange for renovating the entire manor. But until the renovation was completed, using this or any other room was quite depressing.

Alistair remembered that Anna Marlet had almost walked back out of the reception room earlier. He had heard the bell and had met her just as she was reaching for the door. Would it have been better to let her leave? This case was definitely baffling, even somewhat monotonous. *Definitely*, he thought, *it's time for tea.*

Back in his chair, drinking his tea, Alistair thought of the other two offices yet to be renovated. The smallest, the one he was using for storage was devoid of anything. Only concrete floors and walls that were unfinished plasterboard. The other room was just as dismal with dirty green shag carpet from fifty years before. The walls were even worse; painted a lime color. Alistair looked about his finished office, quite pleased with his choice of colors and furnishings. He guessed he needed to have the entire reception area renovated next. One day he might even have a receptionist, he smiled.

He recalled Anna Marlet's comments about following her dream. Like her, he hailed from the Hamptons; he, too, could live comfortably without a career in law enforcement. And, he, too, had always dreamed of being a detective. But—at what cost?

He finished his tea and his daydreaming at the same time. He needed to formulate a plan of action. Although this case seemed to go nowhere, he recalled a case of a similar nature. It revolved around a woman who was found guilty of pretending to be a teenager online. She had been accused of seducing a young, teenaged boy who had eventually committed suicide.

"I need some help. This has me confused," he said aloud. No sooner were the words out of his mouth then he recalled a Bible verse that reminded him that God was not the author of confusion. Yet, his mind argued, where was God when his wife, Ellie, was murdered? Maybe not a God of confusion then, but certainly not one that was helpful. Alistair's faith seemed to be as run down as his suite of offices.

CHAPTER THREE

ALISTAIR NEEDED help and there was only one person he knew he could count on: his ex-partner and best friend, Wade Owens. Alistair had been meaning to get in touch sooner, but as the saying goes, better late than never. He made the call, ignoring the two-hour time difference between New York and Arizona. Wade answered on the second ring.

"Owens here."

"It's Hawk," Alistair said, using the nickname Wade had tacked on him when they first became partners in the NYPD.

"Hawk, you sure do take your time calling. Are you back from your *rest* in Florida? Pretty neat doctor's prescription if you ask me," Wade laughed.

"Yeah, I got back six weeks ago. And it wasn't as neat as you might think. I had doctor's appointments every day and was in the rest home for the entire time."

"So, you're back and just now getting around to calling? What were you doing in all that time?"

"Opening a detective agency in Groveland Hills. I bought the old Greystone Manor. Needs a complete re-do. The Greystone family sold it to Hillsboro Construction who hoped to move their business here, but then the company had to put it back up for sale. The city officials denied their requests to bulldoze most of it since it's on the National Register of Historic Places. They built three offices downstairs with an open area for a reception room, kept the kitchen, took out cabinets and added a couple of restrooms down a hallway. They left it a mess, but they did manage to leave the integrity of the building intact."

"Wow," Wade managed to get in.

"I had my personal office finished first and some of the men from the renovation and construction crew are working today. I plan to have the second floor renovated into my living quarters." Hawk took a breath, and asked "How about you? What are you doing? Once you moved out there, I thought you and Linda would have stayed together. Sorry about the divorce."

"I'm sorry, too, but I'm leaving that in God's hands. Meanwhile I'm still working with the County Sheriff's Department. Homicide detective. I work days; you caught me on coffee break. So, you've opened a detective agency huh? After having to resign from the NYPD, are you sure this is the way to go, Hawk?" Wade sounded concerned, but Alistair didn't let that sway him.

"I'm much too young to retire," Hawk chuckled, "and you know how I thrive on the work—which brings me to this phone call."

Alistair related his earlier meeting with Anna Marlet and the fact that the person calling himself Ted Ashby was in Wade's area of Arizona, according to his FriendsPage account.

"So, you can understand why I thought of calling you. I could use your help."

"Well," Wade seemed to hesitate, "it's a closed case, so I'm not sure I will be able to help you officially. But you know I'll do what I can on my own time. What did you have in mind?"

"There's a few women that were online friends with both Jill and Ted: one in Portland, Oregon, two in Las Vegas, and another in

Seattle, Washington. I'd like to have them interviewed. I want to pinpoint this "Ted" character."

"Send me copies of all you got and we'll go from there. Meanwhile I'll check out a couple of ideas and get back with you. Who's your secretary?"

"Don't have one, yet."

The noise of an electric drill coming from the kitchen all but drowned out Wade Owens' voice on the other end of the phone, but Alistair was able to formulate the beginning of an investigative plan with his friend. The drill stopped its droning, and a workman opened the door that led to the kitchen. "Hey, Mac. Ya wanna check these kitchen cabinets?" he said.

Alistair, finished with his call, dropped the receiver in its cradle as he stood. Stepping into the kitchen he was happily surprised at how well the cabinets looked. "Just right," he remarked to the workman.

"Okay, Mac. We'll get on with the rest and you can get on with your work." The gruffness of the man wasn't lost on Alistair, but they were doing great work in record time, so he opted not to complain. Although the reception room should have been the next room to renovate, he chose the kitchen instead. Since he would be putting in long hours in the office, a fully equipped kitchen was more important.

Closing the door behind him, Alistair walked back into his office, over to the rear window. He stood there, stroking his chin, as he generally did when he was thinking. Looking out at nothing in particular, he tried to get a handle on how the suspect's mind might work. Yes, Ted Ashby was now a suspect in Alistair's book. What was Ashby's goal in the online game he had played with Jill Evans? An idea popped into his head. Online. Yes. He would open an account on FriendsPage for some of the investigation.

———

THE PHONE RANG JUST as Alistair finished his account. "Hawk here," he said.

"I've enlisted an attorney friend of mine, Drake Dumont. He married a gal from Portland and moved his practice there. Anyway, he can spare a paralegal who will do a little gumshoe work for us." It was Wade Owens calling back.

"Fast work, my friend. I like that. What did Dumont think of the chances of proving criminal intent?"

"He was intrigued with the idea and thinks it may be possible."

"So, Dumont's on board. Good. Who's the guy doing the gumshoe work?"

"Sorry, Hawk, you'll have to settle for the female variety—one Stephanie Edwards."

Alistair was hesitant to involve a woman in this particular job. Wasn't that why he took the case, so he could keep punks like Ashby from preying on women? He voiced his concern. Wade assured Hawk that Miss Edwards was good—*very* good—at what she did. "Dumont says that she's probably the one person who could get blood out of a turnip," Wade laughed.

Alistair reluctantly agreed to Miss Edwards of the Dumont Law Firm and promised to have all information and names he'd acquired to Wade by the end of the week. He turned back to his FriendsPage account to review the profile he had created.

PROFILE:
Name: *Alistair Hawkins*
Status: *Widower*
Age: *I'll take the 5th on this*
Body: *6' 2"/Athletic*
Ethnicity: *White*
Religion: *Christian*
Occupation: *Detective*
Something About Me:
My nickname is Hawk. My wife was expecting our first child when she was murdered 18 months ago. I'm what you might call a freelance detective. I've worked all over the country with various law enforcement agencies. I'll work

on cold cases, and cases where the outcome is in doubt. Murder is my specialty. The word on the street is "beware of the Hawk." It's okay that I'm on FriendsPage and allowing this info to be public. There is always a reason for what I do. I may even be investigating you. But don't be afraid to be my friend; you might even assist me in solving a crime. Feel free to ask questions. I always do.

Just enough info, he thought. Then Alistair thought of all the paper work, computer messages, and phone calls he had in front of him, not to mention in person investigations. Perhaps Wade is right; it is time to get a secretary, or at least hire a receptionist. But who would work in an office that was in the middle of renovation? He needed someone who could handle any job he sent her way. Is that a receptionist or a secretary? Hawk wasn't sure. He also wasn't sure if he had put enough thought into the idea of opening his own detective agency, especially since his resignation from being an NYPD detective was not his choice.

CHAPTER FOUR

WADE WAS JUST FINISHING his third cup of coffee when he heard the knock: overnight delivery from Hawk. Thursday, he supposed, was close enough to being the end of the week. Signing for the delivery, he smiled. The package was larger than he thought and when dumped out on his desk, Wade was surprised by the amount of information it contained. Police report, autopsy, email correspondence between the dead girl and her online lover. But added to that were more emails from the online lover to a few of Miss Evans' friends—those in NYC, Portland, Seattle, two in Vegas, and one other, a co-worker, in Paris. Hawk also included information from the initial contact he had had with his client, Miss Marlet. Was it quite thorough or a bit extreme? That remained to be seen.

Wade immediately got comfortable in his overstuffed recliner, preparing for a long read. He was glad it was his day off so he wouldn't be disturbed. An attached note from Hawk suggested Wade open an account on FriendsPage. "Since my client came to me with what may be considered to be an online crime, perhaps we can bait Ted Ashby by opening various accounts," Wade read. Working with

Hawk again now seemed like old times to him, except the fact that he was in Arizona instead of New York City.

Thoughts of his failed marriage invaded his mind. He sat, with some of the paperwork still in his hands, and looked about the spacious living room. Linda's touch was still here; wall-to-wall beige carpet she preferred over stone tile, heavy beige drapes, dark walnut furnishings. You could take the girl out of NYC, but not the city out of the girl.

With their children, Dean and Sara, in college, Wade had hoped he and Linda could repair their marriage. His work as a detective in NYC was more than Linda could handle. When Hawk's pregnant wife was murdered, Linda almost fell apart. And having Hawk as his partner didn't help. It only seemed to make matters worse. Wade immediately quit his job, sold everything, and moved Linda to Arizona. He returned to NYC just long enough to see Hawk through the trial of the man who killed his wife. When he returned home, it appeared that Linda had adjusted to his new detective position with the Sheriff's Department. But after a couple of months, her stress had not lessened. She filed for divorce and moved back to New York to be near their children.

————

THE RINGING of his cell phone woke Wade from his doze in front of the television. "Did you get the package? Have you sifted through it all?" It was Hawk.

"It arrived about eight this morning," Wade replied. "I finished a few hours ago."

"Good. What's your take?" asked Hawk.

"With the information you have on the people out this way, especially the victim's cousin, I'd say we do need to do some interviews. That's where I'd like to involve Dumont's paralegal, Miss Edwards.

"Set it up. I'll make arrangements for the funds. Hate to cut it short, Wade, but I need to get home; it's almost midnight here. Call me tomorrow when plans are in place." Wade heard a click and then— dead air. Hawk had ended the call.

———

ALISTAIR WASN'T LOOKING FORWARD to a midnight drive back to Manhattan. He guessed it was time to think about getting the second floor renovated for his living quarters as soon as the entire office suite was finished. He walked to the window and closed the blinds. Handling a few minor cases as well as the Marlet case would keep him busy for quite a while. But even a busy man needed a decent night's sleep. Yes, he decided. Not only would he would have the upstairs done, but, instead of waiting, he would have it started tomorrow. Meanwhile, he figured his office sofa would be his bed tonight.

———

THE INCESSANT RINGING of a phone somewhere in a remote corner of Alistair's mind found him disoriented and rubbing his eyes. Suddenly he realized he was in his office and it was the desk phone. He stumbled to answer it just as it went dead. He looked at his watch: 7 AM. Then his cell phone went off. Who could be calling at this hour? Caller ID showed A. Marlet.

"Hasn't anyone told you about banker's hours?" he joked.

"I got a call about midnight; it was Ted," Anna remarked breathlessly. "I couldn't wait any longer to call you."

Alistair was wide awake now. "What did he want? How did he get your number?"

"He wants the purple teddy bear. He said Jill promised that to him. I guess he looked up my number, or Jill gave it to him."

"Hmm… the purple teddy bear. What did you tell him?' Alistair asked curiously.

"I told him I'd look for it, and asked for his phone number. He told me he'd call back in a few days," Anna said. "Caller ID showed Rosie's Bar." She gave Hawk the number, with an area code the same as Wade. "What should I do?"

"When he calls back, tell him the police still haven't released all of her belongings. Meanwhile I'll have my contact in Arizona check on Rosie's Bar and see if we can get some answers."

"Now? Today?" Anna sounded frantic.

"Miss Marlet, calm yourself; I *will* get to the bottom of this. Be patient, please." Alistair tried to soften his words. "I'll call as soon as I have something. Trust me." With that, he ended the call. Alistair thought about the last two words he spoke to Anna: *trust me.* "Isn't that what you asked of me, Father? I did trust You, but what good did it do? Ellie still died. And the baby? No. I won't go there again!" Was he actually praying after all these months? No. He guessed he was still angry at God.

———

DO I REALLY HAVE A CASE? Can I even find a solution? He questioned himself. On one hand, I have Anna Marlet who is so certain that her friend wouldn't commit suicide; on the other, the police report ruled it suicide. *What am I missing here?* He wondered. Then Alistair remembered the time difference and set the alarm on his cell phone. He would call Wade in a couple of hours and give him the info on Ted's phone call to Anna, and have him check Rosie's Bar.

On his way to his newly finished kitchen for a cup of tea, he picked up Jill Evans' file, reading as he walked. What was it that Jill had said to Ted about that bear? "Ah, yes, here it is," he smiled. Ted had written that he was using his favorite picture of Jill as wallpaper for his cell, and wondered if she thought that silly. Jill's answer explained the purple teddy bear.

No, I don't think it silly. In fact, I'm flattered. And besides I printed your pic out and my favorite teddy bear is holding it, almost like having it in a frame.

I have to tell you; the teddy bear is purple. It's my favorite color. Hope you don't mind. Have I told you lately that I love you? Well I do... soooo very much. Can't wait for the year to go by. Your Jillybean. Mauh!

Returning to his office, tea and file in hand, his thoughts were on the missing picture. She had printed his picture out, but there was no mention of it in the police report. So where is it? Not in this file. Thumbing through the file, he decided to reread the newspaper clipping.

BEST FRIEND FINDS MODEL DEAD

An aspiring model in the Stella By Starlite Agency, Manhattan, was found dead. Anna Marlet, another model from the same agency, and best friend of the dead woman, found the body. Jill Evans was pronounced dead on the scene by the coroner as an apparent victim of suicide.

Hawk continued with the article; he was so engrossed that he jumped when he heard the bell from over the reception room door.

To Alistair's surprise, a vision of beauty stood amid the rubble of the reception room. She was tall and willowy, with long tresses of highlighted blonde pulled back in a ponytail. She looked like an angel that had just come from a jog in blue tights, walking shorts, tank top and matching running shoes.

As she met Alistair's gaze, her beautiful gray eyes seemed to be taking in everything that was falling apart in the room. Her lips, glazed with a light shimmer of pink, spread into a beautiful smile.

"Good morning," the angel spoke. "Wade told me to come see you; you might need some help. And from the looks of this office, I'd say you do."

"The day hasn't really begun and already I have critics," Alistair joked. "Wade sent you? So, who are you? And why does he, and evidently you, think I need help?"

"May I sit down somewhere? Surely the rest of your digs is better than this one room," the angel quipped. Alistair ushered her into his office and heard her emit a long, low whistle.

"Wow! What a difference," the angel said as she looked around. She flopped down on the sofa Alistair had only just vacated an hour before. Seeing her sitting on what he perceived as his bed, he invited her to take the chair by his desk. Moving to his favorite spot by the window, he maintained his usual standing position, and stroked his chin. "Okay, answer time," he said as he turned to face her.

The angel was one step ahead of him. "My name is Jamie Miller. I live in Manhattan. I met Linda and Wade several years ago. I was fresh out of high school, looking for work and they needed someone to work in Linda's Boutique shop. I kept that job until Linda decided to sell the business. Even after the divorce, we have all stayed in touch. I've had odd jobs since then, but I've been looking for steady work. Wade figured you needed help," Jamie paused as she popped a stick of gum in her mouth. "Come on, Hawk; if any of the other rooms are like the reception room, you really do need help. Even the outside is a mess. Wade figured you'd be holed up in a dump, but this room? Wow."

"Are you quite through, Miss Miller?" Alistair interrupted. "I don't usually entertain rude guests, especially at this hour in the morning."

"Hey, forget it. Wade only wanted to help you and me. I mean, I do need a job," Jamie said, as she stood to leave. Alistair crossed the room, stopping her before she reached the door.

"I'm sorry. Between a new case and not much sleep last night, I'm a little irritable. Shall we start over?"

CHAPTER FIVE

TUESDAY MORNING HAD ALL the makings of a beautiful Fall day when Jamie unlocked the Greystone Manor office. A little over a week into the job and Jamie felt the title of receptionist just didn't cut it. She sat around half the time and cleaned the other half: receptionist or janitor? Maybe a *janrecep*. She laughed at her own pun.

Jamie looked away from the computer screen, her eyes scanning the newly renovated room. The décor suggested elegance. The walls were painted smoky-blue, with mahogany molding and baseboards. The old wooden entrance door had been replaced; the second door had been removed completely. The door's frame and wall ended in a beautiful arch. A medium shade of oak flooring and a glass chandelier gave the room a finished touch.

To Jamie, the focal point was the staircase to the second floor. *It's beautiful*, she thought, *even if it is mahogany. And the Oriental rug on the stairs with those metal doohickeys is kind of cute*, she thought. Although she preferred modern metal office furniture, she was beginning to get comfortable with the mahogany that Hawk was so insistent upon.

The reception room had undergone a great transformation in just a week, but Jamie wondered just how many people she might ever see walking through the door. Her boss seemed a little out of touch with reality. He was certainly not the man Wade described. The way he dressed didn't seem normal either, at least to her way of thinking. The fine elegant Italian silk suit was okay, but why not the popular office blue instead of a charcoal gray? He wore a long, dark gray scarf and a gray Fedora, but no tie. If it wasn't for the silk dress shirts being a different color each day, she'd swear he was wearing a special uniform. Hawk surely was different than anyone she'd ever met.

Getting up from her desk, Jamie decided it was time to think about cleaning and straightening up the office they were using for storage.

"Oh my!" she yelped when she opened the door.

There were boxes upon boxes, lamps, rugs, odd pieces of furniture, various framed paintings and who knew what else. How would she ever get this mess straightened up? After opening a few boxes only to discover books and more books, she wasn't sure there was any place to put them. Hawk's office bookshelves were jammed full. Maybe they could go in the other office. But then another box caught her eye; it had one word written on it—DISHES—in big bold letters. She peeked in the box and sure enough: dishes. Forgetting the books, Jamie carried the box of dishes to the kitchen. She proceeded to wash and store them in the cabinet above the sink. Not a full set, but enough for the office and the occasional lunch, she thought.

————

JAMIE HAD FINISHED with the dishes and decided to give up on the storage room until she talked with her boss. She was seated back at her desk when the door opened, and Hawk came blustering in with a huge smile on his face.

"Well, it's official. Greystone Manor is all mine," he boasted. "It took longer than I hoped, but we finally closed yesterday afternoon. Anything happening here yet this morning?"

"Nada. But I did finish getting my account set up on FriendsPage. I listed my job as an exotic dancer in Las Vegas and I invited some people as friends to make it look legit. I also put in a request to Ted. I found him easy enough. Just waiting to see if he responds."

"Good. Did you get my interview set up?"

"Yep—ten this morning. Just got off the phone with that Marlet woman. It sure wasn't easy getting the people you want to question all together at the same time. They'll meet you at the theater—where two of them work—during a rehearsal break. Name of theater and people, plus the address—it's all there," replied Jamie as she handed him a piece of paper.

Hawk looked at it a moment, tucked it in his shirt pocket, went to the kitchen, no doubt for his morning cup of tea.

"A thank you would have been nice," she said to the doorway. "Oh, well."

Jamie heard Hawk rattling in the kitchen cabinet one minute; the next, he was around the corner from the suite's hallway looking like a lion ready to pounce on its prey. He held a cup from the set of dishes Jamie had found.

"What in the world... is this... those... dishes doing in there?" He stammered, pointing towards the kitchen.

Suddenly angry, he threw the cup in the direction of the storage office. It hit the wall, smashing into pieces. Hawk rushed to the broken cup, fell to his knees and picked up the pieces. Quickly he retreated to his office and, a moment later, reemerged.

"I'll deal with you later," he gruffly remarked, passing Jamie on his way out.

She stood in shock at the scene she had just witnessed. *The man is unhinged,* she thought.

"That's it!" Jamie screamed into the room. She picked up the phone, not thinking about the time difference, and punched in Wade Owens' number. "Wade, it's Jamie. Just listen," she barked. "I've had it here. You told me Hawk would make a great boss. Well, you're wrong. He's crazy, unhinged, off his rocker, bonkers and any other adjectives you can think of. I can't work for him, even if he is your best friend." Jamie steamed, near to tears.

"Is that tears I'm hearing? Calm down! Tell me what this is all about, Jamie. What happened?"

She pulled herself together and related the scene that had just taken place and Hawk's words to her as he left the office.

"If you're standing, sit down," Wade said, "I guess I need to give you a little background." When Jamie assured him that she was sitting, he continued. "About eighteen months ago, Hawk's wife, Ellie, who was pregnant, was murdered. It about did him in. Those dishes belonged to her."

"Oh, no," Jamie moaned. "No wonder. Does he know who killed her, and why?"

"Some guy named Tank Doogan. He thought he was Mister Big Shot. He had pulled a grand theft robbery about ten years ago; Hawk was the one who helped put him behind bars. After serving eight years he was out for good behavior. He always said he'd pay Hawk back. And he did, by taking down Hawk's wife and unborn child."

"Oh!" Jamie gasped, "now I think I understand. Do you think he should be doing this kind of work anymore?"

"Yeah, he can handle it. In fact, it'll probably be good therapy for him."

"Uh... ok," Jamie replied. "I'll be more careful around him and just stick to my job. Thanks for clueing me in, Wade. I'll put the dishes back, too."

"No, Jamie. I think you better just leave them alone for now," Wade cautioned. "Let Hawk make that move."

CHAPTER SIX

AS ALISTAIR WALKED down the theater aisle, he couldn't help but think of Ellie's dishes and Jamie touching them. He thought of firing the girl. But, no: that wasn't the answer. The incident had put him in a foul mood, letting his temper get the best of him. Smashing Ellie's cup beyond repair hurt. And he wasn't sure why. *It's only dishes*, he thought. Maybe questioning this motley looking group sitting on the stage would get his mind off the dishes, and Jamie, *and* back on the case.

He wondered which one, if any, felt inconvenienced. Too bad if they did: inconvenience is sometimes part of the job of catching a killer. Killer? Alistair questioned himself. Killer implies murder, not suicide. He shook the thought off in order to get to the business at hand. From the description Anna Marlet had given him, Alistair was certain he could put the names with the faces in the group.

He noticed Miss Marlet was in animated conversation with the man sitting next to her, Liam Harchol, a wannabe boyfriend of the dead girl. Next to him was a cocky young man sporting a half-shaved look, Matt Hudgins. Next to the Hudgins kid was a pretty little blonde named Ginger Goodling. The stunning dark-skinned woman next to

Miss Goodling was another good friend of the dead girl. Simone Devereaux had been her co-worker when they both modeled in Paris a few months ago. Now, she was living in Montreal, Canada, with her family. The Reverend Whitacker was the last of the group. He, too, had been in Paris at the same time as Mrs. Devereaux and Jill Evans.

Time to get this started, Alistair thought, a little anxiously. *First case since... well, I'm just not going there today.* As he stepped onto the stage, he heard a voice behind him.

"How fitting. Just like a dime store detective novel, gathering all the suspects together in one place... and in a theater at that. But then you always were a bit dramatic, Hawk." At the sound of his nickname, Alistair turned.

"Well, if it isn't my old boss, Detective Donavan. I guess word gets to you fast."

"It always does, and," Donavan sneered. "I have to tell you Hawk you are way off base. That case is closed. It's suicide, not murder. The murder you're seeking revenge for was eighteen months ago. We caught the guy and he's serving life. Justice did prevail."

Hawk knew Donavan was referring to Ellie's murder and the words stung. He wondered what Donavan had against him. *The man has always tried to get into my cases and outdo me*, Hawk thought. *It's not the way to be head of detectives as far as I'm concerned. And how he has lasted as long as he has is beyond my comprehension.* Hawk pulled the reins on his thoughts as Donavan continued.

"Now if you don't want to be run in for creating a disturbance in a closed case, and lose your license, I'd suggest you send these people on their way."

"No!" Anna Marlet screamed, "No way. I've hired Detective Hawkins to find out the truth," Anna was now sobbing. "There is no way Jill would have killed herself... just... no way," she managed to say between sobs.

"As I already told Detective Hawkins," Donavan said, "the case is closed."

"Hey, what harm can there be in a few questions?" added Matt

Hudgins. "We're already here and this guy," he said pointing to Hawk, "is on the clock."

"Detective Donavan," Reverend Whitacker spoke up. "I, too, think there is a lot more to this than a simple suicide. You see, I was Miss Evans' Pastor when we, Miss Evans, Mrs. Devereaux, and myself were working in Paris."

Donavan paced a few steps away from the group, paused, and turned. "Okay. But since this is my jurisdiction, I sit in on the group interview. Got it?"

All heads nodded... all heads... except Hawk's.

"Well, Hawk," Donavan asked, "what about it?"

What is it with this man? Hawk thought. As he stood, legs astride, and stroking his chin, he figured it wouldn't hurt to keep on Donavan's good side. Never know when he might come in handy. Looking at his old boss, "I guess it will have to be," he said.

———

"AS I UNDERSTAND IT, this is a fifteen-minute break. So, who needs to get back to rehearsals first?" Hawk asked the group.

"Actually, I should be working right now. I work on set building," Matt piped up.

"Okay, let's begin with you. And just to let you know, this will be recorded. Rather than ask a lot of questions, how about you telling me what you know about all this and about your involvement with Jill and Ted?"

Click. Donavan's recorder was on. Alistair wasn't sure if he liked that idea or not, but said nothing as he pressed his own recorder.

"Well," Matt muttered, "not much. I was an online friend to Jill, but not to Ted. Jill and I were part of the gang that would get together for eats; sometimes she'd ride on the back of my Harley. I didn't really know much about Ted, except what Ginger told me."

"That it?" asked Alistair.

"Yeah... guess so. I kinda wondered why you wanted to ask me questions."

"You never know. You're excused, but if I think of anything else, I'll get back to you." Alistair paused. "Who's next?"

"I guess I am." It was Ginger. "They'll be back to rehearsals soon."

"I have a couple of questions to ask Miss Goodling, Hawk. I'll handle her and perhaps you can gather the others toward the back of the theater," suggested Donavan. "Don't worry. I'll see to it you get a copy of the interview."

Hawk was beginning to steam. Who did Donavan think he was? The idea to move to the back of the theater was fine, but to talk with the Goodling girl alone? Hmm. Losing his cool wouldn't get him anywhere, except maybe on the wrong side of Donavan and that wasn't where he wanted to be right now. Reluctantly he allowed Donavan to have his way.

Hawk led the way to the theater lobby instead. There were a few areas that provided comfortable seats. Choosing one, he asked, "Okay, who's next?"

"Mind if I go next?" asked Reverend Whitacker, "I'm also working today." Hearing no objections from anyone, Hawk asked Whitacker to tell what he knew.

"The first time I met Jill... uh... Miss Evans, was when she came to Paris to work for Monique, where Mrs. Devereaux was the manager. She... Miss Evans... decided to attend the American Christian Church where I was on mission to pastor for a year." The Reverend hesitated, seemingly getting his thoughts together.

"And?" Hawk prompted.

"I'm trying to figure out how to tell what happened, what I actually know and not just hearsay."

"Maybe I better give you a rundown on the events, since they involved the studio," Mrs. Devereaux spoke up.

"Alright. That okay with you, Rev?" asked Hawk.

"Yes, I think that would be best. Then I can tell you of my involvement."

"I think I'd better interrupt." It was the quiet guy, Liam Harchol. "I have no idea about any of this. Today is the first I've heard about Jill. I lived in Jersey until about a month ago. I have a business here in the city and when I got a divorce, I decided to sell my house and move here to be close to my work. I met the gang and found myself interested in Jill, but she wouldn't give me a tumble. Said she was in a relationship. I found out from her friends that it was online. Still she wouldn't go out with me. That's it, people. Nada. So how about it; can I blow this joint now? Don't worry. I won't leave town; you can always reach me if you need to."

"Go," Hawk said. He also felt like telling him to take his attitude with him. After Harchol left, Hawk listened to Mrs. Devereaux explain about Jill coming to work for Monique, and signing legal documents. If Jill decided to quit, or if she refused modeling jobs, she would be fined in the amount of five thousand dollars. Hawk registered the information, but in the back of his mind, he wondered what was taking Donavan so long.

"The day Monique decided Jill was to do a shampoo ad in the nude was the day Jill decided to quit. She called her parents for the money so she could get out of her contract and get home, but they refused. I was with her when she made the call. I advised her not to raise Monique's ire. I also told her I would see what I could do to lessen the idea of a full nude shot."

The Reverend interrupted to add that Jill had also come to him for advice about breaking her contract.

As Simone Devereaux continued, Hawk began to wonder if this would be a case, or if the Marlet woman was only acting in her grief. "Mrs. Devereaux," Hawk interrupted, "I fail to see where this connects with Ted Ashby."

"I'm getting to that. Everyone, it seemed, thought Jill to be prudish, and some, including me, were upset with her. I thought she should have known what she might be in for before she accepted the contract, but I don't even think she read it," Mrs. Devereaux sounded perturbed.

Hawk could understand that she was, since she made the trip all the way down from Montreal, leaving her family and business. But she continued speaking, adding that she was able to get the shot to show only Jill's back.

"Then, about a week later, the police showed up at Monique's. One of the other models had been working the red-light district; unfortunately, that job also included drug running. I saw this as an opportunity to get Jill out of her contract," she continued.

Just then, Donavan slipped in and took a seat. He seemed quite intent on learning what Mrs. Devereaux had to say, Hawk noticed.

"At that point," Mrs. Devereaux was saying, "everything had to go fast. Monique dissolved Jill's contract. As soon as she showed for work the next morning, Jill was paid. She rushed back home to pack. And this is where the Reverend Whitacker comes in," she finished.

The Reverend picked up with the details. "I made the arrangements for her flight, and since she hadn't been in Paris very long, most of her boxes were still packed. I met Mrs. Devereaux and her husband, Jacque, at Miss Evans' apartment to assist. He and I took all of the packed boxes to the church office to be shipped from there. After that I drove her to the airport and waited until she boarded," the Reverend finished.

Hawk chanced a look at Donavan to see if he looked as bored as Hawk was feeling. To his surprise, Donavan was intently studying Anna Marlet who was fidgeting with the rings on her fingers. Hawk's gut told him something was beginning to turn upside down. The interviews were going nowhere, and he imagined Donavan was going to repeat his earlier warning of this being a closed case and telling him to back off.

"I still fail to see the connection," Hawk addressed both Mrs. Devereaux and the Reverend.

"Jill not only wanted to return to the states," Mrs. Devereaux went on, "she hoped to go to Arizona and meet Ted. But Ted told her no; he said that they needed to give their so-called relationship a full year."

"And Miss Evans told you this, or did you see an email?" asked Hawk.

"She told me."

"Mrs. Devereaux," Donavan stood as he addressed the woman, "what I'm hearing seems to point to the fact that this a suicide. Nothing else."

"Doesn't anyone understand?" Anna screamed, "Jill would not, could not, commit suicide!"

The Reverend Whitacker shifted in his seat. "I have to agree. Miss Evans was a Christian. I don't think she would consider suicide as an option even if she was upset, extremely unhappy, or depressed."

"Look," Mrs. Devereaux interrupted. "I didn't drive seven hours to have some guy with a badge say I wasted my time," directing her remarks to Donavan.

Hawk broke in, reminding them that the interview was not a police inquiry, only fact gathering for his client's case. He encouraged Mrs. Devereaux to continue.

As she began to talk, his mind started to wander. Was he so anxious to be back in law enforcement that he had accepted the first client that walked through his door? Was he really cut out for this work anymore?

If he was still a praying man, he just might be calling on God to help him sort all this out. He missed the times he and Ellie shared in prayer and Bible reading to start their day. On that last morning he and Ellie had read from Ecclesiastes about a time for everything. They were especially drawn to the verse about a time to give birth and a time to die, a time to plant and a time to uproot what is planted. They discussed the joy that would be theirs and the Lord's when their little girl, Emily, was born. Becoming a father after thirty-seven, Hawk was glad it was going to be a girl. He wasn't sure he'd be able to keep up with a ten-year-old boy at forty-seven. Although Ellie was twenty-seven, she was still young enough to be involved in the little one's life. She had laughingly told him she'd never be too old for shopping.

The day Ellie chose to shop for Emily's crib, she had asked Hawk to go with her. As usual, his work had priority. "It's not like you need me to carry anything; they do deliver," he had teased. Hawk regretted that decision a hundred times over. If only... could he have saved her life? It wasn't her time to die, or for Emily to never be born.

Trust Me, he seemed to hear a voice say. He shook it off, along with the memories that were creeping back. He willed himself to pay attention to what Mrs. Devereaux was saying.

"We got away from Paris on that Saturday. Monique and a few of her *girls* were arrested and the studio closed down. It was a bad time. I didn't know anything about her extra *business*, and yet I had been calling Jill naive. I wanted her to work for me in Montreal, but she went back to Stella's." Mrs. Devereaux stood. "Look, I need to get home. If I leave now, I can be home before ten. I would like to see my children before they go to bed."

"Yes, go ahead," Hawk said. "If I think of any questions, I'll call. Same for you, Rev. Miss Marlet, since I already have your statement, there's no need to detain you any longer.'

"Perhaps," said Donavan, "but I have a couple of questions if you don't mind. How long were you and Miss Evans roommates?"

"Ever since we moved from Long Island and went to work for Stella...about three years ago."

"And you were living as roommates the night she died?" Anna only nodded. "Tell me about that night, Miss Marlet."

Anna looked to Hawk. He was stroking his chin, but nodded for her to continue.

"Well, Jill was upset because Ted seemed to be pulling away. He was also upset with a few of Jill's friends."

"Oh, and why do you suppose that was?"

Hawk listened as Anna mentioned friends, including Ginger, who kept emailing Jill with advice to drop Ted. They reasoned that he might be married, and that he didn't appear to be a Christian.

"Plus, she had found out he had other women online to whom he told the same things. He smoked, he drank," Anna continued. "All those things were against everything Jill stood for; we were trying to set her straight. I could not understand why she was so adamant about a relationship with this guy."

It appeared to Hawk that Anna was becoming agitated. He wished Donavan would leave it alone. In fact, he wished Donavan would leave. He might not be his boss anymore, but Hawk could sense that Donavan's jealousy of Hawk's abilities was still there. He was certain that Donavan still acted as the big shot who supervised his officers.

By opening an office in Groveland Hills, Hawk had hoped to avoid him. But with Jill Evans' death happening in Donavan's precinct, Hawk guessed he couldn't avoid him altogether.

"So, what did you and she do that evening?" Donavan continued.

Again, Anna looked at Hawk; once more he nodded.

"I think I succeeded in convincing Jill to give up on Ted. I suggested that we celebrate her freedom," Anna began to sob. "Little did I realize it would be her ultimate freedom." Composing herself, Anna continued. "I always keep a bottle of sweet red wine on hand for when I need to relax. I'm not... ah...I wasn't as strict as Jill when it came to having a drink now and then. But I did manage to get her to have at least one glass of wine. Just to toast."

Was that actually a smile? Hawk noticed it slide across the bright red lips of Anna Marlet. For a model who was not working the day, she certainly was decked out. Her long blond hair fell smoothly over bare shoulders, and the strapless dress of bright navy was seductively short. Her make-up seemed too heavy for daytime hours. Her mascara was very black; the eye shadow matched her dress. Her cheeks were blushed with dark pink, almost clownish in his estimation. Oh, for the simple beauty Ellie had exuded.

"We also had cheese and crackers and finished with Jill's favorite, Godiva dark chocolate truffles. Though she never drank, she did have a few more glasses of wine. But she wasn't drunk! She seemed fine when she went to her room."

"And you didn't check on her the next morning?" asked Donavan.

"There wasn't any need. Her shoot wasn't until two, so I figured she would want to sleep in."

"One more thing Miss Marlet: did you and Miss Evans have a fight that night?"

"No," Anna snapped. "She was my best friend. Why would you ask such a thing?"

"Ok, I'm done here. Hawk? My office—three o'clock." Donavan left in a blur, leaving a surprised Hawk to wonder what was up.

CHAPTER SEVEN

THE DAY HAD BEEN EXCEPTIONALLY long, and Wade was glad to be home. He went to his small office off the kitchen and had just sat down when his phone rang.

"Owens here," he answered. "Hey! Drake, how's it going?" Wade began doodling as he listened to Drake Dumont. Funny, the sketch was beginning to look like Hawk. "What? Yeah, I'm listening," Wade quickly recovered. "Yeah, okay. I'll be looking for it and when did you say she'd be in Vegas? Next Tuesday? And both girls are there? And what about the one in Seattle?" After being assured they all would be interviewed, the call was ended. Almost immediately Wade's email pinged. *Well, here was the info from Portland. The first interview completed.* Next, he needed to get his undercover female officer, Sargent Gloria Parker, on the job, but not on the department's clock. Hawk was paying for this, or at least his client was. Wade wasn't sure he agreed with doing some of the investigation online, but that was Hawk's decision.

WADE HAD BEEN DISTURBED by Jamie's call; he couldn't get it out of his thoughts. He remembered how he pondered just how much he should tell her. When Jamie asked who had killed Ellie and why, he had hesitated a moment, then figured he could tell her that much. But he found himself sweating in hopes she wouldn't ask any more questions. After all, it was Hawk's place to tell her the whole story, not his. Was Hawk having an emotional relapse? He supposed this investigation could trigger one. When Jamie questioned about Hawk investigating this case, Wade had taken a deep breath, hoping his answer of it being good therapy would prove to be true.

He thought back to the first day of Doogan's trial. After getting Linda settled here in their new home, he returned to New York to be with his best friend as the case went to trial. He had tried to convince him not to go to the courthouse that day, but Hawk had insisted, saying he wanted to see the creep in cuffs and irons. Wade knew he had no choice but to go with him, especially since Hawk appeared to be very agitated.

"I really don't think this is a good idea," Wade had ventured to say as he and Hawk leaned against the wall near the transport door.

"I do," Hawk replied. "I didn't come this far not to see him. I want Doogan to know that I know." Their conversation was interrupted; the transport door opened. And there he was. All six feet of Tank Doogan; shaved head, mustache, and a beard that almost covered the scar running from his ear over his cheek. He was in prison garb, with handcuffs and leg irons in place. He surveyed the room with a cocky look on his face. Then his eyes lit upon Hawk. "Gottcha. Just like I said I..."

Hawk was away from the wall and on Doogan in seconds. His muscular hands went straight to the man's burly throat, and he screamed, "I'll kill you! I'll kill you!"

Wade heard the snap of handcuffs and realized they were on Hawk. Doogan was coughing, and his cocky look was replaced with fear as he was ushered into the courtroom.

Wade tried to approach his partner and best friend, but was

restrained by Detective Donavan. "We don't need a total breakdown. Get him over to Bellevue for evaluation and counseling. *And,* we keep this away from the press," Donavan said, loud enough so all his officers understood. As two of the officers led Hawk out of the building, he looked back, and Wade saw the forlorn look in his eyes.

CHAPTER EIGHT

THE DEPARTMENT HADN'T CHANGED in the past eighteen months, but Hawk had. This wasn't when or how he planned to re-visit his old precinct; when Detective Howard Donavan barked an order, the recipient usually jumped. But Hawk wasn't jumping anymore. He just wanted to see what his old boss was up to.

The door closed slowly behind him as he stood in the middle of the booking room. The same old greenish-gray walls stared back at him. The metal and chrome desks and chairs still sported a cold look; the tile was even more yellowed than he remembered. Immobilized by a fog of memories he watched various police personnel pass, feeling that all eyes were on him. He began sweating as he waited for the taunts, but they didn't come. It was just as the doctor had predicted.

"Hey, Hawk!" a voice called from somewhere in his fog. "Hawk," the voice sounded again. "Can I help you?"

Come on, Hawk, he thought to himself; *shake it off.* "Donavan... appointment," was all he could manage as he moved forward.

He remembered the last time he had been here. It was an official order, coming right after Ellie's killer was brought to trial. Being here only reminded him of the day God had let him down... again.

Donavan had given him a choice. Take a year's sabbatical in the healthcare facility the department offered and resign at the year's end, or... be fired.

———

DONAVAN'S HAND WAS EXTENDED. "Glad you made it, Hawk; have a seat. I'll get right to it. I had Miss Goodling's interview edited, and after listening to her statement a few times, I've decided to reopen the case. There may be more to it than a simple suicide as we first thought. Possibly it *is* homicide."

Hawk let out an audible sigh, thinking he just might get his life and career back on course. He looked around the room. Framed certificates, various awards that either the precinct or Donavan himself had received, covered one entire wall. The rest of the walls were cream-colored, and white metal blinds were on the two windows that overlooked the parking lot. Yet the proverbial gunmetal gray desk was also in this office. This surprised him; his old boss kept bragging about the nice oak desk he wanted. *You'd think he would have it by now*, Hawk thought.

Then Donavan dropped his bombshell. "Looks like Anna Marlet might need to hire a lawyer instead of retaining you, Hawk."

"What?"

"She's my number one suspect," Donavan gloated. "Since we're reopening the case, the department will be investigating. You might want to think about giving up the idea of being a detective in the private sector," he chuckled.

Ever since Donavan had stuck his nose into the interviews at the theater, Hawk had sensed Donavan would step on his toes again. But this?

"Before I make that decision, I'd like to hear that tape."

"Suit yourself," Donavan said and pushed the play button.

"...Yeah, they were best friends, they grew up together, both of them from wealthy families on the Island." Hawk knew about that, thinking of his own parents and his growing up on Long Island.

"I remember one fight they had," the tape of Goodling continued, "and it wasn't that long ago. Just before Jill went to Paris." Hawk remembered that Simone Devereaux had also mentioned a big blow-up between Jill and Anna. He listened more closely. "I think Anna was jealous of Jill. She told me as much one time when we all met for a party at Bailey's Bistro. But this fight had Jill in tears and wondering what she'd done to upset Anna. ...No, I wasn't present, but they didn't speak again until Jill came back from Paris." Hawk wasn't hearing anything that could implicate his client in homicide. It seemed to him that Donavan was just blowing smoke.

"Hmm, what was it about?" Donavan had left his question on the recording.

"Well... Jill said Anna screamed at her about always thinking she was the prettiest and best, and how she always got the better modeling gigs. But I think there was a lot more to it."

Click.

"There's more, but does that sound like Miss Goodling's talking about a caring and bereaved best friend?" asked Donavan.

"There's nothing there to implicate my client. You hearing something that I'm not?"

"Let's put it this way, Hawk; it's given me pause to think that maybe—just maybe—there's more to it than a simple suicide. And," Donavan added, "I'm almost certain Marlet's hiding something. Call it my cop's instinct, but something's missing."

"Whatever you call it, I don't hear it. Besides, Miss Marlet has given me information that shows a much darker story, and it doesn't involve her."

"But does it include info on her own mental breakdown six months ago?"

CHAPTER NINE

HAWK'S DECISION TO return to his Manhattan Condo was two-fold. He wasn't ready to deal with his receptionist yet. And, he needed to get his head around the bombshell Donavan had dropped on him. *Was Anna hiding something?* She certainly didn't kill Jill, no matter what Donavan thought. Yet she didn't mention her hospital stay or the fights she had with the dead girl. It was time for a cup of tea and another opinion.

———

DRINKING HIS TEA, Hawk waited for Wade to answer. "Leave your message; oh—and your name and number. I'll get back to you soon." A disappointed Hawk left his message and slammed his cell on the table. He began pacing, stroking his chin as he contemplated. He was agitated, doubting himself. *What's going on here? I don't need this garbage. Maybe I'm in the wrong business. Maybe the time away wasn't enough. Maybe if Ellie hadn't died. Why, God, why?* His thoughts screamed inside his head. His cell phone brought him back to reality. Seeing Wade's name, Hawk collected his emotions and answered.

"Hey, buddy; thanks for calling me back so soon."

"So, what's up?" asked Wade.

Hawk related the theater interviews and his visit at Donavan's office.

"The old precinct, huh. And it sounds like he hasn't changed at all," mused Wade, "still interfering and playing the big shot detective. Almost like old times, except you no longer work there. Don't let him get to you, Hawk, and don't forget—you were the best detective on the force. Donavan was always jealous of that, and he probably is still. I don't doubt that he would try anything, within his legal power, to pull you down."

"Guess I am letting him get to me. Guess I'm missing Ellie right now, too. Guess I need to get the renovation going on my living quarters above the office. Guess I'm doing a lot of guessing."

"Speaking of your office, I need to share a phone call I received from Jamie this morning." As Hawk listened, he realized just how much he was letting things get to him. To the point of affecting others. "That doesn't sound like the Hawk I know. You always had it together, and people could depend on you. You got the job done and then some. When was the last time you picked up your Bible?"

Hawk had to think about that one. Leave it to Wade to get to the heart of the matter. "If I'm honest, probably not since Ellie's death. Me and God have been a little estranged."

"Everything I'm hearing sounds like you're still looking for revenge. But Doogan's away for life. Exacting vengeance isn't in your job description, Hawk; it belongs to the Lord. I'd say it was time to pick up your Bible again. Maybe you should start with Psalm 139. Give all of this to God. Let Him handle it and close the gap between you and Him."

"You sure know how to lay it on the line, Wade—no holding back," Hawk chuckled, halfheartedly.

"Hey, what are friends for? Okay. Now my thoughts on the bombshell Donavan threw at you. Call Marlet out on it. Tell her to lay all her cards on the table or you can't help her."

"You're right," Hawk conceded.

"Meanwhile," Wade continued. "I should have the other interviews in another two weeks. And, my undercover gal, who by the way is working for us on her days off, opened an online account and has tried to invite Ted to her FriendsPage. So far, he's not biting. But if he does, she'll try to set up a romantic meeting with him. We do have his location narrowed down. It's within a twenty-mile radius north of Scottsdale. You're on the right track, Hawk. Just get Marlet to open up, and you can stay ahead of Donavan," Wade concluded.

"As usual, you're right, on all accounts. You always did keep my feet on the ground. I miss my partner and best friend. It's good to have you working with me on this case. And, as soon as I get back to my office, I'll talk with Jamie."

––––––––

JAMIE HAD JUST SHUT the computer down when Hawk returned to the office. Passing her desk, he called over his shoulder, "Come in my office." He was sitting behind his desk when she entered. "I know it's time for you to leave, but we need to talk. Have a seat,"

She was almost sure she'd be getting the ax; if not today, then tomorrow. Yet there was something in Hawk's voice that now made her wonder.

"First off—let me apologize," Hawk began.

"Nah, that's okay, my fault," Jamie interrupted.

"Please, Jamie, let me finish. I had a call from Wade, and he told me about your call to him and what he revealed to you." Hawk seemed to be having a rough time. She didn't know what to say or do so she just sat there waiting for him to continue.

"Someday, when I'm able, I'll tell you the rest of what happened." Jamie just nodded, not wanting to throw Hawk off track.

"Seems we keep getting off on the wrong foot with one another," Hawk gave a nervous laugh.

"Yeah, we sure do," she said, snapping her gum. Jamie didn't like the fact that her remark sounded timid to her ears. *I can't let him intimidate me, whether I keep this job or not,* she thought.

————

HAWK WALKED to the window and stroked his chin. He looked at a peaceful scene of the sun falling behind the jutted Palisades across the river, and wished he could feel that same peace within himself. But peace would only come when he rid himself of the anger. Tamping down his bitterness was a start. Hawk turned back to face Jamie before he spoke again.

"About the dishes. Tomorrow, before you come in, stop and pick up whatever you think is needed to furnish the office kitchen. I don't care where you shop or about the cost: just get them tomorrow. Then please repack Ellie's dishes and return them to the storage room. Then set up an appointment with Anna Marlet for ten Thursday morning. Okay, I guess that's it."

"Does this mean I still have my job?" Jamie asked as she rose to leave.

"Yes. You're a good employee. Wade was right to send you here. I want you to stay. I'm not trying to make any excuses, but I have been stressed. I plan to work on that…and my manners."

Hawk watched as Jamie left his office and collected her things. He noticed the smile on her face and heard her say, "Good 'ol Wade," as she left.

CHAPTER TEN

"I'LL KILL YOU! I'll kill you!" Hawk awoke. Once again, the nightmare had hit like a whirling tornado. Jumping from the bed, he wondered what could have triggered it this time.

Knowing he wouldn't be getting back to sleep, he dressed, threw a few things in an overnight bag and, at four in the morning, headed for Groveland Hills and his office.

———

A FRUSTRATED TURN of events was not what Hawk had envisioned, especially when it involved Donavan and his smug, superior attitude. He looked at his watch for the umpteenth time: only two hours since he had left his condo. Time was still crawling—just like his thoughts, dense and thick as smoke, curling their way around his mind. Lingering, then dissipating. He hoped that the meeting with Anna Marlet, later this morning, would make things clearer.

Hawk meandered to his favorite spot at the window and noticed that sunlight was hinting at an appearance. With the night fading away, his garden would soon be in full light. As he stared out the window, whispers of doubt crowded Hawk's mind as he thought about Wade's advice on closing the gap between himself and God. But how could he expect God to forgive him when he had not forgiven Ellie's killer? Or, for that matter, was he still blaming God? He was tired of thinking. He needed sleep, but it eluded him like wind whipping through the trees. Staying in the condo was no longer inviting. He'd sleep on his office sofa until his new home was completed.

After brewing a cup of tea, Hawk decided to check on the work being done upstairs. He hadn't been up there since he had spoken with the foreman and laid out the plans. Looking over the renovation would help pass the early hours.

Tea in hand, Hawk took the staircase slowly, opened the door, and felt for a light switch. Entering the room, he first noticed the bay window, which would eventually have padded seats, at the far end of the room. Facing west, the window provided an even more spectacular view of the garden and the Hudson River beyond. Someone had left one of the windows partially opened, and the soft morning air bore the cool fragrance of late autumn. Hawk stood mesmerized by the beauty of the awakening dawn.

Surely God is in this place. The thought came unbidden but comfortably. "Yes, Lord, I'm sure You are here," Hawk whispered, "but I'm not sure that I'm ready."

He stood, choosing not to dwell on God's beauty, and decided to see what else had been finished. Walking through an open doorway, Hawk was in his new kitchen. Another light switch and the beautiful mahogany cabinets were bathed with soft lighting, as were the marble counters below them. Up-lights placed above the cabinets danced across the ceiling, and the Italian stone flooring was exquisite. A cozy dining room opened off the kitchen.

Inspecting both bedrooms and baths made Hawk realize that the renovation was completed in record time. It was a job well done. All that was needed was paint and carpet. He hoped that would be done today; then the interior designer could get to work.

Feeling an urge to get on with life, courage coursed through Hawk's being at that moment. In this new home, maybe, the nightmare would be a thing of the past. Glancing at his watch again, he was happily surprised that another hour had passed so quickly. "Yes, this place is going to be good," he spoke to the ceiling.

Bam! Bam! Bam!!

CHAPTER ELEVEN

BANGING ON THE DOOR, Anna couldn't understand why Hawk wasn't answering. She had tried the doorbell, but evidently, it wasn't working. With the outside of the old Greystone Manor fixed up—new shutters, doors, eaves, and maroon paint instead of that awful black— you would think the doorbell would be working as well. She tried knocking again but to no avail. His car was here, so he must be also. Anna had arrived early, planning to wait until Hawk came in for the day. This new development couldn't wait. The side of her fists were hurting and turning a bright shade of pink. About to try a shoe, she heard the deadbolt.

"Are you trying to wake the dead?" Hawk's defensive stance made Anna shiver. "Our appointment is for ten. What are you doing here at this hour?"

Hawk didn't move. Anna was getting more frustrated. She had been banging on the door for what seemed to be at least ten minutes, and the early morning air was beginning to chill her. Not answering his question, Anna attempted to push past him, yet he still didn't move.

"Look, mister, I'm paying you good money for a job you don't seem to be doing. Now let me in." Again, Anna tried to enter, and this time, Hawk stepped aside.

"You could get me a cup of that coffee, too." Anna was still on her tirade as she stepped into the reception room.

"I could, but it's not coffee," Hawk said, sounding amused.

Anna turned. She wasn't ready for whatever game he might be playing.

"As long as it's got caffeine in it, I don't care what it is."

"It's tea, Miss Marlet, and there should be enough left in the teapot for another cup. The kitchen is through the open doorway."

Anna stared, open-mouthed, as Hawk walked past her into his office. The coffee or tea could wait, she decided and followed him.

———

STANDING AT THE WINDOW, he heard Anna stomp into the room. He turned to see her sit on the client side of his desk. "What? No tea, Miss Marlet? It really is very good."

"I don't care about your tea, Detective Hawkins. What I do care about is that you are making a real mess out of this case, ...a case I hired you for, which means you are supposed to be working for me. Instead, you've allowed Detective Donavan to get involved. He's now suggesting that it might be murder. He even had me in the station for questioning late yesterday."

"You yourself said Miss Evans 'just couldn't have killed herself.'" Hawk shot back. "Didn't you say you expected to be questioned?" Hawk reminded her. He placed his now empty teacup on his desk.

"Yes, but not to be the one accused of killing her," Anna screamed. "So why aren't you doing the job I hired you for? I thought you were the best."

———

HAWK USED to think that too. Up until Ellie was killed. Now even he wasn't so sure. This was not the first time that he doubted his abilities. Why *did* he take a job to investigate a closed case? Well, he had gotten himself into this, so he had to see it through.

"...so why do you let him?" Anna was asking. Hawk's thoughts and lack of sleep were probably contributing to his inability to concentrate. Especially with what a screaming woman in his office, at this early hour, was saying.

"Let who do what, Miss Marlet?"

"Were you not listening to me? Accuse me of murder! You let Donavan boss you around as though you were still working for the NYPD."

Hawk slapped both his hands down on his desk and leaned forward.

"Do you actually have any idea what I do for a living, Miss Marlet? I'm a detective, and I detect that you're not being honest enough with me so that I can do the job that you're paying me good money for." Hawk was not about to let Anna Marlet get the upper hand in this encounter. He sat down as he continued.

"Now, why don't you tell me about your fight with your best friend, and your breakdown: the one you saw fit to tell Donavan about, but not me—the detective *you* hired!"

CHAPTER TWELVE

DETECTIVE HOWARD J. Donavan. The gold letters glistened on the frosted glass of his office door. He pushed it open and headed straight for the file on his desk. Donavan. Yeah. He liked being called Donavan. He thought he might have the Howard J. removed. It just didn't fit who he was: a tough, no holds barred type of guy. As head of the precinct's detectives, he took no guff from any of his men or women. And he didn't plan to take any from Hawk, either. Detective Hawkins may not work for the NYPD anymore, but this case was still in Donavan's precinct. And since Hawk decided to open this can of worms, Donavan was going to work it, even if it meant finding Hawk's client guilty of murder.

Looking through the file, he remembered how upset Anna Marlet had become when questioned about her breakdown, her fights with Jill Evans, and her movements on the night her roommate died. Marlet's answers about the breakdown were honest. They were consistent with the hospital report he had secured. Yes—she was hospitalized for a month. Yes—the diagnosis was "extreme stress and depression." Yes—she was put on a prescription and a dietary regimen she has followed for the past six months. What caused the breakdown? Donavan remembered asking the question *and* Anna Marlet's hesitation in answering. Nervously, she stated the same thing Ginger Goodling had told him that day at the theater. She was jealous of the dead girl's popularity, the fancy photo shoots, her beauty. *People have killed for less,* Donavan thought.

But Anna Marlet's answers to the question about the reasons for the fights didn't quite match what the Goodling girl had said. Marlet stated the reason was simple. She'd had a boyfriend problem, and Jill was trying to help, but because she was so stressed, Anna refused her help. Goodling had said "The big fight was that Anna got mad, told Jill that she had "brown-nosed" for the Paris job and that she, Anna, was moving. Of course, she didn't, because she got put into Bellevue Hospital."

The very next day, Jill Evans left for Paris, and Anna Marlet quietly allowed her doctor to admit her to Bellevue's Psych unit.

"Contact with Jill was not possible," Donavan read Marlet's words, "and I was ashamed and embarrassed that anyone might know where I was. By the time I got out, Jill was back from Paris. Things had gone badly for her over there. Things were bad with her online love affair, too." The Goodling girl had stated that Anna was gloating and happy that things went sour for Jill.

Donavan never liked a case that involved too many women. The cattiness always seemed to surface. Marlet sounded jealous of the dead girl, and of Goodling, too. And Goodling seemed just as jealous of Marlet. The whole file read like a cheap novel.

Donavan's office door opened; Sargent Belton entered with his coffee. There was another woman he had issues with, but at least she still brought his coffee to him. He motioned her in as he glanced back at the file, not wanting to make any eye contact. As she set down the mug of steaming hot black coffee, he waved her back out, not once taking his eyes off the file. Yet something on her face caught his peripheral. Was that a sneer? He jerked his head up only to see her back, head held high, as she exited the room.

Donavan knew she had put in for a transfer, and that was fine by him. In fact, it couldn't come too soon. He only hoped her replacement would be a male. Maybe he could get the other two female officers to ask for transfers as well.

Donavan continued reading about the events on the night Jill Evans died. But it was Anna Marlet's story, with no one to substantiate or refute it.

————

JAMIE HAD ARRIVED for work just a few minutes after eight and was surprised to see Hawk's car already there, along with another vehicle she didn't recognize. She wondered if she had forgotten an appointment for Hawk. Or was this one he made without letting her know? Either way, she was sorry she was running late, and she wasn't in the mood to get chewed out again.

After stowing her purse, Jamie began her day at the computer. She didn't look up from the keyboard as Anna Marlet stormed out of Hawk's office. But she did jump when she heard the outer door slam violently.

So, Anna Marlet changed her appointment from ten to early morning, or... no. Jamie decided not to follow that line of thought. The question now was whether she should inquire if she was needed in her role of receptionist. That was answered when Hawk stepped out of his office with a recorder.

"Here," he said, handing it to Jamie, "I want you to transcribe Miss Marlet's... ah... we'll call it her testimony... about her movements on the night of Jill Evans' death and on the next morning. She told me this is exactly what she told to Donavan, who, by the way, is trying to accuse her of murder. She may be a little over the top, but she's not a murderer."

Without giving Jamie a chance to respond, Hawk retreated to his office.

"Wow! What a case! And he's trusting *me* to hear a testimony and transcribe it," she voiced to the room.

A moment later, Hawk opened his office door, only to add, "Miss Marlet will be returning with Miss Evans' laptop. Be sure to give her a receipt, and if she asks, I'm in conference. Once in a day is all I can handle of her."

For a split-second, Jamie wondered if Hawk required an answer. She knew he didn't when he walked back into his office and closed the door.

CHAPTER THIRTEEN

IT WAS TUESDAY, and Wade had the day off. He decided to drive out of town for a few hours. He could leave the thoughts of work behind and make some decisions about his future. He was headed south when a sheet of orange dust enveloped his car before he knew what hit him. Uttering a quick prayer, he pulled the car as far off to the right of the road as possible. Cutting the engine, he set the emergency brake and waited. He felt the wind buffet the car and prayed it wouldn't be turned around or... worse yet... turned over.

He could remember only one other time he had been caught in a dust storm. Linda had been with him; their divorce had just been finalized. He recalled thinking that on the way to the courthouse, she was his wife; now, returning to the house they shared, she was his ex-wife. That dust storm was a kitten compared to the one he was sitting in now, but it had caused far more damage. Linda's resolve to move back to New York had only strengthened.

Wham! Crash!

Something came through the rear window, but Wade wasn't waiting to find out what. He released his seat belt and dove for the floor just as another strong gust lifted the front end of his classic 1957 Chevy Bel Air.

"Lord," Wade's voice cracked, "I'm trusting You to be with me through this storm. Thy will be done."

The car dropped with a jarring bounce, slid sideways, and smashed into an immovable object. Wade felt something wet on his forehead as he tried to steady his hold on the door's armrest. The car itself seemed to hold on to the object it had smashed against, yet the wind still pounded with a vengeance.

Soon orange dust began filling the car's interior. Wade searched for his handkerchief, crushed it against his nose and mouth, and tried to hold down the fear that was beginning to build in his gut. Another strong gust pulled the car loose and sent it side over side until it hit another unseen object. The car snapped back on its wheels and Wade could only pray that what had felt like a hump wasn't a person.

Dazed, unsure of his injuries, he waited for the next gust. Nothing. The worst seemed to be over. Or was this just a lull? Keeping the handkerchief over his nose and mouth, Wade used his hold on the door's armrest to pull himself upright. That's when he noticed thin shafts of sunlight slicing through the dissipating dust.

————

NOT WANTING to leave his car, Wade argued with the sheriff's deputy and the EMT's, as they tried to convince him that he needed to go to the hospital. Not until the deputy in charge assured him that Troy's Classics had been notified and that someone would stay with the car, did Wade consent. In the ambulance, he began to relax as he noticed he was hooked up to all sorts of tubes. No doubt one of them held the potion that was easing his pain. As he tried to stay awake, his thoughts went to Hawk's case. What he wouldn't give right now to be sitting at his home desk with every scrap of paper concerning his part of the investigation spread out before him. That was his last thought as he finally allowed himself to be lulled into a light sleep.

BANDAGED, and with prescriptions for antibiotics and pain relievers in his lap, Wade sat in a wheelchair, waiting for his ride with Deputy Carson. He was glad the officer had agreed to stay the night. Wade didn't want to be admitted for observation. The doctor had told him to stay off work for a week and light-duty the first week back. That was okay by him, as he was sore all over. Yet he knew he wouldn't be content just lying around the house. Wade rubbed the scruff of a beard as he thought about what he would, and could, do at home. Certainly, he needed to call Hawk with the results of Dumont's interviews, such as they were. Not that there wasn't enough information, just that the information wasn't enough; at least, not enough to incriminate Ted.

Wade understood the frustration that Sargent Gloria Parker was feeling. She had reached a dead end. Playing a real estate agent on FriendsPage, and using a picture of a model in a swimsuit, she had invited Ted to be her friend. No response. In fact, he had actually disappeared off the Internet, as though he was afraid of being found.

WADE COULD SMELL the coffee as he headed for the kitchen the next morning. He wondered if Carson had the flunky's job of making coffee at work or was just being thoughtful. "Morning, Carson. Coffee smells good."

"Good morning, sir. I hope you don't mind, but I needed a cup and thought you might like one too. I blended the hazelnut I found in one of the cabinets with the regular grind you had in the canister. Hope you like it."

Hazelnut coffee had been Linda's favorite, not his. But Wade figured it might be a good idea to keep that thought to himself and just drink the coffee. He was sure the kid meant well. Maybe drinking the brew would help him to sense Linda's presence.

"Thanks. There's some donuts over there in the breadbox," Wade gestured as he sat, and then laughed. "We need to dispense with the "sir." By the way, which one of us is the newest kid on the block?"

"Well, sir... uh... I mean... I've been with the department three years now, but I don't usually have contact with the detectives. I work the night shift."

They sat in silence as they drank coffee and ate donuts. Wade was glad the doctor had asked Carson to stay only one night. He was secretly hoping the kid would leave after the coffee and donuts. He certainly couldn't work on Hawk's case with him hanging around.

"Uh... sir?" Carson broke into Wade's thoughts. "I wonder if I could, uh, well, I want to become a detective and thought maybe, uh, well, maybe you could give me some advice."

Wade couldn't hide the smile that flashed across his face, realizing that "sir" was just part of the kid's lingo, and that he wasn't going to get rid of him as soon as he had hoped. "So, you want to be a detective, huh? How old are you?"

"Twenty-four, sir," Carson answered.

"Are you married?"

"No, sir, but I do have a girl named Linda."

Strong memories came so quickly that Wade nearly knocked his chair over as he rose and rushed out of the room. Picking up Linda's photograph from his desk, he hugged it to his chest, as though in doing so, she would materialize in his arms. Between her coffee and the fact that the kid had a girl with the same name, it was more than Wade could bear.

"Uh, sir... are you alright?" the voice behind him said.

"Yeah, yeah, kid. Go on back to your coffee. I'll be there in a minute," Wade said, without turning around.

He heard Carson step back into the kitchen as he felt a tear fall on his cheek. He still ached for his wife. Correction: ex-wife. But at least he could hope to see her again. Perhaps even hold her once more. How did Hawk handle it, knowing Ellie would never return?

AFTER CARSON HAD GONE, Wade realized how tired and sore he was. He had spent the last couple of hours with the kid, giving him information, and his personal thoughts about becoming a detective. As he gulped down pain medicine, Wade recalled that he was about Carson's age when he first joined the police force in New York City. It was only six years ago that he had become a detective. Twenty years as a law enforcement officer, and what did he have to show for it? Nothing: just a broken marriage. And all because he had a passion for the work. A job that Linda hated, especially after Ellie was killed.

His thoughts returned to his children back in New York. He missed his family. Wade didn't believe in divorce; and, he knew God didn't approve. He was still praying that Linda would return and want him once again. But the likelihood of that happening was slim. He knew he would have to be the one to make a change.

Although the papers on his desk cried out to be organized, and he needed to touch base with Hawk, he opted for some rest in his recliner.

WADE WAS ROUSED from sleep by his cell phone. Reaching for it, he realized he had slept for three hours. Without checking the ID, he groggily answered. "Yeah?"

"Have I caught you at a bad time?"

It was Hawk. Wade related the dust storm, the ambulance ride to the hospital ER, and Carson's stay with him.

"I came away blessed, though, Hawk. Nothing broken. Just a slight concussion and three stitches in my forehead."

"I'm sorry to hear that." Hawk paused as though he was searching for the right words, but instead asked, "Anything I can do from long distance?"

"Maybe. Give me another day, and I'll be ready to wrap up this end of the investigation and get all the interviews and information sent off by Friday," Wade answered.

"Don't push yourself. Take a few more days to rest," Hawk insisted. "We'll talk again Monday. Some interesting twists have developed here. Miss Marlet has not been completely forthright; Donavan is thinking she may have killed her friend." Hawk hung up.

CHAPTER FOURTEEN

SITTING in church for Saturday evening Bible study, Wade reflected that Hawk's advice was right on target. Surprised at himself, Wade felt much better from resting over the last four days. Clearing up Hawk's case and returning to Bible study was better medicine than the doctor had prescribed. The praise and worship team had just finished, and people were greeting one another as Pastor Ray made his way to the lectern.

"Good evening, everyone. Before I begin, I'd like to offer a prayer of thanks for all those who survived Tuesday's dust storm with little harm or damage." Pastor Ray hesitated, and added, "We're glad to see Wade Owens with us this evening. I believe he was the only member who needed to visit the hospital. Let us pray." Wade disliked having attention called to himself, but he knew the pastor meant well.

Troy Classics had called Wade on Friday to give him the estimate about the damage to his car. The repair work wasn't cheap. He smiled and wondered if Pastor Ray's prayer would help his car *and* his wallet. A Real Estate sign from someone's front yard was the culprit that broke the rear window. As the car kept sliding, it met the concrete base of a light pole that pushed the rear fender into the trunk. The somersaults that ensued had caused minimal roof damage. The "hump" Wade had felt turned out to be a low concrete wall that brought the car to a halt. Had it not, his head injury could have been worse.

"...in the name of Jesus, amen. You may be seated."

It wasn't like Wade to let his mind wander during prayer. He asked God's forgiveness and opened his Bible.

———

HAWK AWOKE Sunday morning to welcomed sunlight peeking through the bedroom window blinds. It was the first day of sunshine since he had arrived at the summer cottage that he and Ellie owned on Montauk beach. It wasn't his usual time of the year to be here, but Hawk had decided to take as his own, the advice he had given Wade about rest, and this seemed to be the best place to get away from it all.

When he had arrived Wednesday, the weather was as gloomy as his mood. If the saying *A real man cries* was true, then he was a real man. Being here without Ellie, remembering all the happy times and happy plans made in the cottage, brought on gut-wrenching sobs. These were the first real tears that Hawk had been able to shed since her death. Anger had been a dam holding them back. Did this mean his anger was subsiding, that he could be a decent human being once again? He could only wonder.

He considered venturing over to his parents in East Hampton to attend church with them. He hadn't spoken to them since Ellie's death; he was pretty sure they would question what he wanted. He imagined his parents were still blaming him for not keeping her safe. After all, he was the law.

Hawk's father had asked him many times to come into the world of real estate development, affectionately called "the family business." But he didn't believe that being on the Forbes list was as important as the career of his dreams. Ever since he was a little boy, reading Donald Sobol books about the boy detective Encyclopedia Brown,

Hawk had wanted to be a detective. The family business might be nice and safe, but nice and safe wasn't what Hawk wanted. Ellie had accepted that fact.

No, he guessed he wouldn't be going to his parent's home or to church for that matter. It was too soon, he thought again, for either of them.

Hawk looked around the bedroom, drinking in the signs of Ellie's touch. There weren't many left. He had moved what he wanted to their condo in the city. Whatever remained, except for the furniture, he had given to Ellie's family. He realized that the time had come to sell their summer home. Stark reality settled over him when he realized that perhaps he was looking at the place for the last time.

———

DALE ROBERTS WAS in when Hawk called the realty office. As Dale was familiar with the cottage, it didn't take the realtor very long to arrive with a contract and lawn signs. Dale assured him it would be a quick sale. He had a waiting list of buyers from the Hempsteads and a few from upstate, all looking for a place on Montauk. As Hawk handed Dale the keys, he took one more look around. As he closed the door behind him, he felt a tear fall.

"No, not now," he said under his breath. Chapters were ending in his life, but he knew that he needed to be strong and get on with living. At least, that's what the doctor had told him. *Easy for him*, thought Hawk. The doctor hadn't lost the love of his life.

———

NOT HAVING to return to his Manhattan condo would make it easy to get back to Groveland Hills. He could take the interstate most of the way. Hawk was beginning to feel some accomplishment. He now had the cottage and condo with realtors. He had even managed a day last week to move the rest of his personal belongings from the condo to his office storage. Then he contracted with Teri Brown Realty to handle the sale. Teri thought it would hasten the sale if Hawk sold it furnished and he agreed.

The miles were zipping by as fast as the thoughts that were running a race in his head. Hawk had left Jamie in charge of seeing that the interior designer would have his living quarters above the office finished by the time he returned. He had also given Jamie the job of assuring Anna Marlet that he was still on the case even though he was out of town.

He had invested in a pre-paid cell phone, deciding it would be used only for Jamie to reach him. And on penalty of death, Jamie was not to give Miss Marlet the cell number. In other words, he could not be reached. Hawk had also decided not to tell Jamie exactly where he was, in case she would let that information slip. Fortunately, she didn't have occasion to call him at all. He realized that Wade had sent him a good receptionist, after all. But she was becoming more than that; she was his right hand, his girl Friday. It was a cliché, but that was fine by him.

Two and a half hours had blurred past; he was approaching his exit.

PULLING INTO THE DRIVE, Hawk was surprised to see Jamie's car parked in her usual spot. *Guess her old clunker finally gave out and she left it here for the tow truck,* he thought. Hearing a noise as he unlocked the door, he instinctively reached for his shoulder holster. No gun. No holster. Hawk let out an uneasy chuckle. Old habits never die. But maybe it wouldn't be a bad idea to carry his weapon once more.

There it was again. Something or someone was inside. As he threw open the door, a blood-curdling scream met his ears, and his eyes stared into those same beautiful gray eyes of a month ago. "I... I didn't expect you b... back... yet," Jamie stammered. "I was just leaving."

"What are you doing here?" Hawk asked cautiously. "It's not a workday. And even if your church has Sunday evening services, you're running late."

Jamie turned back to her desk and sat down. "I came in after lunch to catch up on a few things. I had had trouble with the car Friday and was very late getting in. I had made plans that night and couldn't stay after hours. Besides, I'm not too keen on being here at night, especially alone."

The girl is nervously rattling on, seemingly without taking a breath. *What is she trying to hide, or am I getting overly suspicious of everyone?* Thought Hawk.

"On Saturday I had already planned a day out at the mall with my best friend. So, I figured I'd work today since I don't go to church. I sleep in on Sunday mornings and then just lie around the rest of the day, so it was perfect for catching up," Jamie concluded.

"So, what was so important that it couldn't wait until tomorrow morning?" Hawk realized he was dancing around the issue. After the emotional time he'd had the last few days, putting the cottage up for sale and closing another chapter in his life with more finality than he thought possible, he guessed he didn't want to be alone right now.

"Let's forget that question, Jamie," Hawk said as an idea formed. "Since you're already here, how would you like to earn some overtime?"

He could kill two birds with one stone, as the saying goes. Get help with transferring the items from the storage office *and* not be alone.

"I'm caught up here; whaddaya have in mind?"

"I assume that means you also made certain that the upstairs was completed?"

"Yeah, of course," she said, snapping her gum. "The only thing left to do in this whole building is that room." Jamie pointed toward the office that Hawk had been using for storage.

"Well, that's what I have in mind. I could really use your help to move all that stuff upstairs and find a place for it all. What do you say?"

"Uh, Hawk, your interior designer asked if you had any personal pieces, and I let her look in there. She's already moved everything except a few boxes of very personal items. And no. I didn't let her touch Ellie's box of dishes," Jamie quickly added.

"Well, then," Hawk hesitated a moment, walked to the storage office door, and turned to face Jamie; "I guess we could get those boxes upstairs and see if we can find a place for what's left."

"Sounds good to me, Boss; but do you think we could send out for pizza first? I'm starved."

CHAPTER FIFTEEN

IT FELT good to wake up in a new bed instead of his office sofa. Hawk was favorably impressed with the superb job the designer, and her crew had done with his new home. She had managed to work his choice of brown, in various shades, throughout his new home. Even Jamie remarked as they worked last night, putting away the contents of the last few boxes.

"I couldn't believe you wanted brown," Jamie had said, "But seeing what that gal did with so many shades, it looks good. She told me it was called tone-on-tone. Weird name, but it still looks great."

There was a sense of permanence and graciousness that filled Hawk's new home. It exuded warmth, along with strength and endurance, which he felt matched his masculinity. Yet there was a touch of elegance that Ellie would have loved. The few pieces of their saved furniture melded comfortably into the overall design. The results conveyed a relaxed atmosphere.

It had taken only a few hours last night to put things away and eat a pizza delivered from Georgios, but it had been enough time for Jamie to convince Hawk to put Ellie's dishes in his kitchen. He remembered her words and how they had jolted him.

"Boss, if you leave these dishes in the box and hidden in the back of a closet, it will be like burying Ellie's memory, too."

When did this girl get so smart and when did she start calling me boss? Hawk wondered.

"I can't bury her again," he had barely whispered. "Go ahead. Wash them and find a place for them." Enough thinking. Time to get downstairs and begin the new work week.

———

JAMIE ARRIVED JUST as Hawk slipped into his office. He figured she would be busy for at least a half-hour and that would give him time to check through the Emerson case and the other files on his desk. His work on the Marlet case was quite time-consuming; having other cases at the same time was mind-boggling. It was time to consider a partner. His thoughts went to Wade, but what would it take to get his friend to move back to New York and work for him?

Building cases and investigating were incredibly grueling, especially if they were homicides, but Wade's passion to provide justice for the victims matched his own. Hawk also recognized the toll this had on the lives of them both. Yet in spite of Ellie's death, Hawk intended to persevere, always, in the darkest of situations, calmly peeling a case apart until the solution was found and the guilty party apprehended.

———

"MORNING, BOSS," Jamie stuck her head in the door. "You ready for me?"

"What do you have, Jamie?"

"A few phone messages," she walked to his desk. "And yeah, a few are from that Marlet woman. Is she ever gonna let you work the case or is she gonna keep trying to tell you how to do it?" Jamie laughed.

"She only wishes," Hawk replied. "Did the morning paper arrive yet?"

"It wasn't here when I came in. I'll go check."

Funny how the small-town daily newspaper had already become a habit, Hawk smiled to himself. Living here was growing on him. Maybe the small-town idea could woo Wade back. Linda might consider coming back… if Wade was here instead of in the city.

Hawk heard Jamie simultaneously slam the front door and let out that blood-curdling scream of hers. Hawk jumped up from his desk and hurried to the reception room. "What is it? Are you all right?"

"It's, it's… it's…" Jamie sat down, slammed the newspaper on her desk and, not able to speak, pointed at the headline. MURDER HITS GROVELAND HILLS.

CHAPTER SIXTEEN

ANNA QUIT HER PACING; her eyes looking around the apartment before they settled on Jill's closed bedroom door. Her throat tightened, and hot fresh tears filled her eyes. Forcing the tears to abate, she walked to the window and edged it open. Her nostrils filled with diesel and gas fumes from cabs and buses, evoking a nostalgic sensory experience. There was a strange blend of aromas from food vendors and the emission of fumes from slow-moving traffic. Anna thought of the many times she and Jill watched as the city began to come alive with early commuters. Honking horns, police whistles, and sirens, all joined together for the symphony of a Manhattan morning.

Anna closed the window and walked away, realizing that looking down on the city had done nothing to resolve her frustration. *Why hasn't Detective Hawkins returned my calls?* She thought.

She shuddered as she passed Jill's closed door. How could she rid herself of the rage, terror, and grief she was feeling?

She wandered into the kitchen and mindlessly poured herself another cup of coffee. Staring at her cell phone, she willed it to ring. *Surely Detective Hawkins would be in his office and received his messages by now,* she thought.

Anna jumped, spilling coffee on her dress when the doorbell rang. Anxiously she opened the door and there stood the paperboy, hand out for payment, and the paper tucked under his arm.

———

IN A CLEAN DRESS and with a fresh cup of coffee, Anna settled on the sofa to page through the paper. A small item on page eight caught her eye. Perhaps it was the answer to why her hired detective seemed to be avoiding her. A murder had occurred in Groveland Hills. Not bothering to read the story, she tossed the paper to the floor and began to pace and think once more.

Pacing… thinking… pacing… thinking. Detective Hawkins would probably jump on that murder, letting her investigation slide to bottom of his caseloads. There had to be something else she could do besides waiting for a phone call. Yet two fearful questions kept niggling in the back of her mind. *What if the man who murdered Jill is out to get me, too? How safe will I be trying to solve the mystery myself? No, better let the professional do that.* Still, she felt she needed to do something to keep Detective Hawkins moving.

———

IT TOOK LONGER than Hawk had wanted to spend to calm Jamie down and convince her she was safe. Hawk had read the account, and the killer was already behind bars. It was a jewelry store robbery gone sour. The jeweler was dead. The robber, just a kid, was in shock, with the gun still in his hand when the police arrived. It was an easy case to close. And that was a good thing. The GHPD wasn't equipped for a full-fledged homicide investigation. Since there hadn't been a murder in the town in over five years, the city council had seen fit to eliminate the one homicide detective they did have. They also didn't see a need to hire additional personnel or purchase more modern equipment, and Hawk doubted that the jewelry store case would be enough to change their minds. Chief Elliot Fields tried to convince the council otherwise, but it appeared that he was fighting a losing battle.

———

JAMIE HAD SETTLED on Hawk's office sofa, while he stood astride at the window, stroking his chin. "Okay, Jamie," he said as he turned around. "It's like this. I can't have a hysterical woman working for me. I know it's not the prettiest of jobs, but it's a good one. I can't promise you that it won't get nasty at times, but it's not as ugly as working in the big city could be. There you would actually see a lot of crime and low life. So, you have a choice to make. Grow up to this job and not let it get to you, or get a different job. I want you to take the rest of the day off and think about it. Give me your answer in the morning."

"I'm... so... sorry," Jamie sniffled.

"Just go home, or someplace. Relax and decide if you can handle all that goes with this job. Put the phone on voice mail, and I'll see you in the morning." Hawk escorted Jamie to her desk and then watched her leave. He heard the old rattle-trap she called a car, start-up; then, locked the door and returned to his office. Plopping down in his chair, elbows atop the desk, he wondered if he himself could handle the job, and, all that went with it.

Hawk felt in a worse state than he had in several days. There had been too many changes in his life in the past two years. Ellie's death was the toughest. He was starting a new phase of life, and he wondered if this new home would really help him move on. Was he even ready to move on? Perhaps going back into law enforcement was the wrong decision. Why all these doubts again? Jamie and her hysterics certainly didn't help. She was a good worker, and he found her trustworthy. She just needed to get the drama out of her work life; then maybe the office would seem more settled. All these thoughts were beginning to smack of self-pity.

"That's it," he said to the room. "Enough of self-doubt and pity." He slammed his fist on the desk, grabbed the Marlet file, and set to work —hopefully without interruption.

————

HAWK SPENT close to three hours poring over emails and instant messages between Jill and Ted when the office phone rang. He ignored it. If it was that Marlet woman, as Jamie had put it, she could leave a message. Marlet needed to realize Hawk had other cases besides hers. The phone quit ringing. Then his old cell phone rang. He ignored that letting it go to voice mail. Bleary-eyed from reading; he stood to stretch and make a cup of tea.

————

BACK AT HIS DESK, his new cell rang. Only Jamie had that number. Perhaps she was ready to give him her decision before morning. Without looking at caller ID, he answered, "Hawk here."

"You're a tough guy to get a hold of. Why didn't you give me this number? I tried the office, voice mail, then the other cell. It rang and rang, then voice mail. I called Jamie to find out what was going on. She gave me this number. She figured you wouldn't mind, since it was me," Wade chuckled.

"Sorry, I was trying to get in some uninterrupted work."

"Why a second cell phone?"

"Marlet. But let's not talk of her. Have you got something for me?"

"Yeah, but I doubt you'll like it. I think we've hit a dead end. Ted has disappeared, at least from the Internet. He closed his FriendsPage account, and we can't find him anywhere on the Internet. We thought we had him narrowed down to north of Sun Point, but there's no Ted Ashby. Hawk, are we even sure he used his real name online?"

"Hmph," Hawk grumbled. "That's a good question. But what else do we have to go on? I just spent the last hour re-reading the chats and emails from him to Jill, and there's nothing there to indicate an address. Nothing seems to piece together. And I see nothing in the transcripts from Miss Evans' friends to indicate anything but suicide. Even her laptop was void of anything incriminating."

"I thought Donavan had decided to reopen the case because it might be a homicide. He must have something if he's thinking murder."

"Yes, he has. But it's because Anna Marlet wasn't fully forthcoming with all she told me. She was fearful it might incriminate her. When Donavan got from her, what she should have told me, he got suspicious or..." Hawk hesitated, "he's out to try to..."

"Donavan always has been jealous of you," Wade interrupted. "You're good. You were the best detective that precinct ever had, and he couldn't handle that. But he's not the one in charge. God is. And you need to turn this *stuff* over to Him. Including Donavan. Don't let the guy get to you. By the way, have you read that Scripture I mentioned?"

"Not yet, Wade; I need more time," Hawk reluctantly answered. "Maybe you can help me," Hawk said, quickly changing the subject back to the case. "Something is kind of screwy about this case. Jill chatted with Ted about a purple teddy bear. She mentioned in her note that the bear was to go to Ted. But the bear is nowhere to be found. I've been wondering if the purple bear might hold a key to solving this case if only we can find it."

———

JAMIE HADN'T BOTHERED to tell Wade that Hawk had given her an ultimatum; she just said she was at lunch. That wasn't a lie. She was having lunch or at least trying to. After sitting in her car at Riverside Park, doing some deep thinking, she was now sitting in a booth at Georgios. She never went home. In fact, she never left town. She really liked Groveland Hills. She had even applied for an apartment at Wood Hill Apartments. And she really did want to keep her job. She couldn't help being a drama queen. Or could she?

"Miss, is there anything wrong with the hamburger?" the waiter asked.

"Uh, no. Sorry. Guess I was daydreaming," Jamie flashed him a smile. "Could I have another root beer?"

"Sure thing," he said. "You're not from around here, are you?"

"No, but I hope to be soon. I do work here, though."

"Oh? Where?" the waiter inquired.

Jamie hesitated in answering, wondering if she could meet Hawk's requirement of a non-hysterical woman. Meanwhile, the waiter took her glass for a refill. By the time he returned with her drink, Jamie had made up her mind. She would give up her drama queen status and grow into the job like Hawk said.

"Here you go. By the way, my name is Preston, Preston Valetti. I hope you'll come back for lunch again soon." He started to walk away.

"My name is Jamie Miller. Nice to meet you." She extended her hand.

"Yes. Me too," Preston said as he turned around and took her hand.

"I'm sorry I didn't answer you. I was thinking of my job. I work for a private detective."

Dropping her hand, Preston stood with a surprised look on his face. "You mean the guy they call the Hawk? Over at Hawk Detective Agency?"

"Yep. That's the one."

"Fantastic! You'll have to tell me all about your job sometime. That has to be a jammer!"

"Jammer?"

"Oh. Some of the kids from the high school come in for lunch, usually on Thursday and Fridays, and use that expression a lot. I must have picked it up from them. Hey! Want me to warm your burger?"

"Na, it's okay. I can eat now. I got my job all settled."

CHAPTER SEVENTEEN

IT WAS a good feeling having things work out so well in the past week. Jamie was glad she had *"womaned"* up to the job. She was moving into her own apartment: no more roommates. Hawk had given her the day off, and Preston and his friend were going to help. After one date, Preston was ready to help Jamie with anything. Her friend and roommate, Rebecca Holland, had planned to help. But, as owner of Becky's Florist in the Bronx, she had a noon deadline to deliver. A knock on the door and Jamie's heart did a flutter. Preston was early, but that was okay. She was anxious to see him again.

"Come on in. It's opened," she hollered.

But what she wasn't ready to see was a man with a stocking over his face. Before Jamie could let out a scream, he had one gloved hand over her mouth and the other around her waist. A second man had his blue tee-shirt pulled up over his nose. Whatever object he had in his hand, she knew he intended to use it.

A vision of nighttime hit Jamie as the blow to her head buckled her knees. She sensed the release of *stocking guy's* hands and tried to call out and roll from his clutches. But the sleazebag that knocked her down was now on his knees pulling, something like duct tape, across her mouth. A sharp kick to her ribs kept her from rolling away and the tape from screaming for help. Then, another kick.

———

WAITING FOR HIS FRIEND, Jerry Malone, to arrive, Preston knocked on Jamie's door for the third time: still no answer.

Something must be wrong, Preston thought. He tried the door, and it opened. Hearing a moan, he ran straight ahead and found Jamie lying on the floor, covered in blood.

"Hey!" a voice called from the doorway.

Jamie moaned again. Preston turned around as his friend approached; he appeared to be frozen in place, as Jerry knelt next to Jamie.

"What happened?" Jerry asked. He looked at Preston, then leaned over Jamie as she moaned. She tried to speak, but it was only a whisper.

———

"JAMIE MILLER?" Hawk asked. He flashed his ID at the ER nurse as she mouthed fifteen and motioned down the hall. As he approached room 15, he saw two men outside the closed drapes. "Which one of you is Preston? What happened?"

"That would be me," Preston replied, "and we really don't know what happened. She was beat up pretty bad. They're going to admit her to the ICU."

Hawk looked from Preston to the other man.

"Oh, this is a friend. Jerry Malone," Preston added by way of an introduction. "He was planning to help me move Jamie."

"Jerry." Hawk nodded, then turned back to Preston. "Did Jamie say anything?"

———

JERRY STOOD in a cloud of fear, a question circling his mind. Had Preston heard what his girlfriend had said? She had spoken in a broken whisper that he himself almost missed. He held his breath as Preston spoke to the detective.

"No, not really. All she did was moan a few times, and then she was out. I didn't wait. I called 911 immediately. It took me a while to find your number. Sorry."

Jerry watched as Hawk nodded, then turned as he saw the ER doctor walking toward the little group.

The fear that had been lurking in Jerry's thoughts disappeared as attention focused on the approaching doctor. His plan was still intact.

———

HAWK ARRIVED at the Bronx Police precinct that was handling Jamie's case. He checked in and was about to sit when he heard his name called. It was Peter Williams, the officer who was heading up the investigation.

"Hey, Pete. Just the man I want to see." They shook hands, and Hawk followed Williams to his office.

"Have a seat, Hawk," Pete invited. "It's been a while."

"Not since I tried to strangle Doogan." Hawk gave a halfhearted chuckle.

"Yes, well, I'm not too sure that Doogan isn't through with you yet."

"He's up for life. What are you saying?" Hawk frowned as he stroked his chin.

"Word's already on the street that a member of his gang, the guy they call Link, did that number on your secretary."

"What? He already got the best of me when he killed my pregnant wife."

Hawk stood with a calmness that belied the churning he felt in the pit of his stomach. "I'll get him," he almost whispered.

"Sit on it, Hawk," Pete said in a gruff voice. "You may be a Private

Eye, but you're also a private citizen when it comes to this case. You don't take the law into your own hands no matter how many years you spent on the force. And... the grapevine has it that Donavan is aware of what happened, and that he's just waiting for you to make another stupid move."

"Well, I can't just sit around and do nothing," Hawk spit out. "Just last week I told Jamie I couldn't promise the job wouldn't get nasty... but not like this. Not Jamie."

"Hawk. Work with me here, okay?" Pete softened. "Work on the QT if you must, and if you do find something, let me know. But for goodness sake, don't do anything that will rile Donavan. I think he's sorry he didn't put you on report that day at Doogan's trial. I'm just saying watch your step. I actually think he'd like to see you dry up and blow away."

CHAPTER EIGHTEEN

THREE DAYS LATER, Hawk watched a wino stagger from parked car to parked car, trying each door as he did so. It wasn't Hawk's job to pull his ID here in the Bronx and stop the guy. Hunts Point wasn't really where he wanted to be. He wouldn't be here now except that one of his old informants told him where Link was hiding. It was a rundown tenement building near the Farmers Market.

Parking at the market, Hawk decided to walk the rest of the way. His case or not, there was no way he'd let this punk get away with hurting Jamie. As he approached the building where Link was supposedly holed up, Hawk noticed that the old tenement appeared vacant, except for the low life of the area. He took a few steps inside, hoping it wouldn't take long for his eyes to adjust to the dark.

"Hold it right there, mister," a voice came from the dark recess of the building. "I got me an itchy finger." The voice came closer, and Hawk could make out the shadow of a hulk of a man. Not as big as Doogan, but one who would certainly be a contender.

"Tank sure had you pegged. Said you'd come looking for me right off. Now we gotcha," the voice cackled.

So, this was Link, Hawk thought. One look at the man and he knew he had to come up with a plan, and quickly. He ducked and started back toward the light of the entrance when two more thugs blocked his way, one of them putting him into a stranglehold. Hawk fought him off and tried for the entrance once more. Again, his way was blocked, and the blow to his jaw knocked him to his knees. He staggered to his feet, hatred, and revenge, giving him a reason to keep moving. As he turned to try a different direction, he came face to face with Link.

Whack!

Hawk, once more, fell to his knees. He struggled to stand but felt himself sinking into a dark bottomless pit. He tried to fight his way back to the light, but it was futile. Hawk finally succumbed to a hopeless tangle of pain and blackness.

———

HAWK REGAINED CONSCIOUSNESS; it was still dark, except for one small window. A tiny ray of daylight fought to shine through to the broken glass on the floor of what appeared to be a parking garage. His head felt as though it was ready to explode with pain. He wondered how long he had been out. Trying to move, he found that Link had him hogtied. The rope was coarse and biting around Hawk's wrist and ankles. The stench from the slime on the cement floor was turning his stomach. He wished they had gagged him; then he wouldn't have to taste the filth. He tried to turn on his side, which only caused the rope to bite more.

Hawk watched a rat scurry across the broken glass a few inches away. A *pop* echoed. The rat blew up, splattering blood and flesh in his face and on his clothes. Moving backward, Hawk heard a deep bellowing laugh come from somewhere in the darkness.

"Target practice," a sluggish voice said. "When Link and the rest of the boys get back from the pickup, we're gonna have us a party. So, stay still, or the next one's yours."

No one would hear, with that silencer. They thought of

everything, realized Hawk. *So, it's just me and the guard. But for how long? Williams warned me, but did I listen? No. So who's going to get me out of this jam?* Hawk asked himself.

"I am," the voice said.

It was loud enough to knock Hawk off his feet if he wasn't already on the ground. Wallowing in slime wasn't what he had planned for the day. He tried to move a few more inches. Another shot, but the bullet hit the wall.

"I told cha to shtay 'till." The voice was even more slurred than before.

His guard was either drinking or snorting. Maybe both. Hawk could only hope the guy would pass out so he could reach the glass to cut himself free.

"Trust me."

This time it was a whisper. Then Hawk knew. But how could he trust again after Ellie? *"God, that's too hard,"* he answered silently.

"Trust me."

He felt the tears well up in his eyes. *"How can I?"* he asked again.

"Trust me."

Hawk's heart felt raw. *Lord, I can't do this. I need Your help to trust again.* He felt anguish course through his body and then... a calmness he hadn't felt since before Ellie died.

Thud!

The guy was down, but was he out? Hawk decided to trust. He snaked his way toward the broken glass before Link, and the rest of the gang could return.

CHAPTER NINETEEN

UNLOCKING THE OFFICE DOOR, Hawk stormed toward the steps leading to his apartment but stopped short when he saw Jamie at her desk. Instead of a ponytail, she had allowed her long hair to hang loose; she was dressed in jeans and a long-sleeved blouse. He was certain she was trying to cover the bruises on her body.

"Jamie! You shouldn't be here. I'm sure work is not what the doctor had in mind when he released you from the hospital yesterday."

"Whoa! Boss. What happened to you? You look like you had a ride in the back of a garbage truck," Jamie said. "I really can't do anything in my apartment," she demurely added, "and it's too boring to sit around. So, I came in. Sitting at the computer is easy, and the Doc is okay with that."

Hawk winced when he saw Jamie's face. The swelling was still prominent; the black eyes she sported in the hospital were now blue. He could see the stitches on her chin and the corner of a bandage under the hair that hung over her left eye.

"Hey! Boss. It's okay," Jamie broke Hawk's stare. "I mean, you did tell me you couldn't promise it wouldn't get nasty."

"Yes, well, uh... I'm going up for a shower. We'll talk when I get back down."

————

TOWEL DRYING HIS HAIR, Hawk punched in William's direct line and put his phone on speaker.

"Officer Williams."

"Pete. Hawk here. I have Link's location."

"Yeah, so do we," Pete replied. "Bronx PD busted a drug ring about a half hour ago, and Link was one of them. Seems they were having a party, but without what they called their guest of honor. The officers found an area with pieces of cut hemp, as though they had had somebody tied up. You wouldn't know anything about that now, would you, Hawk?" Williams asked.

"It sounds like something Doogan would have his boys do," Hawk answered.

"You're evading my question, Hawk."

"Is it actually relevant?" Hawk asked as he slipped into his loafers.

"Is there anything Forensic might find at the scene to point to you?"

"No. I covered my tracks."

"What guarantee do you have that Link won't squeal?"

"How about he's in enough trouble already?"

"Hawk, work with me here. I can't be left in the dark," Williams pleaded.

He relented and told Williams of his encounter with Link.

"Hawk, the Department could have a field day if they connect you with this. "

"You're right. Going there wasn't one of my brightest decisions. But at least you have Doogan's gang, or what's left of it, off the streets."

"Hmm, let's hope so."

"How about keeping me posted on whatever happens."

"Yeah," Williams said, "just like you kept me posted? Instead, you went against procedure. I'll take it from here. And you, Hawk, stay out of it." Williams voice was stern. "I will try to keep you up on any developments. But like I said, stay out of it. If you do hear something, then let me know. Don't take matters into your own hands again."

———

JAMIE HAD WONDERED about coming back to work so soon, but she really couldn't be fixing up her new apartment until she felt stronger. That would take more of an effort than sitting at the computer. It was so nice of Preston and Jerry to get her moved that day in spite of her being in the hospital. When Rebecca was finished with her work, she saw Jamie for a few brief moments at the hospital, then went with the guys to show them where to place everything in the apartment. Jamie was glad she had friends that were there for her when she needed them.

Hawk's apartment door closed, and she saw him carrying a white trash bag down the stairs.

"Hey, Boss. You clean up, real good." She knew she was trying to lighten the mood because she was sure that some heavy talk was on its way. When Hawk set the bag at the bottom of the stairs, Jamie asked, "You want me to put that trash out back for you?"

"No Jamie; it's the clothes I changed. They need to go to the cleaners. But before I do that, we need to talk."

Yep, she knew it. Maybe this time, it would mean the end of her job. She followed Hawk into his office and sat in front of his desk.

"No, Jamie; sit on the sofa. You'll be more comfortable." Hawk paced as Jamie moved to the sofa. Now he did have her concerned

"I'm so sorry about the beating."

"Hey, Boss, it wasn't your fault," Jamie interrupted.

"Oh, but it was. You see the guy who attacked you did so under instruction from Tank Doogan. The guy that killed my Ellie."

Jamie's mouth opened, but all she could say was, "Oh."

"Doogan got word to his gang, and two of them attacked you. The gang had a drug ring going also. The officer working your case is Pete Williams. He and the Bronx PD are handling it. Knowing it wasn't my case, I did something foolish that almost messed up the whole investigation."

Jamie listened as Hawk retold his tale. She couldn't believe he'd put himself in that kind of danger for her. She also wondered if Preston or anybody else knew about his day. When Hawk finished, she asked.

"No one, except Williams. And I really rather that the story wasn't repeated."

Hawk paused long enough so Jamie could assure him she wouldn't say a word.

"Now I know you have every reason to quit, but I really would like you to stay. I still can't make any guarantees, but I doubt there will be a repeat performance like this. Once you get moved, it should be better."

"It's already done. My friends moved me in. They couldn't do anything for me in the hospital, so they figured they could at least move my stuff. And I do want to keep my job." Changing the subject quickly, Jamie asked, "Now can I talk to you about work?" Hawk nodded.

"Although Ted never answered my request on FriendsPage, some other guy requested me as a friend. I accepted, and we began chatting. It sounds like some of the stuff Ted said to Jill and a couple of the other women. Do you think Ted could have opened a new account under a different name?"

"Whoa, girl," Hawk smiled. "First things first. You're almost sounding like a PI. Yes, do keep up the friendship with this new guy online, in case he is Ted, but meanwhile, you need to go home and rest. I'm going back upstairs to do the same."

"Okay, Boss," she said.

The outer door slammed.

"I'll see who it is. I just hope it's not that Marlet woman," Jamie smiled.

Opening Hawk's office door, she let out her bloodcurdling scream as she came face to face with Detective Donavan.

CHAPTER TWENTY

IN A FEW LARGE STRIDES, Hawk was at Jamie's side. He figured she was still skittish with surprise encounters. Donavan pushed his way past them both into the office. Hawk encouraged Jamie to be on her way.

"Jamie, would you mind taking care of the bag of garbage on your way out?" he asked, hoping she would understand.

"Sure, Boss," she answered with a wink, as she left.

Hawk closed the door and watched Donavan as he walked around the room.

"Nice... very nice. Ever thought of taking on a partner?"

"Can't say," he replied, although he had been thinking of that a few days prior. He was hoping to convince Wade to move back to New York as his partner.

"Have a seat," Hawk remarked as he sat down at his desk. When Donavan was seated, Hawk asked, "What can I do for you?"

"We need to talk." Before Hawk could ask about what, Donavan continued, "Actually, I need your help."

"Help?"

Hawk was more than curious. So, Donavan wasn't here about his encounter with Doogan's men. Or was he teasing his way into the subject?

"Yeah. Help. I have another charge lodged against me, causing Internal Affairs to investigate."

Hawk felt a laugh trying to bubble its way out. Instead, he coughed and leaned back in his chair, stroking his chin.

"Go on," he said

"Sargent Teresa Belton has brought some trumped-up charge against me, sexual harassment and all. That lady doesn't even know what harassment is." Donavan sounded peeved. "Seems there are a couple of other female officers with complaints too, as well as," Donavan paused, "your client, Marlet. I'm on suspension until further notice."

Hawk was really beginning to see the humor of his nemesis' situation. He remembered how upset Anna Marlet had been because she believed Donavan had reopened the case only to pin the murder charge on her.

"Isn't this the third time this has happened?" Hawk asked.

"Third time. Big deal. These broads shouldn't be in law enforcement anyway."

Hawk didn't remark about women on the force. After all, didn't he himself think they should be protected, not out there doing the protection? But of their capability, he had no doubt. Even Jamie was showing her strong side. God knew what He was doing, and His promise to protect was for all, men and women. So why wasn't He there for Ellie?

Hawk's fist involuntarily came down on the desk, causing him to blink back his thoughts.

"And just what do you think I can do?" Hawk asked before Donavan had a chance to remark about his fist punching his own desk.

"For starters? Get your client off my back; get her to drop her charges. Then come to the hearing as a witness in my defense." Before

Hawk could answer, Donavan continued, "After the protection, I gave you back at Doogan's trial, you owe me, Hawk."

Hawk did indeed remember that it was Donavan who lessened the chances of charges being brought against him by not putting him on report. But he also remembered it was Donavan who had him cuffed and removed to Bellevue's psych ward. Donavan was out to get him even then, but without a blot on the department. Donavan gave Hawk the choice to retire from the NYPD, or be put on report. Hawk leaned forward, arms on his desk.

"Tell you what Donavan. First, I'll pray about this situation; then I'll talk to my client."

"When did you start praying again?" Donavan asked with a smirk.

Yes, thought Hawk, *when* did *I start praying again?*

"That's something I've been remiss in doing: it's time to get back to God." Although he said it, he wasn't sure if he meant it.

"Okay, you do that, Hawk. But don't forget—you owe me one."

"I'll let you know. When's the hearing?"

"Monday morning at ten, and I expect to see you there," Donavan sternly remarked. "I have to get going," he said abruptly. "My lawyer managed to fit me in at dinner, but only if I buy." Donavan stood to leave. Hawk stood also and watched Donavan walk out.

———

JAMIE FELT her lunch was perfect since Preston was able to take his break at the same time. Monday wasn't busy in Georgios, so it gave the couple some alone time. Sitting in a back booth, Preston said he was still concerned about the attack on her earlier in the week. "Has Hawk found anything out yet?" he asked.

"Well, kinda, but I really can't talk about what's going on."

"Oh, come on, Jamie, it's me. You can tell me anything. I'll keep it quiet. After all, I'm a lawyer, or would be if the right law firm would hire me."

Jamie longed to be able to talk to him about her job, but confidentiality was a trust she would not break. Not only that, she sure didn't want to take a chance on losing what she now considered a great job.

"Sorry, Preston, I just can't. I tell you what; why don't you come by the office, meet Hawk, then ask him yourself."

"You're no fun when you don't let me in on what's happening," laughed Preston as he got up to refill their root beers.

Jamie thought about how much time she and Preston had spent together since they met. It was as though she was in a dream world. Preston was the most handsome guy she'd ever dated. His dusty black hair had a hint of curls and was cut just above his collar. Jamie's heart fluttered a little when Preston looked at her with his warm, chocolate brown eyes. He also had a sparkling smile that sat above a gorgeous square jaw. Oh, he was good looking all right, she thought.

Jamie looked to see where Preston was with their root beers. That's when she noticed him in deep conversation with a guy; she'd seen here a couple of times before. "Hmm," she murmured. Maybe she should have Hawk check Preston out before she allowed herself to get too serious about him. Golly, here she was getting suspicious of her new boyfriend. *Job hazard?* She wondered.

———

HAWK LEFT his office door opened so he would hear Jamie as soon as she returned from lunch. Since she had bought a different used car and wasn't slamming the front door anymore, it wasn't always easy to tell when she arrived at her desk. She seemed to be growing into the job just as he'd requested. Yes, Jamie was still bright and bubbly, but she was also taking on an air of professionalism. She'd even quit gum chewing on the job.

"Hey, Boss." Jamie still managed to sneak in. "I saw your door open; is everything okay?"

"Yes, fine. I'm thinking of leaving it open during working hours unless I have a client. After you hang up your coat, come on in. There's some business we need to take care of."

Hawk made a cup of tea and saw that Jamie was sitting on the sofa when he returned. Her face was looking better. The swelling was down, and the bruises were all but gone. The bandage had been removed above her left eye, but the stitches on her chin were still there. She still wore her hair down and continued to wear long sleeves. Although Jamie seemed to be taking it all in stride, Hawk was having a rough time accepting the fact that Link could have killed her.

"Let me begin with a fact," he said as he sat down. "You have a good head on your shoulders, Jamie. And I can see why Wade thought of you to work for me. You are proving yourself trustworthy, and I'd like to give you more responsibility. But I will also need to caution you from time to time."

"Caution? About what, Boss? Oops, maybe you'd rather I didn't call you that?"

"No, it's okay."

"First thing," Hawk continued, "thanks for taking out my *garbage* Friday." They both laughed. "Fortunately, or not, Donavan wasn't here about the Hunt's Point incident. In fact, I'm not sure he knew of my involvement."

"So, what did he want?"

"My help."

"Wow." Jamie seemed very surprised. But then Hawk remembered how surprised he was. He related to Jamie his meeting with Donavan.

"So, are you going to help?"

"I called Miss Marlet and left a voice mail. Then I called the modeling agency. She's been on a two-week model shoot out of town. Guess that's why she hasn't been barging into the office. She's due back Sunday evening."

"So ya can't ask her to drop the charges," Jamie was smiling.

"No. I can't, and I don't think it would look good for our agency if I were to show up for the hearing. There's no subpoena, and this is his third time for the same charge."

"Three strikes and you're out," Jamie laughed.

"Enough of Donavan. Back to caution. What do you really know about this Preston Valetti?"

"Yeah, I was thinking about that at lunch," Jamie told Hawk how Preston had questioned her about her job. She included her concerns about the guy Preston had been talking to. "I was getting suspicious."

"It's smart that you are," Hawk said. "To be honest, we really don't know who Ted is. He might be here in New York, even though he said Arizona. He could be Preston. Want me to run a check on him?"

"Wow! Boss, I was thinking the same thing. But I know how busy you are."

"I want to know too, Jamie; besides I would send it Williams' way with the possibility it could be connected with the attack and the fact that Preston might even be Ted."

"Maybe ya better, Boss. He seems real nice, and he's a hottie, but so was Ted Bundy."

"Now I need your take on Marlet's interview, the one you transcribed."

"My take? Uh, Boss, you're the PI."

"Don't be surprised, Jamie. Sometimes a woman's point of view is helpful. Ellie used to give me feedback when I could share a case with her, and she didn't work for me. You do."

CHAPTER TWENTY-ONE

"DETECTIVE HAWKINS IS VERY BUSY, and you don't have an appointment." Jamie insisted.

"It's okay, Jamie," Hawk said from his office doorway, "just hold any calls while I'm in conference with Detective Donavan."

"Guess you didn't hear. I'm no longer on the force. No need to call me Detective anymore." Donavan sounded angry and dejected when he took a chair in front of Hawk's desk.

"And where were you?"

Hawk ignored the question as he noticed Donavan's arms at his sides, hands balled into fists and the flinching of his jaw. News had traveled fast to Hawk's ears. Word was that it took Internal Affairs only two days to reach a guilty verdict on his nemesis. Yet he didn't get the euphoric feeling he was hoping for. It was too bad. Donavan had good instincts; he belonged in homicide, or, at least, in some capacity of law enforcement. Now he wouldn't even have that. He'd lost his job. Yet, as sad as all that might be, at least he wouldn't be breathing down Hawk's neck and trying to accuse Anna Marlet of killing her best friend. Even that case was re-closed with the verdict of suicide standing. But he was doubtful that that would stop Miss Marlet, and he was sure he would be hearing from her today.

"Yes, I heard, but it doesn't change the fact that you are a detective, and as far as..."

"Glad to hear you say that, Hawk," Donavan interrupted. "I still think you need a partner and I'd be just the guy for it. Remember, you owe me. You didn't show up at the hearing, so the least you can do is give me the job."

"Sorry, Donavan," Hawk began, "this is not the time for me to have a partner. Next, I don't owe you. If you think what I did to Tank Doogan was something to be charged for, then you should have done it at that time, and not try to blackmail me now."

Donavan stood and tried to interrupt, but Hawk, not liking his threatening tone, sat him back down.

"Let me finish. My credibility would be out the window with the NYPD, and my client list would most likely be non-existent. I can't do it. Why not contact that security company upstate that wanted to hire you a few years back?" Hawk ventured to suggest.

"I could still report you and..."

"No," Hawk interrupted, "leave it. It's over. The department would only see it as an act of revenge by trying to pull someone else down with you. Besides, I've given you enough of my time. As Jamie told you, I *am* very busy." Hawk stood as a way of dismissing Donavan.

"Yes, but not with the Marlet case," he smirked as he stood. "That's been closed again, and it's still suicide."

Hawk didn't answer as he watched Donavan stomp out of his office. Like a little boy who didn't get the cookie he wanted, Donavan slammed the outer door behind him.

"Wow! what was that all about?" Jamie asked as she entered Hawk's office.

"He can't get what he wants from me, *and* he's not happy because he can't do anything about it," Hawk laughed. "I really shouldn't be laughing at his expense, but his visit has set me free."

"So, does that mean we don't have the Marlet case anymore?"

"No. In fact, I think she'll be even more determined. I expect we'll hear from her soon."

CHAPTER TWENTY-TWO

GAZING at the small white clapboard church with its soaring steeple, Hawk still wasn't sure if he was ready to attend. Yet he knew God was dealing with him ever since his encounter with Link and the rest of Doogan's old gang.

Approaching the red double doors, Hawk noticed the sign above. *Groveland Hills Community Church established 1801.* Stepping inside, the warmth felt good after the blustery wind. The uncertainty of attending made him late, leaving him no choice but to sit in a pew near the front.

With praise and worship music over, the pastor began his sermon. Hawk tried to listen, but his thoughts began to drift back to his meeting with Anna Marlet on Wednesday. He was right; she was more determined than ever to prove her case. Thankfully she seemed calmer, probably because Donavan was out of the equation. She was also a little more forthcoming about her and Jill Evans' friendship.

Although they had their disagreements, they were still best of friends—more like sisters, ever since childhood. They both came from money but had had dreams of becoming models. And they both accomplished their dreams. They also moved to the city and became roommates, working for the same modeling agency.

Hawk knew the feeling of following your dreams. Wasn't he from the Hamptons also? Didn't he have enough funds so he could live comfortably without having to be a detective? Yet this had always been his dream.

Marlet had gone on to tell Hawk, "My breakdown was because of stress in another area of my life. I just took it out on Jill. I, too, had a man in my life," Anna continued, "and it didn't work out. I took it hard, very hard."

Hawk could understand about a lost relationship and just how hard it was. "What about the night she died?" he had remembered to ask Marlet.

"Jill seemed obsessed with Ted, but I think she had begun to realize he was playing her, so we decided, or maybe it was at my suggestion that we have a breakup party, just the two of us. We had some red wine and dark chocolate truffles. Donavan tried to say I cut open the chocolate balls and inserted the liquid from her sleeping pills so she would OD."

"...and unforgiveness will eat at you."

The word from the pastor brought Hawk out of his thoughts. Unforgiveness.

"It's not an option," the pastor continued. "Jesus commands us to forgive others. In Mark 11:25, we read: 'When you stand praying, if you hold anything against anyone, forgive him, so that your Father in heaven may forgive you your sins.' And Ephesians 4:31-32 tells us to put away bitterness, anger, and to forgive as God forgives us. Is it easy?"

Hawk had the answer for that one. Not only was it not easy, it was impossible! *There is no way I can forgive, Lord; not now, not ever. Don't ask it of me*; he almost blurted aloud. Hawk grabbed his coat and all but ran out of the church. He knew he couldn't handle another minute of the pastor's sermon.

By the time he got to his car, the cry of his heart was so loud he was sure it could be heard back in the church. Getting in, he slammed his fist against the steering wheel and screamed out loud, "God, don't do this to me. Just give me Ellie back!"

———

HAWK STOOD IN HIS GARDEN, looking north, up the Hudson. Sing-Sing Prison sat only a short seventeen miles away, but it was a trip he wasn't planning to take, ever. This morning was the first time he had been back in church since Ellie was killed, and it had to be a sermon on forgiveness.

"No, it isn't going to happen," Hawk said to the wind, as though it would carry his words to Tank Doogan's cell. Just as soon as the words were out of his mouth, a Scripture crawled into his thoughts. *Forgive them Father, for they know not what they do.*

"The creep doesn't deserve forgiveness; he deserves the chair," Hawk argued out loud with his thoughts. But somewhere in the back of his mind, he was afraid he would lose this argument. He couldn't deal with this now, so he walked the garden path back to his office and a cup of tea.

———

BUSY. *That's what I need to be—busy*, thought Hawk. He remembered Jamie didn't attend church. Maybe she'd like some more overtime. He finished his tea and rang Jamie.

"Okay, ya got my number, leave yours. I'll call ya later," her voice mail said.

"Call me on my cell when you can. Not urgent," Hawk recorded and snapped his cell closed. Before he could lay the phone down, it rang. *That was fast*, he thought. Without looking at caller ID, he answered.

"Hawk here."

"What's wrong with Alistair or Mr. Hawkins?" the caller said.

It was a voice Hawk well recognized, one he had not heard since Ellie's funeral.

"Is finding fault with me all you can do, Dad?"

"I didn't call to argue, boy," his Dad said.

"Then what did you call for? You and Mom haven't bothered since Ellie's funeral."

"Now, boy, you can just simmer down."

"And you can quit calling me boy. I haven't been a boy in years. I'm a man. Maybe not the one you expected me to be, but still a man." Hawk was pacing, stroking his chin, and wondering how much worse this day could get.

"No, you didn't turn out the way I wanted, but there's not much I can do about that now. I'm not calling you that foolish nickname you insist on using," his father continued, "you have a good strong first name; you should use it."

"Then why don't you, instead of calling me, boy?" Hawk wasn't in the mood for an argument with his father, so he changed his tone. "Dad, I'm tired. What do you want?"

"Okay, boy... er... Alistair. What are you thinking of, putting Ellie's summer home up for sale?"

Great, thought Hawk, *how do I explain my reasons to a man who never understood my career choice?*

"It's time."

"What do you mean it's time?"

"Dad, if that's all you called about..."

"I would think," his father interrupted, "you would want to keep Ellie's memory alive. Plus move back to the Island instead of moving further away."

Evidently not far enough, Hawk thought. "The memories are painful, and I can't do my job from there, Dad."

"Yes, that is another thing, Alistair. Why in the world would you open a detective agency after what happened to Ellie?"

"Dad, it's what I do."

"You don't have to. You can come home and join the firm."

"No! I told you a long time ago this is what I want to do with my life. Ellie didn't have a problem with it, so why do you?"

"Because it's that kind of work that killed your wife and my granddaughter."

"Are you getting emotional on me, Dad?" As incredulous as is might be, Hawk had to ask.

"Of course not, boy! Guess I'll just have to buy the place myself."

"No... Dad?" But it was too late. Hawk's father had hung up.

———

MAYBE IF HAWK got to the realtor before his father did, he could prevent what he saw as a disaster. After finding the realtor's card, he picked up his cell when it rang in his hand

"Hawk here."

"Mr. Hawkins, Dale Roberts calling. I hate to bother you on a Sunday, but we got a cash offer on the Montauk place."

No, Dad, no, thought Hawk. Evidently, having to look for the realtor's business card was just enough time for his father to make his offer. And it would be just like him to offer cash, something Dale Roberts would advise not passing up.

"Mr. Hawkins, are you there?"

"Sorry. I guess the cash offer took me by surprise."

"Well, it did me, too."

"Who made the offer?" Hawk braced for the worst, trying to formulate a good reason to refuse. He knew his father would meet the asking price and probably throw in the closing cost just to clinch the deal.

"A family from Buffalo, a Mr. and Mrs. Townsend, and their children. They are in my office as we speak. After seeing the place, they wanted me to call you right away."

Not realizing he was holding his breath, Hawk exhaled, feeling more than relieved.

"So, what do we do next?"

Dale Roberts told Hawk what Mr. and Mrs. Townsend offered, and the fact that they would like to spend Christmas there, instead of in Buffalo. The offer was less than the asking price, but doable. And it would keep it out of his father's clutches.

"I accept. How soon can we close?"

"We need you to sign the offer to accept. Then we set up a closing date. What day can you make it out here?"

Hawk was anxious to get this over with so he asked if an electronic signature would suffice. It would. One down: one to go. Hawk could only hope his father didn't find out that he also had the Manhattan condo up for sale.

———

SUPPER WAS LESS THAN INTERESTING. Some left-over meatloaf, salad, and a glass of milk. Jamie had returned Hawk's call while he was in his office, awaiting his realtor's email, his cell upstairs. Her message said she and Rebecca were going to a show, and she'd see him in the morning since it wasn't urgent. *So much for staying busy and someone to keep me company*, thought Hawk.

———

MONDAY MORNING and Jamie was surprised that Hawk was an hour late coming down to work. He looked as though he hadn't had much sleep. Passing her desk, without even saying good morning, he went straight to his office and closed the door. Strange, Jamie thought. She wasn't sure what was going on with him, but she had business that needed tending. Gathering up phone messages, emails, and a courier delivered envelope, she marched into Hawk's office.

"Okay, Boss, I got a lot for ya this morning." Jamie plopped down across from Hawk. She decided to ignore how tired he looked and refrained from making any remarks or asking questions.

"These calls aren't in a hurry," she said, as she handed him the messages. "But these few may need attention right away." She handed those to Hawk also but kept one to herself.

"And what is that one, Jamie?"

"A strange one. It was on voice mail. Came in 5:30 Friday evening. Some guy saying the message was for Alistair Hawkins the third and that he was Alistair Hawkins the second. "

"It was my Dad. He called me back. The matter was personal. All taken care of." Hawk let out a sigh. "This one from Dale Roberts—when did it come in?"

"It had to be about fifteen minutes before you came down. He wanted an appointment. I told him that I could set one, but he insisted on setting it with you personally. He wouldn't say what it was about."

"He's my realtor on the Island; it's about the closing on some property I have for sale out there. Also, personal, so I'll handle that. Anything else?"

"Yeah, this." Jamie handed over the sealed envelope. "The report on Preston, or at least I think that's what it is."

"I know you're anxious, Jamie, and I'll get to it as soon as possible and then let you know."

"One more thing, Boss. Greg Oliver, the guy we think may be Ted —we've been chatting. Of course, he thinks I'm an exotic dancer in Vegas. He says he'll be in Vegas on business and wants to meet."

"Have you answered him yet?"

"No, I just got the message this morning. He left it last night."

"Maybe we need to get a meeting set up and see if it is Ted. I'll call Wade to get his female undercover to take it from here. You will need to give Wade all the info and the password so she can use the site."

"That's okay by me. But won't it be dangerous?"

"That's the reason for an undercover cop on the job, and not you."

The phone rang; Hawk told Jamie to answer it at his desk.

"Hawk Detective Agency. How may I help you?"

Hawk watched Jamie's face turn white as she listened to the person calling. This was the closest he had seen her to hysterics since

Donavan surprised her. He only hoped she didn't start screaming again.

"Calm down. He's here; just a minute." With that, she handed the phone to Hawk as she mouthed *Marlet.* Hawk was impressed; Jamie was getting better at staying calm.

"Miss Marlet, how..."

"He's called again, asking for the purple teddy bear," Anna interrupted. "He doesn't believe the police still have it. He thinks I do. He has threatened to come here and take it by force. What should I do? I can't find the bear anywhere." She was screaming hysterically.

"What I don't understand is why he's so interested in the bear?"

Anna quieted down but was slow to answer. "I think because it belonged to Jill...plus, she called him Teddy Bear. I'm sure you read the email where she said she slept with the bear and would dream of him. Anyway, as crazy as it may seem, I think Ted really loved Jill. Yet in some weird way wanted her dead."

"You scare me, Miss Marlet; you're beginning to make sense," Hawk gave out a halfhearted chuckle.

CHAPTER TWENTY-THREE

TWO HOURS on the phone with Hawk, and Wade was torn between working the case or getting to New York. He heard the anguish in his friend's voice, especially when he spoke about attending church. Wade could use seeing Dean and Sara for Thanksgiving as an excuse, and maybe—just maybe—he could see Linda. Wade was certain God wouldn't let him down on that. He was also certain that it was time to bring the sheriff in on this case, and get Parker on it officially.

———

AFTER A BUSY DAY, Hawk decided to leave at four and perhaps pick up a bite to eat at Georgios. As he started upstairs, the phone rang, and he mouthed to Jamie that he wasn't in. He noticed she shrugged her shoulders and put the call on hold.

"It's Wade. I thought you'd want to take his call," she said.

"I'll get it in my office. Thanks."

———

"HAWK, it's official. The Sheriff's Department is now involved. They have had two women, locally, lodge a complaint about Ted Ashby for the same reasons. He sent a few porn pictures to one woman's page. We have Sargent Parker set up to meet him in Vegas Wednesday night. Tell Jamie, thanks for doing her part."

"I will. She was more than happy to give up the FriendsPage site."

"It may be another dead end, but it's the first real lead we've had here in a while. One we intend to follow, as far as it goes."

"We may have another lead here, also," Hawk spoke about Marlet's latest phone call from Ted. "I'm having a trace run on her cell and, hopefully, we'll pinpoint him."

"Okay, sounds good. Now, how about putting me up a week or two? I'm coming to see the kids for Thanksgiving and—hopefully —Linda."

The words were no sooner out of Wade's mouth that Hawk felt a stab of pain. He knew he would still have a tough time during another Thanksgiving and Christmas without Ellie.

"Sorry, Hawk. I..."

"It's okay. I'm just glad you'll be here. Not only will I put you up, I'll put you to work."

————

WADE SAT, the phone still in his hand, thinking about Hawk's last words. Put me to work? He mulled that idea over. He had given thought to returning to New York; after all, that's where family and friends were. What he would do for work was the question. Had always been the question. Having always been in law enforcement, he really didn't know anything else. If he went back to the NYPD, there would be no chance for him and Linda at all. He wondered what work Hawk had in mind.

Wade dropped the phone receiver to its base and headed out the door. The sun was bright, and the temperature warm. No jacket needed here, except at night. It was beautiful in Arizona, and he could have lived here for the rest of his life if Linda had stayed. Yet he missed the seasons. He enjoyed the winter snow—when he didn't have to work in it.

Driving to his office, Wade opened the windows of the rented SUV. Troy Classics had his '57 Chevy Bel Air repaired and painted, and he planned to pick it up after work, anxious to have his *baby* back.

It had been his father's car, bought new. His dad always kept it garaged, in great shape, and shiny. As a kid, Wade had enjoyed riding shotgun when it was just the two of them going for a ride through Central Park. He really loved that old car. But when he was ten, his dad got a better job and bought a new car. He garaged the Bel Air at Grammy's house upstate. When Grammy passed away, Wade was a senior in high school, and the house went to his Dad and Mom. On the day Wade graduated, his dad surprised him with the Bel Air as a graduation present.

———

FINDING his parking space open for a change, Wade pulled in and cut the engine. He sat with his hands on the steering wheel, staring at the sign in front of him. Reserved. Detective Wade Owens. It didn't mean anything, though. People parked there if they wanted, and no one enforced the reserved sign.

He got out and looked around the parking lot. No, he really wouldn't miss it here. Was it time to put the house up for sale? With only a year's equity, he wasn't sure. He hated the thought of taking a possible loss.

———

NO SOONER HAD Wade sat at his desk than Sargent Gloria Parker walked in.

"It's all set. I have my reservation at the Las Vegas Hilton; I'm to meet Greg, alias Ted, at the bar at eight, Wednesday night. I leave in the morning."

"Did they get a GPA tracker on your car?"

"No, I don't want it. I can always be tracked through my cell, if necessary."

"I wish you'd reconsider working with Vegas PD and wear a wire."

"Not a good idea. This guy just might get wandering hands and find it. Too chancy. I have a recorder in my purse. It will pick up enough, and I'm taking my laptop."

"The whole thing is risky, especially since the picture Jamie used doesn't exactly look like you."

"I've got a good line for that. In fact, I already told him that the pic is ages ago and that I look even better."

"I'm still not sure I agree with the setup. I'd rather see a uniform go in, arrest him, and then question him."

"You know we can't do that. Without a good cause, we couldn't even get the Vegas police to help. And I want to do this. You know my ambition to become a detective; this may help me get that advancement. See you next week, and I'll be calling in on Thursday."

"Yes, but..."

"Quit worrying, Wade," Gloria said as she left his office.

———

HAWK WAS tired of going over the Evans' suicide file and was glad for the diversion his other cases gave him, especially the background check on Preston Valetti.

"Jamie," Hawk called through the open door.

"Yeah, Boss?" she said as she came to the door.

"I can imagine you've been a little anxious, waiting for me to get to Preston's background check."

Jamie inched her way toward Hawk's desk.

"Yeah, I have." Hawk could hear the concern in her voice.

"It's good, Jamie, so sit down and breathe."

Jamie didn't just sit; she plopped into the chair, letting out an audible breath as she did.

"It's all good. He was born in Bayberry, a suburb of Syracuse, and moved to NYC when he was two. After high school, he attended Syracuse University College of Law. He was a member of the Criminal Justice Society and the Christian Legal Fellowship, two of the many student organizations. Preston also managed to get into the International Law program and did a summer internship abroad in London. He majored in Criminal Law and Procedure. And passed the New York State Bar, first time. Quite impressive. The rest you can read for yourself. At least he's on the right side of the law."

"Then what's with him talking so often to this guy who looks like a bum? They seemed like buddies, but so secretive."

"Did he mention to you why he's working at Georgios and not with a law firm?"

"Yeah. Seems he had a lot of offers through the school, but none of them were where he wanted to be."

"That's curious," Hawk said as he stroked his chin. "Tell you what. Closely observe the two of them the next time you see them in conversation. Then ask Preston about the guy. Who he is? Then let..."

The office phone interrupted Hawk in mid-sentence.

Jamie reached over and answered, "Hawk Detective Agency. How may I help you?" Hawk waited.

"Let me see if he has a time slot for then. Hold on." Jamie put the call on hold. "It's Anna Marlet; she wants to meet with you Thursday morning."

Hawk looked at his planner. "Guess I need to see her sooner or later. Tell her eleven."

"Miss Marlet? He has an eleven that morning, would... okay, you're down for eleven on Thursday the eighteenth." Turning back to Hawk, Jamie smiled. "I'm taking an early lunch Thursday."

———

ANNA WAS NERVOUSLY BOUNCING her legs, while her fingers echoed *tip-tap* on the purse in her lap. She was trying to listen to what Hawk was saying, but all she could think of was that maybe hiring the Hawk had been a waste of money. He didn't seem to be any closer to a solution than when he started two months before. And from the sound of things, he might give up and rule suicide, too.

"We really have to wait and see what Sargent Parker finds out after her meeting with this guy who calls himself Greg. We'll find out if he really is Ted," Hawk was saying.

She heard him, but it wasn't registering. Nothing was. Anna was growing weary of it all. She couldn't understand why it was taking so long to find Ted, and she told Hawk so.

"Miss Marlet," Hawk began when there was a tap on the door. Jamie stuck her head in to say there was a call from Detective Owens, and she was leaving for lunch.

"This may be the break we've been waiting for," Hawk said as he answered the phone. "Hey Wade, what have you... oh?"

Again, Anna had to wait. She hated waiting. She watched as Hawk turned his chair slightly away from her direct vision. He held the phone in one hand while stroking his chin with the other. *Why doesn't he just grow a beard and get it over with,* she thought. Hawk wasn't saying anything, so she hoped that the other detective was saying that they found Ted.

"Yes, yes," Hawk turned back toward the center of his desk. "Yes, I understand. No, you need to be there, but let me know the minute... yes, okay."

Anna watched as Hawk ended the call and leaned forward at his desk.

"Well?" she asked.

"Another wrinkle. Sargent Parker is missing."

———

GOING to Georgios on Thursday when the high school students were there wasn't the way Jamie wanted to lunch, especially having to listen to *"jammer"* a dozen times or more, but she wanted to see if the bum would be here today. The place was crowded, and she couldn't get a table or a booth in Preston's station. Her waitress wore way too much makeup; trying to look younger, Jamie supposed. The woman's hair was more yellow than blonde, a poor coloring job. Her nametag said Maxine, and she was snapping gum when she took Jamie's order. In the center of the room, Preston was balancing a tray above his head as he maneuvered around students in his way. Then Jamie saw the bum, sitting at the counter, hunched over what could be a cup of coffee. She wondered if she'd have a chance to talk to Preston this lunch. Maybe she could eat real slow.

———

HAWK WASN'T EXACTLY happy with the way Anna Marlet took the news that the undercover cop was missing; he was even more concerned how Jamie would take it. Would she turn hysterical on him again? He didn't care for the idea of involving females in this kind of work. But not like Donavan, who didn't believe women couldn't handle law enforcement work. It was the danger; he knew what could happen. Ellie was killed because she was married to a law enforcement officer. Jamie was beaten because she worked for one. All Hawk could do was pray that Gloria Parker would be found soon.

———

JAMIE BOUNCED in and plopped herself on Hawk's office sofa.

"I found out who the guy is. It wasn't easy getting Preston alone. I didn't even get him for my waiter. I had some ditzy chick, trying to look as young as the teens who come in on Thursday and Friday. Egad, her hair was..."

"Get to the point, Jamie. The man. Who is he?"

"Oh. Yeah. He's Preston's father. Long story. Preston says he'll tell me another time."

"His name, Jamie?"

"Oh, right. I'm just so excited that he isn't some creepy criminal."

"Jamie!"

"His name, yeah, sorry, it's Nick. Nick Valetti."

"Hmm, that name sounds familiar. I think I'll have Williams run a background check on the dad, too."

As she rose to go to her desk, Hawk asked Jamie to wait. "Please sit. I have some disturbing news, and we need your help." Jamie sat on the chair that Anna had so recently vacated.

"What news? And why do you need my help?"

"Gloria Parker is missing. She didn't report in as scheduled. When Wade contacted the hotel, he found out that she never checked in. She doesn't answer her cell. But he doesn't want to leave a message in case she and the guy are still together. Wade put out an APB for her car, and they're tracing Parker through her cell phone."

"Oh, my gosh. Oh, my gosh. And she took my fake ID on FriendsPage. What can I do?"

"We need you to get on that site and see if there has been any activity between her and the guy named Greg or, possibly, a coded message from her."

"I'll do it now and let ya know as soon as I bring it up."

––––––––

WHILE JAMIE GOT busy on the internet, Hawk made a call to Williams. "I need another background check. It's the father of the Valetti kid. His name is Nick Valetti. Think you could get it by tomorrow?"

Hawk knew he was being pushy, but the way things had been going he figured it would be a nice change for something to happen so quickly.

"Better than that, I can give it to you now. Nick was one of our own," said Williams. "I don't know that you ever met him. But surely you have heard of him. He and his partner were on an armed robbery call. His partner, Alec Romero, was taken down. Nick got shot up pretty bad, but he lived. Walks with a limp now. He was in rehab almost a year, along with counseling. He has a clean background and a good record with the NYPD. The incident caused him to end his career with the department, though. Nick didn't want to be a desk jockey. I heard he was doing yard work, maintenance, gopher type jobs for some rich family in Syracuse. He was from there, so I guess he didn't mind going back. I heard, too, he's getting decent pay with room and board. Do you need anything on paper sent over?"

"No. That's all the info I need, and I do recall that incident."

"Is he in any trouble?"

"No. His son's girlfriend is my receptionist, and she kept seeing them huddled together. She got a little suspicious. Guess this job is growing on her," Hawk chuckled.

Williams laughed. "I was going to call you later, but now will do. We ran that trace on the number Marlet's cell phone company gave you. It came from BJ's in Sun Point, Arizona. It's a bar on North Rattle Snake Road."

"Okay, got it. Thanks. I'll get that info to Wade and let him follow it up. But I have a feeling it's going to be like the first call Miss Marlet received. Thanks again."

———

HEY, Boss! You finally off the phone? I have FriendsPage up," Jamie hollered from her desk.

"I think," said Hawk, as he walked to her desk, "it's time for us to get an intercom. Let me see what you have."

"It's nothing really. She sent Greg a message on Tuesday night saying she was looking forward to meeting him the next night. But nothing else, and he didn't answer."

CHAPTER TWENTY-FOUR

HAWK HAD a cup of tea and was relaxed in his recliner, about to watch the late news when his phone rang. He checked caller ID. Wade.

"Hey, pal. At this hour, and on a Saturday, it's got to be important."

"Parker is dead. They found her body yesterday, twenty miles north of Sun Point."

"I don't get it. Wasn't the meeting set up for Vegas?" he asked Wade.

"That's what we're investigating. The manager at a little wayside motel is an amateur ham radio operator. He heard the APB on his police scanner and remembered that a woman of her description had checked in Tuesday night. He looked up her registration card. Her license tag number matched."

Hawk had emailed Wade the information about Ted's call to Anna Marlet only two nights before and now this. Were the two incidents connected? Was the investigation getting too close for Ted's comfort? Or, perhaps it wasn't Ted meeting Gloria, but actually, the guy calling himself Greg.

"What's been found out so far? Why was she there and not in Las Vegas?" Hawk asked.

"We still don't have the answer to that. Her cell phone is missing, along with her recorder, ID, and gun. After the attempted sting, whoever did this, is probably on to us," Wade's voice sounded dull.

"How was the murder, uh… how did Ted do it, Wade? Assuming it was Ted."

"That's another question. Was it, Ted? Or was it really this guy calling himself Greg? The last time she was seen was when she checked in, and no one saw her with anyone. Yet sometime between check-in and finding her body, she evidently got in her car, either alone, with someone, or she may have picked someone up along the way. Tire tracks prove the car was driven to the spot where her body was found." There was a pause, and it seemed Wade was trying to compose himself.

"As to how she was killed. We believe there was a struggle. I don't know what was she trying to prove. How could she imagine she'd have any power over the guy? Evidently, she was knocked unconscious, possibly with the butt of her own gun. She was..." Wade paused. "Well, let's just say it wasn't a pretty sight when I identified the body."

"Why you?" Hawk asked in amazement.

"Had to, Hawk. She didn't have family close; plus, I felt responsible. Parker wouldn't take my suggestions for a wire or a GPS tracker. I should have insisted, or called the deal off."

"Hey, pal, don't do that guilt trip on yourself. Take it from one who knows. It doesn't help, and it sometimes makes it worse. Besides, if anyone is to blame, it would be me. I'm the one who asked for your help." Hawk hesitated, then asked, "Was she raped?"

"No, but..." Wade sounded addled, and that's when the phone went dead.

———

THE SHAKING FINALLY STOPPED. Wade wondered if he'd ever get the scene out of his mind. It was only yesterday, but he felt the rawness of it as though he was still standing in the morgue. He remembered clearly when he was asked to identify Parker's body. Except for the cord mark around her throat, she could have been sleeping; she looked so serene. All her dreams of promotion were just as dead. *Did she think she could bring the guy in without following the rules?* If there had been a change of venue on the part of the man calling himself Greg Oliver, it should have raised a red flag. *Was this the reason her body lay on the cold slab in front of him?* He felt anger roiling within, anger at himself. He never should have put her on the case. Having identified her body, Wade turned to leave when the attendant touched his shoulder.

"Sorry, sir. There is one more thing you need to see."

That's when Wade noticed there were three separate sheets covering the body. The one covering between her waist and thighs was the one the attendant removed. Wade knew he was going to be sick. He turned away, and then it came. Like a drunken man, he staggered in his own vomit, groping for a handhold.

CHAPTER TWENTY-FIVE

HIS THOUGHTS ROILING, Hawk descended the stairs to the reception area rather slowly. He couldn't understand why Wade seemed to break down over Parker's death. He also had to break the news to Jamie.

"Morning, Boss. Beginning of a short week. Do I get the day after Thanksgiving off, too? I'd like to get out of town for a few days."

"Sure. That could be nice for you," Hawk stopped at her desk. "Anyplace in particular?"

"Not sure. Rebecca and I are trying to figure it out."

"Uh, Jamie," Hawk started.

"It's okay, Hawk. Wade called me last night. I'm so sorry. And no; I'm not gonna do the drama queen thing. I'm startin' to understand. This kind of work is sometimes ugly and dangerous."

"Thanks. It makes it a little easier all around."

"Yeah, sure. Uh, Boss, have you ever thought of hiring a groundskeeper or a janitor?"

"You certainly changed the subject quickly. Come in my office. I can tell that you have something brewing in that head of yours."

They both sat down, and Hawk leaned back in his chair. "Okay, spill."

"I don't know if you know it or not, but Preston lives in the same complex I do. His Dad just moved in with him. Mr. Valetti's job with those rich snobs ended Friday, and he didn't have any place to go. He hasn't found a good job yet. I just thought, well, maybe you could hire someone to be here every day."

"Hmm," Hawk stroked his chin and leaned forward.

"Preston did get his boss to hire his Dad as a temporary, part-time busboy. But he really needs a better job full time," Jamie added.

"Is he working today?"

"I think so."

"Then let me take you to lunch."

HAWK HAD ONLY BEEN to The Embers, the other restaurant in town. Never to Georgios. But it was clean, and the aroma of food nestled in your nostrils like an invited guest. Booths lined the walls, and tables were well spaced throughout the dining room. Tablecloths of blue were on the tables, and there was floral wallpaper from the top of the booths to the ceiling. The color scheme and the soft background music made for a relaxing experience, he supposed. He couldn't envision teens gathering here though, he thought, as Jamie led the way to a back booth.

"This okay, Boss?"

"Yes, just fine. Is this Preston's station?"

Jamie didn't answer, seemingly intent on catching Preston when he came on the floor. It didn't take long, and he was ready to take their orders.

"Hey, Preston. Hawk wants to meet your Dad," Jamie blurted.

"My Dad?" Preston asked. He seemed a little surprised. "He's washing dishes, but let me see if he can take a break. Root beer for you, Jamie. How about you, Detective Hawkins?

"First, call me Hawk. And I'd like hot tea, with milk, not powdered cream. Thanks."

Preston was gone only a few minutes when Nick Valetti, drying his hands, limped toward Hawk and Jamie's booth.

"The Hawk, as I live and breathe," Nick extended his hand. "You can't know how great it is to finally meet you. Of course, I had hoped it would have been sooner. I always thought we might have been able to work together at some point."

"Knowing of your background with the NYPD, it's good to meet you, also."

Hawk shook the man's hand and invited him to sit down. Preston returned with drinks, including a coffee for his Dad and his own root beer.

Hawk began. "Speaking of work, I have a proposition for you. I need a full-time employee for the grounds, some janitor chores in the office, and who knows what else. It would pay well, and I can offer you the caretaker's apartment above the garage. It needs renovating, but I can have that done this week. I think most of the furniture is still there, too."

"Did these kids put you up to this?" Nick sounded miffed.

"Jamie mentioned it. But it's something I had planned to do down the road. There's no reason not to do it now before I lose you to another job. Come to the office when you get off work. Take a look around at the grounds and office. What do you say?"

Nick seemed to be thinking; Hawk waited and sipped his tea.

"Okay. You've got yourself a caretaker. No need for me to look around. I've seen the Greystone Manor before. When do you want me to start? I do need to give notice here."

"I'll have your quarters finished this week. You can start any time after you give notice."

"Deal. I'll go give 'em notice now. Thanks, Hawk."

———

HAWK WAS PLEASED at how his detective agency was growing. When Nick gave his notice the day before, they told him he could leave anytime; he reported to work this morning. Hawk had him out checking through the shed and organizing everything to suit himself. The construction crew was also able to get started on the renovation. At least something was moving along smoothly. Nick would stay with his son until the crew was finished.

"Jamie," Hawk called her to his office.

"Yeah, Boss?"

"I'm checking in to getting Nick a slightly used pick-up truck to use on the grounds and for short errands. That aside, I'm thinking maybe we could use Preston here, too. We've turned down quite a few jobs and/or referred them to attorneys in the city. Maybe we should have our own attorney on board, and then we could take on those clients also. What do you think? Would Preston be interested?"

"Oh, my gosh! That would be great! He could have that office behind me."

"No, he would be offered the old storage office. I'm saving that one with the hopes that Wade will take me up on my offer to come back and partner with me. When Larry is finished with Nick's quarters, I'll have them start on that room. Then we should be all finished with Greystone Manor except for the storage room over the garage and outbuildings. What I would like you to do is set up an appointment with Preston in the next day or two, but I don't want you telling him why. Can you do that, Jamie?"

"Will that mean I can't see him if he accepts the offer?"

"No, I'm a little more liberal than that, but I want this offer to come from me."

"Okay, Boss. You got my word. I'll set it up and tell him he needs to find out from you what it's all about."

CHAPTER TWENTY-SIX

WADE PACED THE OFFICE, his face a beet red. Faster. Faster. Then he stopped short, almost slamming into Carson. Three other officers stood alongside Carson, waiting.

"Can't anybody give me an answer? Why is it taking so long to find Parker's stuff? The books list at least three other cases with this same MO: women who have made *careers,* using their bodies for modeling, exotic dancing, prostitution… they're found alone, unconscious, strangled, the body between their waist and hips mutilated, as if with a butcher knife. We're dealing with a sick serial killer."

Wade stopped for a drink of water and looked at his men. Three were seasoned detectives, except Carson, who had just been promoted. What a case for the new *kid.*

"We haven't had the first clue on the others. But this time it hits home; it's one of our own. She had contact with someone, and we're privy to some of that contact. So why… is it taking so blasted long?" The frustration went all the way down to Wade's toes. He needed a break, or he'd blow up. "I have a conference call. Johnson will take over. Any questions?" Hearing none, Wade dismissed the men.

———

WADE KNEW the conference call was an excuse, but right now he needed some air and time alone with God. Grabbing a mug of coffee from the break room, he walked outside. Ruthie, the dispatcher, was on her break, but on her cell. He nodded and kept walking. No need to talk. The way he felt right now, he could walk all the way to New York and right into the arms of Linda. He ached for her. And although she disliked his job, she had always managed to comfort him when he was in the middle of a difficult case. For now, he would sit and invite the Holy Spirit to give him comfort.

The bench felt harder, and the sun seemed hotter than usual today. Wade wished he'd brought his Bible from his desk to seek God's Word on this case; then a Scripture from Ecclesiastes came to his mind. *A time to be born, and a time to die...* Maybe it *was* Gloria's time, but it seemed so unfair. Wade thanked God that she was a believer and was now with Him.

"Detective Owens. Sir?" Wade turned to see Carson excitedly running toward him.

"Yeah. What's up?" Wade asked as he stood.

"They found two cell phones and some other stuff." Carson was already heading back to the door he had just exited. "It's in the first interview room," he called over his shoulder.

Wade followed and realized that fifteen minutes were indeed enough time for God to answer his prayer for peace.

As he reached the room, he noticed officers looking over the bagged evidence. Seven bags, Wade counted, ranging from two cell phones to a piece of hair. Everything was laid out in a neat row on the table. He picked up a bag with one of the cell phones, preparing to open it.

"Hold it, Owens," Johnson said. "Forensic hasn't had a go at it yet. They thought you'd like to see it first."

Turning the bag over in his hand instead, Wade asked, "Who are *they*? Who brought it in? And, do we have the forensic report on her car yet?"

"Mitchell and Harrison. They combed a ten-mile radius where Parker's body was found and brought the evidence in. I placed the car report on your desk. Disappointing, though: hours of going over the car, headlight to taillight, turning it inside out. Nothing. Not even her fingerprints. The car was wiped clean."

"So, do we know whose cell this is? Or this one?" he asked, picking up the other bagged phone. All heads shook, and someone mumbled no.

"Not till Forensic," voiced Johnson.

"Then get these bags to them. Now!" Wade barked, as he left the room.

———

JAMIE HAD INVITED HAWK, Preston, Nick, Rebecca, and Jerry to her apartment for a Thanksgiving meal. It was nice, but Hawk couldn't get away fast enough. Even after a year and a half, memories of Ellie continued to grip his soul. He still felt raw from her absence.

Now, the day after, the office closed, Hawk decided to work. He needed to stay busy and pulled out the file Marlet had given him the day she hired him. Glancing through it again, nothing jumped out to give him any indication as to why Ted might have closed his account on FriendsPage. Then he got to the other file that Dumont's Law Firm had compiled from the interviews Stephanie Edwards had conducted. There it was. The gal in Seattle, Washington, a former model, had an account on FriendsPage. She had Ted and Jill listed as friends. Hawk reread the message the woman had sent to Ted, *after* Jill Evans' suicide.

Ted, what has happened to Jill? She doesn't answer my emails & I haven't seen her online. No one else seems to know anything either. Do you? Email me.

That must have triggered a warning to him to delete his account. *Guilty as charged?* thought Hawk. He also wondered if Wade had picked up on this.

"Speaking of Wade, it's been almost a week since I heard from him," Hawk said aloud. *When did he start talking to himself*, he thought, as he dialed Wade's cell? Hawk was sure he had given him enough time to get through the meltdown he apparently had last Saturday. Death was part of the job and not always a pretty sight. Why was Wade so upset about this one? There were other coworkers who had been taken down in the past. And Parker wasn't even his partner; or was there something else going on?

"Couldn't be anybody but Hawk," Wade said when he answered.

"You would know, especially when you have caller ID," Hawk laughed. It was good to hear Wade laugh as well.

"I know I owe you an explanation, Hawk. I've been working up to calling you." Wade didn't give Hawk a chance to say anything and went on to tell him about the killer's MO.

"We're dealing with a sicko, Hawk; a killer who's knocking off women who make a living as dancers, models, or such. And he uses the Internet. It's like an online shooting gallery. Only this guy doesn't shoot. He strangles and mutilates."

"Sounds that way. But is it only one guy? Is it Ted? Or do we also have another man, by the name of Greg Oliver?"

"We're not sure. It's possible we're dealing with a copycat. Or it could be Ted, using a stolen persona. We may be getting too close for comfort. But we're still running down all leads. Sounds like he may have some kind of vendetta against women in that line of work. There were three other females here in the county killed over the past year, same MO, but cold cases. We went back to their files and evidence. Fortunately, their computers were still stored in the evidence room."

"Don't tell me. They all had contact with Ted."

"You got it, Hawk."

———

HAWK WALKED to the garden's edge. It was cold, and the brisk air felt good. Again, he looked north up the Hudson. "Don't ask that of me, Lord," was his whispered prayer. He turned to see Larry and his renovation crew arriving to work on Nick's quarters. "Morning, Larry; didn't expect to see you here today."

"No problem with that, is there Mr. Hawkins? We work today, and we're finished. All we have left to do is the paint and lay the carpet. By four, we can put the furniture back and be outta here."

"I just thought with the Thanksgiving holiday you would be closed. I'm sure Nick will be glad to know he can move in tomorrow," Hawk said. "When you're finished, come to my office. I'll have a check for you. Then I'd like to have you start as soon as possible on the smaller office inside."

"As I recall, there wasn't that much to do. I can put two of my men on it right now."

"Sounds good."

"And when do you want us to finish the rest of the garage and rooms above it?"

"I want to wait on that. I need my new maintenance man to sort through all the junk and see if anything is salvageable. Once that is done, I'll call you."

CHAPTER TWENTY-SEVEN

MONDAY MORNING DAWNED as dismal as Hawk felt. He closed the file and added it to the stack that was beginning to grow on the corner of his desk. He was glad he was finished with the Emerson case. He only wished that he could say the same about Marlet's. Now that Ted was a suspect in several murders in the vicinity of Sun Point, the county Sheriff's Department had jurisdiction in the case, with Wade heading it up. At least Marlet wasn't pestering Hawk as before, although she did call the office a couple of times a week for updates.

Hawk's biggest concerns for December were Jamie's dejected demeanor and the fact that it was predicted to snow by the weekend. Using the newly installed intercom for the first time, Hawk pressed the button to Jamie's desk to request her presence in his office.

"Yeah, Boss?" Jamie asked as she shuffled to his desk.

Hawk motioned for her to sit, but plopping seemed to be her way lately. She'd even taken up chewing and snapping gum again.

"What's up, Jamie? Ever since Preston said no to my job offer, it seems you have been down."

Expecting an answer, Hawk waited. But Jamie just sat there with her head down, playing with her hair, now back in a ponytail.

"Jamie?" Hawk spoke louder. "Are you with me here?" She looked up and slowly nodded her head.

"Okay. Then let me start by repeating what I said to you when you were playing the drama queen, as you called it. Just like I can't have a hysterical woman working for me, I won't have someone working here who can't keep emotions reined in, either. I don't need a dejected, down in the dumps, negative person in my business. I told you then that it's not the prettiest of jobs. It can get nasty. Well, life does too, and you need to handle it elsewhere. In the office, you are to be professional. And, personally, I don't care to be pulled down by someone who is negative every day. You're good at your job and, for the most part, pleasant to be around. So, it's up to you. Lose the negative attitude, or look for other work."

"Oh, Boss," Jamie finally uttered. "Just when I thought I had a guy who was in love with me, it ends."

"What happened? Did his refusal of my job offer make a change in the relationship?"

"It's… well…" Jamie began to sob.

Hawk, now regretting his harsh words, asked, "Do you need to go home?"

"Nah. It's just… well… Preston had sent his resume to some fancy law firm in Chicago when he graduated. That's where he wanted to go and why he didn't take any other offers. Now, after two years, he finally hears from them." Hawk didn't venture a word; he waited for Jamie to finish.

"He's going, Boss. He's going!" Then Jamie cried.

Hawk kept quiet but handed her the box of tissues he had once offered Anna Marlet.

"Perhaps you should take the rest of the day off. Think things over. Why not go home?"

"No!" Jamie said sternly. "I need to work, to stay busy. And, get out of this mood. I'll be okay." She stood and reached for the stack of files on his desk.

"These need filing." It was a statement rather than a question. Shoulders straight, she walked out of his office.

Hawk knew the feeling of needing to stay busy when everything around you seemed to be falling apart. He let her go. *So, Preston is going to Chicago*, he thought. *I wonder if Nick will follow?*

————

JAMIE WORKED WELL, but quietly, for the rest of the day. She took time to say goodnight, locking up behind her. Hawk was left with his thoughts. Standing in his favorite spot by the window, he watched Nick working in the back garden. The man was staying busy, even in the cold; he seemed to thrive in the weather. Hawk was as surprised as Nick had been when a beautiful stone fountain had been found amid dead bushes in the middle of the garden. It would be beautiful in the late spring and summer. Nick had decided that a sitting area, with an arbor and rose garden, would be perfect to surround the fountain, and Hawk was impressed with the plans he had drawn up. He remembered Nick mentioning it would be a nice place for a wedding. If he was thinking of Preston and Jamie, Nick might have to think again.

————

AS NICK PUT AWAY the last of the tools and headed up to his apartment, he couldn't believe how God had blessed him. To work for the Hawk was almost as good as working with the Hawk. He was praying that his son's decision to take the job in Chicago, instead of the one Hawk offered, wouldn't cause a problem for himself. Preston could work wherever he wanted, and Nick was glad for that. But he wanted to stay right where he was. It couldn't get any better than this.

In his apartment, Nick put a TV dinner in the microwave and made a cup of coffee. He had worked hard today and didn't feel like cooking. The apartment was warm and comfortable but lonely. Yet he should be used to that.

How many years had Preston's mother been gone? Too many to care anymore, he reflected. She had walked out when Preston was four. That meant Nick had to find a nanny since his work hours on the force were so unpredictable. He was proud of Preston becoming a lawyer, and of the fact that his son thought enough of his old man to get him a part-time job until something better came along. Well, it had… and he wanted to keep it. He'd talk to Hawk and make sure he understood that no matter what Preston did, Nick was staying on with the agency. Nick did feel bad for Jamie, though. He knew she had been hoping Preston would accept Hawk's offer.

———

A KNOCK on his door brought Nick out of a short after-dinner nap. *What could Hawk want?* He wondered. Nick was surprised when he saw it was Preston. "Come in, son. Come in."

"Hey! This place is nice, Dad. Are you comfortable? Do you like the job?" Preston sat on the edge of a big overstuffed sofa, just meant for comfort. He seemed edgy.

"Now I know you're not here to see how I'm doing. So, what's up besides Chicago?"

"Dad, you know I care about how you're doing. I mean, if you're not happy, then I'd like to take you to Chicago with me."

"Chicago's not for me. Neither is living with you. Don't get me wrong. I appreciated you helping me out when I needed it, but now, no. I can't think of working for a better person than the Hawk. He was the best; still is. I want to stay here, son, and I wish you the best. It's not like we'll never see one another again." Nick hated that he was rattling on, but he wanted to make sure Preston understood he was set where he was.

"That's great, Dad; but, well… I guess you know that Jamie and I are no longer seeing one another. I mean… I'm in love with her. I even thought of marriage, but you know that can't happen. I won't be unequally yoked. Look what happened with you and my mother."

"Jamie's not like your mother. She may not go to church, but that could change. We've been talking. Yet I do understand what you're saying, and you're right." Nick paused. "So, when do they put you to work?"

"Actually, the letter was just to tell me that a position should come open by spring. Since Jamie thinks I've been offered the job already, I didn't tell her any differently. I decided to go now... find a restaurant job while I'm waiting. I can't stay here and not be with Jamie. I'm leaving for Chicago in the morning, after Jamie is at work. It will be easier. I hope she doesn't blame you for my decision."

"You don't worry about that, son. Just leave everything with the Lord. Things will be just fine with her and me. Now, how about we visit?"

———

HAWK GAZED out his bedroom window as he finished his tea. An earlier than expected light snow fell overnight, turning the grounds into a winter wonderland. He saw Jamie pulling in the driveway. Was he late? He had wanted to be down before she got in this morning.

He stepped in his office when he heard her unlock the front door. Hoping to get her on the right track for the day, he decided to stand in his doorway to greet her, all the while hoping that her mood had improved.

"Good morning, Jamie. This light snow has made our place here look beautiful. How are you?"

"In need of a cup of coffee," she said as she breezed into the kitchen. Hawk followed.

"Isn't your coffee pot working?"

"Well, if you must know, I spent the night at Rebecca's last night, and I took off early enough to be on time for work. I left her sleeping.

I'm not sure which one of us has the bigger hangover, but I figure she'll call me later and let me know."

Hangover is right, thought Hawk.

"Maybe you should go home and freshen up."

Jamie stopped fumbling for the coffee filter and turned to face Hawk.

"Are you now telling me I stink, and can't drink on my own time? Is that another rule to add to thou shall not be a drama queen, and thou shall not be down in the dumps?" She stood there, hands on her hips, with a defiant look in her eyes, waiting for him to answer.

When did he become a tyrant and expect perfection out of others when he couldn't even measure up to what God expected of him?

"No, Jamie. That's not what I'm saying. Perhaps I didn't say it right. I just thought you might like to freshen up and maybe even get a few more hours of sleep. I can handle the office this morning." Hawk paused for a moment. "Actually, I can remember when I would have given anything if my boss would have made that suggestion to me."

"You drink, boss?" Jamie's demeanor changed to one of surprise and amusement.

"No, not anymore. It was years ago, in my early twenties... and then not for very long. One terrible hangover cured me."

"I really don't want to go home," Jamie said more softly. "I don't want to run into Preston."

CHAPTER TWENTY-EIGHT

AFTER GOING over the transcripts of the text messages from both phones, Wade sat in bewilderment. The phone that belonged to Parker had needed a battery. The other belonged to Greg Oliver, the owner of Cars Town Auto Sales. He was a single dad with custody of his twelve-year-old son.

Both phones were found in plain sight, not two feet from Parker's car, as though they were meant to be found. On one phone, there wasn't much texting; the usual chats—where he lived, where he worked, information about his son. There were answers from Parker, using the fake persona that Jamie had created; change of meeting places, due to car failure and that he would be riding his Harley.

Since the battery was missing from Parker's phone, it was no wonder that the trace had failed.

Parker, why didn't you call? Or couldn't you? Wade thought.

This was definitely a change Wade didn't like. If this was a copycat killer, then they were still dealing with Ted. Or, was Ted just who he claimed to be with Jill Evans? Perhaps they would have their serial killer behind bars before the morning was out. Two uniformed deputies were on their way to the car lot to pick up Oliver.

Grabbing a cup of coffee, Wade looked over the rest of the report. The other evidence was of no consequence. The hair, which was found next to the phones, came from a coyote. There was a pen, evidently on the ground for some time: an empty cigarette pack, a comb, and a paperback novel... all with vague fingerprints. But if Oliver's prints match... well, he'd deal with him when the results hit his desk.

———

JOHNSON ENTERED. "They just brought Oliver in kicking and screaming. He's getting printed now. We ran a check on him before they brought him in. Nothing. The guy is clean; no past record."

Wade gulped his coffee down.

"Put him in the small interview room. I'll interrogate him where it's tight quarters. Make him sweat a little. I want you and Price in with me. Buzz me when you have him set."

Wade was ready. He didn't like it, but he was ready. He entered the interview room and was face to face with a man who sat like a scared rabbit, behind a scruff of beard at least as old as the one Wade himself was sporting. Almost three days on surveillance didn't leave a guy time for a decent meal, much less a shave.

Could this be Gloria's killer? Is it Ted, or a copycat? Wade's head ached as the questions galloped through his mind like a pack of thundering horses: questions he hoped to have answered, and soon.

He motioned Johnson to start the recorder as he sat down across from the rabbit. "Okay. Your name again, for the record."

"Guh... reg Oliver and... man, I didn't kill anybody. I'm in the automotive business like I told you. I own Cars Town Motors, here in town. And..."

"Hold it," Wade interrupted, "I ask the questions; you answer them. Nothing extra. Got it?"

"Got it. But I still didn't kill anybody."

"Okay, that's what we're here to find out. A cell phone, in your name, was found near the murder scene along with the cell from the victim. Her phone had text messages from yours. She received emails from you. You planned a meeting in Las Vegas but changed plans via text. What happened? Was the law getting too close for comfort?"

"I didn't text anybody, and I sure didn't send emails to this Gloria woman. Yeah, the phone is mine, but I bought it for my kid. He lost it a couple of months ago and only just told me. Said he was afraid to tell me. I didn't know it was missing, or I would have stopped the service."

"Okay, Ted. Maybe that part of your story is..."

"Why are you calling me Ted?" the rabbit interrupted. "The other guys did the same. My name is Greg. Greg Oliver."

Confidence seemed to be surfacing within the suspect. Wade continued questioning him, yet he couldn't trip him up. He gave it over to Price and motioned Johnson to follow him out the room.

"What have we got here, Johnson?" Wade asked after they sat down in his office.

"We took a chance and questioned the kid at his school, and he tells the same story. He thinks that the last time he saw the phone was in his backpack. That was two months ago, at his Little League baseball practice, after school. Some of the other kid's mothers were there. And we managed to question them, also. But they didn't remember seeing any strange man, or any of the fathers that afternoon. When the kid got home, he went to use the cell, and it was missing. He didn't tell his dad, figuring he would find it before his father found out."

"How fearful was the boy of his father?"

"Oh, the usual. He had lost the phone once before and had several privileges taken from him. He thought it would be easier to do without the phone and still get to do other things."

Carson came in with coffee for both men and a message that the interview was over.

"It's being transcribed. Sounds like a dead-end. Don't know if we're going to be able to hold him," Carson said.

"Yeah, I was afraid of that," Wade muttered. "Carson, you go back, and as soon as that transcript is ready, bring it here."

After Carson left, Wade turned to Johnson, who was trying to get comfortable on a hardwood bench against the wall.

"Maybe we are looking at only one man. A man who stole the cell, and used this guy's name to set up a FriendsPage account after he closed out the one of Ted Ashby."

"I suppose it's possible, but the account in Greg Oliver's name was opened before Ted closed his account," Johnson said.

"He might have opened an account in Greg Oliver's name as a backup. And at the schoolyard, he could have used anyone as an accomplice," suggested Wade. "Let's find out if there was anyone else hanging around, another mother, or a kid that normally wouldn't be there. It's amazing what kids will do for a ten spot or a twenty-dollar bill."

Price knocked on the door and entered. "Can't shake him, sir, and his prints don't match any on the evidence. Let him go?"

Wade thought for a moment, then nodded. "But keep a tail on him."

CHAPTER TWENTY-NINE

HAWK WAS STILL TRYING to get his mind around the fact that ever since Ellie was killed, he had allowed doubt, depression, and bitterness fill him. He was sitting in judgment, not only of Doogan but —it appeared—everyone else. *Lord, when did that happen? When did I decide I didn't need You?*

This revelation was hard to take. He knew he needed to get on the right path, but how? He was still hurting. Maybe he could start with Jamie if it wasn't too late. So, she had emotions, was a drama queen, drank, and didn't go to church. Yet how could he be the one to show her the way when he himself was having a hard time getting back to God?

The intercom buzzed. "Wade on two." Jamie's voice sounded flat and annoyed. *If Wade is on two, she must be on one, probably talking with Rebecca about the ogre she works for.* Not that Hawk could blame her. He wouldn't be surprised if she turned in her notice.

"Hawk here. It's been a while. How's it going on that end?"

Wade brought Hawk up to date. "I'm going to overnight all the info from the investigation, including the transcript of Greg Oliver. I thought we had him, Hawk; I really thought we had Ted. Look it over with those hawk eyes of yours. Maybe you'll see something I missed."

———

AFTER THE DISCOURAGING phone call from Wade, Hawk decided on a cup of tea. He didn't want another confrontation with Jamie, so he used the direct access door from his office to the kitchen. Before Hawk could start the kettle, he heard Jamie softly crying. Then he heard Nick's voice. Having made a mess of things once today, he changed his mind about tea and slipped back to his office. This was one time he would let God take care of the situation.

———

HAWK SAT AT HIS DESK, wondering where he was going when a knock on the door brought him out of his reverie.

"Come in." Thank goodness. It was Nick, not Jamie.

"Sorry to bother you, Hawk, but I need to talk with you."

"Sure. Sit down." Hawk could only hope that Nick had not decided to go with his son to Chicago. "What can I do for you?"

"Preston left today, and he asked me to tell Jamie. Naturally, it upset her, so I suggested that she go home for the rest of the day. I told her I'd square it with you. I didn't mean to override your authority, but I think she needed to get away from here."

"Actually, I tried to talk her into going home this morning, but she wanted to avoid running into Preston. Seems she and her friend Rebecca had quite a night and one too many drinks. I'm glad you were able to convince her." Hawk was impressed by Nick's sensitivity to Jamie's situation and his take-charge manner.

"You know, I offered Preston a job here, but he was set on Chicago. To be honest, I thought you'd go with him."

"I have no desire to live in Chicago. This is where I want to be. I prefer being back in law enforcement, even if it's only vicariously.

Plus, I'm not anxious to be living with my son. I'm still young, even at forty-nine. I'd be back on the force if it wasn't for the leg. I have my private investigator's license, but I'm sure the force doesn't need a bum-legged detective."

"Well then, maybe you'd be interested in expanding your position here. It's something I've been thinking about lately." Hawk knew Wade wouldn't be leaving Arizona anytime soon, even if he could be coaxed into working with Hawk Detective Agency.

"I would need you to handle a few cases at the desk, but also do some leg work. We can always hire someone for the grounds and janitorial work. What do you say?"

"Say?" Nick grinned. "I say, 'Let me at those cases.'"

———

THE SNOW HAD all but disappeared when Jamie pulled into work an hour late. She was surprised that the door was unlocked. She hoped Hawk hadn't been hard on Nick yesterday. Or worse, fired him and was now waiting to fire her. She entered and was doubly surprised to see the back of a man's suit—and the guy in it—going through her file cabinet. *Guess the boss couldn't wait and already replaced me. Or maybe he had been planning this for several days. Might as well get it over with,* she thought.

"Good morning," Jamie said as brightly as she could. The man turned around. *Nick! So, this is my replacement. Hawk couldn't get the son, so he promotes the dad.* "I'm so surprised to see you in here, Nick... and, in a suit."

He looked quite different in a blue suit and tie. They made his blue eyes sparkle. Nick's mustache hinted of the brown hair she supposed he once had, but his eyebrows were still a light brown. His hair was graying on top and had already turned white on the sides. His cheeks were rosy from the outdoors, and a smile was, as always, in place. Funny, she'd never noticed before. Jamie now understood where Preston got his good looks.

"Good morning, Jamie. I'm glad to see you. Here, let me help you with your coat, and then maybe you can help me find the Danvers' file."

"I... I don't understand."

"Hawk has asked me to come on board and do some investigative work. He even gave me an office. He plans to hire someone for the janitorial and grounds work. I'll supervise them. I'm buzzer number three on that intercom thing of yours."

"Oh, Nick, that's great! I thought maybe I was fired," she laughed. "The Danvers' file is on my desk in pending. I'm glad you'll be working on that. Where's the boss?"

"In his office, and he's not to be disturbed. He also asked that I handle anything that comes in today, including Miss Marlet. He received an overnight earlier from Wade, who is hoping that Hawk might see something he's overlooked. And if anybody can, it's the Hawk."

———

HAWK EMERGED from his office a half-hour later. "Jamie, if anyone calls, I'm out of the office. If they want to know where tell them, you can't say, and I'll be in tomorrow sometime."

"What if Wade calls?"

"I told him to reach me at home," he thumbed upwards. "Meanwhile, Nick will handle things until I return." He smiled as he climbed the stairs, two at a time.

The first thing Hawk did after spreading the investigation paperwork out on his dining room table was to make a cup of tea. He always worked better with a cup of smooth tasting English Blend tea, or so he thought.

Stroking his chin, he tried to make some sense of all Wade sent. Nothing seemed to be adding up in Arizona, either. Greg Oliver turned out to be what the sheriff's office had figured: Ted's attempt to frame the man. Evidently, the Oliver kid's phone was stolen over two months earlier, and the time lag made it more difficult. No one saw anything. The kid finally admitted that he wasn't really sure when he last saw his cell. A mess: Hawk was looking at a mess.

He walked to the window to think. Hawk was appreciating the skills of Nick more each day, as he looked over the garden. The man worked hard, and his record with the NYPD was enough to have him working in the office. He was sure Nick would prove to be an asset to Hawk Detective Agency. If he could only get Wade to come back, he'd have a dream agency. The three of them would make quite a team.

Back at the table, Hawk began arranging the information in time sequence. Things needed to add up... and soon. Three other women had been murdered in that county before Gloria Parker. He looked at the dates and spotted a pattern. Each murder was committed in the middle of the second month of each quarter of the year. According to the pattern, the killer wasn't due to strike again until mid-February. His phone rang. It was Wade.

"What's up?" Hawk asked.

"My man Johnson followed up on a hunch; he came up with six suicides this year. They were similar to the Evans girl. I'll email that info."

"Interesting. When did they take place? I mean, what are the dates?" Hawk waited.

"January 9th, March 13th, April 4th, June 19th..."

"And the next was in July, then nothing in September, but picking up again in October."

"Yeah, except for September. You're right, Hawk; there wasn't one that month. But how did you guess that?"

"Not a guess Wade; an MO." Hawk then told Wade how he saw a pattern emerge, both in the murders and suicides.

"What happened to September?"

"One of two things. It was a suicide that looked like an accident, or it mocked a natural death." Hawk thought for a moment. "Hold on a minute; I have a hunch.

———

"I CHECKED THE FILES, and it's just as I thought. September was the month Jill committed suicide. The pattern wasn't broken, just moved to New York. According to the pattern, there will be a suicide this month that we probably can't prevent."

"Hawk, do you really think all these are connected?"

"I'm beginning to. I'm going to get in touch with a professor friend of mine to find out about subliminal messages, or, in other words, brainwashing."

"I've heard of it, but is it possible? How exactly would brainwashing fit?"

"I think it is possible since it's the application of a concentrated means of persuasion. Ted could have sent repeated suggestions to the women in order to produce a specific end. And in this case, the end was death.

It's actually considered romance scamming," Hawk continued. "usually used for robbing a wealthy target: young or old, male or female. Online romances are booming. Some are good, others tragic. Before the Internet, the love con was initiated through lonely heart columns in magazines."

"Do you think this may be the case here?" Wade interjected. "I'm not sure I can believe that someone would commit suicide at the suggestion of another person."

"I know. It sounds incredulous. Yet it appears to be going in that direction. There was a case a few years back, very similar. It was a con perpetrated on a dating site. The woman involved had made contact with a man who was 100% her match. Or so she thought. Normal *get-to-know-you* emails were exchanged. Then they became more intimate. After three months of dedicated persuasion, the con artist got what he was after. He bilked the woman of over $300,000. But what Ted was after was the suicidal death of his target, a sort of 'murder by persuasion.'"

CHAPTER THIRTY

"OKAY, WHICH OFFICE IS HIS?" Jamie heard the man bellow and slam the door at the same time.

"May I help you, sir?" she asked.

"Just point me to Alistair's office." He was still bellowing.

"If you mean Mr. Hawkins, sir, he's out of the office today, but..."

"Never mind the buts, just tell me where he is," he demanded.

"Mr., uh, your name, sir?"

"Alistair Hawkins the second. Now tell me where my son is."

Jamie heard Nick's office door open and felt some relief. Maybe he could calm Hawk's father down. When Mr. Hawkins heard the office door open, he turned around, and Jamie noticed that he froze as he said, "You!"

———

"PLEASE. COME INTO MY OFFICE," Nick remarked, leaving his door open for Hawk's father to follow. He sat at his desk as the elder Hawkins entered, shutting the door behind him.

Nick gestured to the chair in front of his desk. "Please, have a seat."

So, this was Hawk's father. He wasn't sure how this would play out, but he had to see it through. He remembered only too well the last time he saw the man, but he was surprised Hawkins remembered him. Nick never wanted to relive that day, but here it was, staring him in the face, three and a half years later.

———

HAWK HEARD the front door slam and a man's rather loud voice. It sounded a lot like his father. What in the world was he doing here?

As much as he didn't want to take the time to settle whatever was erupting between Jamie and his dad, he knew he needed to spare her this encounter. As he opened his apartment door, he heard Nick inviting his father into his office. *Good*, he thought. Nick could handle his father. Hawk closed his door and returned to the dining room table. Hawk was sure Nick would call if he needed him.

———

IT HAD BEEN a typical late June day in Manhattan; Nick remembered: plenty of sunshine to heat everything in sight and floating mirages on most streets. There was only an hour left on his shift. Then it was home to enjoy a glass of lemonade and cool off with air-conditioning. He and Alec Romero, his partner of five years, were kidding around about who made the best lemonade when the call came in. It was a robbery in progress at a bank, and they were the closest, just one block away. When they arrived on the scene, all the tellers were on the floor—except for one who was pulling money from a safe. Customers were also on the floor, but for one man who had refused.

The robber, so intent on shooting the guy, unless he got down, didn't notice that he and Romero had entered the bank. Nick saw the semi-automatic in his hands and heard the robber. "I count to three, and you're dead if not down. One. Two." Without a second to lose, Nick dove to knock the customer to the floor. Bullets rang out as

Nick took those meant for the stubborn customer. Romero let off a couple of shots, managing to hit the robber in his shoulder. The robber turned, firing, knocking Romero down like a bowling pin. Nick managed to aim his gun and fire off two shots before he blacked out.

It wasn't until he woke up in the emergency room a few hours later that he learned a bullet had hit the femoral artery in his right leg. The quickness of an officer on backup had saved his life. Nick also found out; his partner didn't make it, and neither did the robber. He had thanked God that his life was spared, and he prayed for the Romero family. He also prayed for the robber's family and asked God's forgiveness for causing the man's death. And he learned the name of the man whose life he had saved. Alistair Hawkins.

Nick also remembered how he blamed the Hawkins guy for refusing to hit the floor. Perhaps Romero would still be alive, and Nick wouldn't have been all shot up. He had even entertained the thought that maybe he should have let the robber shoot the guy because he refused to hit the floor. It took six months of rehab and counseling before he could get over blaming Hawkins for the losses. He had written a letter to Hawkins asking for forgiveness as part of that counseling therapy. It was mailed, but Nick never knew if the man had received it. A week after that incident, Nick was able to ask God to forgive him for blaming Hawkins. He had managed, with God's help, to put it all behind him.

But now, here sits Hawkins and he's the father of my boss, thought Nick.

———

SINCE NICK DIDN'T CALL, Hawk settled back to the case. Having made notes concerning the MO he had discovered Hawk began reading the paperwork once again to be sure he didn't overlook anything else. The murders were cold cases; not a clue, no fingerprints, and nothing left at the scene.

The suicides were just that: suicides. Emails to women in the entertainment business contained pledges of love and a promise to meet them within a year, claiming they would then know one another better. One significant item was Ted's "illness." When a woman became too demanding, Ted's health "declined." The word "terminal" was used. There was no mention of cell phone use in any of the other suicides.

Maybe that was a place to begin. He made a note to call Wade. It was frustrating to think that, if the pattern continued, another suicide would happen, and that he would be helpless to prevent it.

The only change in the killer's MO appeared to be with Sargent Parker. Clues abounded. It was as though the killer wanted to be found. Or, was he trying to send detectives in another direction by framing a total stranger? Hawk could only pray Ted would slip up before another death occurred.

The front door slammed again, and Hawk rose to look out the front window. He watched as his father got into his cherry-red BMW and peeled out of the driveway.

———

NICK STOOD at the doorway of his office, looking at Hawkins' back as he stormed out of the building.

"That's one angry dude. What's his problem?"

"Sorry, Jamie, I don't even think *he* knows what it is." Nick turned back to his desk.

Jamie came bouncing in. "That Marlet woman called and... wow! This office is nice. I haven't been in here since we cleared it out. Larry's guys did a good job. But you need curtains to cover those wooden blinds..." she turned, "and these wall-to-wall bookshelves need some knick-knacks. You sure have a lot of books, or are they Hawks'?"

"Some are mine, but most of them belong to Preston. He asked if I would store all his boxed books until he got settled. I thought they would store better on the shelves and help to fill some empty spaces. No curtains for me. I don't do frilly. That's the same reason for the lack of knick-knacks, as you call them."

"At least you have wall-to-wall carpet, and I like the deep gray color. Hmm, multi-striped red and gray wallpaper above guard rails and light gray paint below. It does look good, Nick. It fits you."

"Glad you approve. Now, what about Miss Marlet?"

"Oh, yeah. She's wanting to know what's happening about finding Ted. When I told her Hawk was out of the office and wouldn't be back till tomorrow, she asked for an appointment. I told her I'd call her back when I found out when he'd be in."

"Call her, and make the appointment for two o'clock tomorrow afternoon. It will be with me, but don't let her know that part."

"Okay," Jamie said. As she left the room, she almost ran into Hawk. "Hey, Boss, you're not supposed to be in today," she laughed and returned to her desk.

———

HAWK ENTERED Nick's office and closed the door. He sat down, letting out a long sigh.

"So, what did my father want? Is he still steamed about the sale of my summer home?"

"No... it wasn't that," Nick hesitated.

"Don't tell me he found out about my Manhattan condo?"

"No. He was looking for you. But when he saw me, it turned into something entirely different. To be honest, I'm trying to figure how to tell you."

"The best way is just spit it out, Nick. At this point, I'm beyond surprises."

"Okay. But I'm just not sure where to begin."

"How about at the beginning?"

"First, let me say, I didn't know he was your father. Since I only knew you by Hawk, and then only by reputation, I never gave your last name a thought."

Hawk was more than curious, but he needed to let Nick tell it in his own way and time. Besides, he needed a break from the paperwork upstairs.

"About three and a half years ago in June—the twenty-fourth to be exact—my partner and I were an hour away from ending our shift when a call came in. Armed robbery at Chase on First Avenue. We were on East Fifty Forth, only a block from there, so we got sent, with backup to follow. When we arrived, everyone was on the floor, except one customer who refused. The robber had his gun beaded on the man and was so intent on shooting him, he never knew Romero and I had come in. When I heard the robber's threat, I dove for the customer and took the bullets meant for him."

"Yes. I remember hearing about it when Ellie and I returned from our honeymoon. Although it happened in a different precinct, I was sorry to hear about one of our own going down. I offered my prayers and attended the funeral along with the reps from our precinct."

"When I took the bullets," Nick continued, "Romero shot at the robber, hitting him in the shoulder. Before he could get off another shot, that guy turned and, with a couple of shots, took Romero down. I didn't know he was dead until later. I managed to get off two shots before I blacked out. One of them hit its target good and proper, so our robber was dead. I didn't find that out until I woke up in the ER. All I kept thinking of was the stupid man who wouldn't hit the floor when he was told. Romero might still be alive if he had, and I might not have this limp."

"So, what has this got to do with my father?"

"That was the other thing I found out in the ER; the name of the man who refused to listen to a man with a gun in his hand. Alistair Hawkins. Your father, Hawk. Only I didn't know that's who he was at that time."

Hawk drew in a deep breath. "He never said anything, not a word. Why? Why?" Hawk was out of the chair and pacing. "Why, Dad, why?"

"I'm concerned, Hawk." Hawk stopped pacing, sat back down, and looked Nick squarely in the eyes.

"About what? Did he threaten you, or..."?

"No. My concern is about my job here with you. Will this knowledge change anything?"

"Not on my part, Nick." Hawk sat again. "You saved my father's life at the expense of your own injuries and Romero's life. Did he try to argue with you about forcing him to hit the floor?"

"No. In fact, he asked my forgiveness and actually broke down sitting right where you are now. I think he's been carrying a heavy burden for a long time. Possibly he was concerned about ever meeting me again, thinking that I might retaliate. But I let him know that I had harbored some ill thoughts at one time, but had written to him asking his forgiveness. He let me know he received it but thought it was just a way to get back at him. I told your father that within the week of writing that letter, I had prayed to God to ask his forgiveness. Your father broke down at that point. We had prayer, and he left."

Hawk sat stunned, not saying a word.

"I don't know what's going on between you and your father, Hawk, but this may have had some bearing on it."

Hawk stood. "Yes, Nick, you may be right. At least I hope so. He and my mother were so happy at my wedding. When we got home from our honeymoon, he seemed like a different man. He kept insisting that I quit the force and come into the family business. I just figured it was his usual issue of never understanding my career choice. Maybe the bank incident was, or is still, part of the problem. But it appears he left here angry."

"It will take some time to sink in, Hawk. He's been carrying this for over three years. It's harder to switch gears the longer you carry it, especially if you haven't given it to God. Can you understand?"

Hawk felt a prick in his heart, as it cried a loud "no" within his chest.

"Yes, I do know. The creep who killed my Ellie and our unborn Emily... I still can't forget or forgive him. Pray for me, Nick."

CHAPTER THIRTY-ONE

NICK LEFT the kitchen and returned to his office after a delightful lunch of homemade chicken soup and dumplings, courtesy of Jamie. She was a good person, and Nick liked her. He was sure she'd make the perfect wife for Preston, if only she was a believer. Although she politely refused his invitation to attend church on Sunday, he would pray and ask her again next week.

———

NICK STILL HAD time to make the two needed phone calls in order to finish the Danvers' case and still keep Miss Marlet's appointment on time.

At five minutes before two, Jamie stuck her head in the door. "Marlet is here."

"Show her in at two, Jamie, not before."

"Okay, Boss Junior," Jamie laughed.

Five minutes later, brows furrowed, Miss Marlet entered Nick's office. He was a little surprised when the object of his two o'clock appointment appeared. Hawk and Jamie had prepared him for a much different picture. Her makeup was light, not overdone. The long-sleeved, green knit dress hugged her trim body, and her shoes were black, as was her purse. A simple gold chain caressed her neck, while a matching pair of earrings peeked through her long blond hair.

"Please have a seat, Miss Marlet. My name is Nick Valetti, and I'll be meeting with you since Mr. Hawkins is still out of the office."

"I'm not sure I understand. I thought he worked alone."

"I'm his new partner. We both worked with the NYPD at one time," Nick said, by way of explanation.

"Just how much do you know about my case?" Anna asked.

"Enough to help you today. So, tell me what your concern is and let's see what I can do to help you." Nick set back in his chair and waited for Marlet to process the new information.

"Okay. Since you're his partner, I guess I can talk with you. I want to know three things. Where does the case stand? Have they found Ted? And what can we charge him with here in New York after Arizona is through with him?"

Nick knew she would not want to hear about the dead ends, so he had to come up with enough truth that would keep her calm and satisfied. He opted for involving her intelligence.

"How much do you know about police work? Miss Marlet."

"I... not very much. Only what I see on TV."

"I wish that real-life police work could be as fast and easy as the TV shows portray and that we could solve every case within the hour or two that the show runs. But, as you must realize by now, it doesn't. Yet there is good news. Progress is being made. We have discovered a pattern to the murders and suicides—an MO—the way the killer works. That helps to narrow the investigation and will help in finding Ted sooner rather than later. And, because of you, we will be able to bring a serial killer to justice. The NYPD, and the authorities in Arizona, thank you for your concern in not believing that Miss Evans committed suicide. As far as what the state of New York can charge him with, it's not yet known."

Anna Marlet rose and extended her hand. "Thank you, Mr. Valetti.

You have given me more of an update than anyone. Will you continue on this case?"

"As long as I am needed." Nick rose and escorted Marlet to the door, wishing her a pleasant day. Smiling, he walked back to the kitchen for a cup of coffee. He noticed Jamie grinning too, as he passed her desk.

"Treat you to a cup of coffee, Jamie?"

———

AFTER A FEW HOURS of sifting through the paperwork again, Hawk stood, stretched, and walked to the living room window. There was a light skiff of snow on the ground and walkway. Seeing how well Nick had improved the grounds, Hawk decided he could hire a lawn service as needed, and have Nick full time in the office. He fit Hawk's idea of a PI. But the test was today with Anna Marlet. He hoped she wasn't giving Nick too much of a rough time.

Stepping back to the table, he opened his laptop and got back to work. Although there was an MO, something was missing. Looking over the phone calls placed to Anna Marlet, Hawk noticed that each one came from the business phones of various nightspots in Sun Point. Yet no employee had made calls at the times in question. It appeared someone was tapping into the line from outside. "That's it," Hawk said aloud. He typed that thought in an email to Wade, and hit "send."

———

HAWK WAS DRAWN from fractured thoughts, sprinkled with intrigue, when his home phone rang. Checking caller ID, he picked up and asked, "Did you read my email, Wade?"

"Sure did. I knew you might see something else. Thanks. The local newspaper is cooperating with us. They will be running a story on the killer's MO and the phone tapping idea in their next edition. We decided to shake some bushes with hopes of drawing Ted out. I hope something will break in a day or two. I'll let you know as soon as we have something, or if anything changes."

"As will I. He's about due to call Marlet again about that bear."

"Before I forget, I assigned a few men to search the area around the telephone lines that come in at BJ's and Rosie's Bar. We'll try and lift prints, also."

"They'll be smudged at best, or non-existent."

"Perhaps, but I'm not leaving any stone unturned. A cop killer just doesn't set well with me."

"Is that all it is, Wade, or were you two an item?"

"Hawk, you know me better than that. First, my only interest is in Linda. I pray each day that she will change her mind and come back. I'd remarry her in a heartbeat. Second, if I was looking or seeing someone, you'd have already known about it."

"Sorry, Pal. I just wanted to be sure. You seemed to have taken this to heart."

"That's because I've never sent an officer to their death before."

———

"WELL. HOW DID IT GO?" Hawk said, standing in the doorway of Nick's office.

"Come on in and sit yourself down. It went very well. She purred like a kitten when she left. She seems to understand having to wait."

"Purred? That's not a word I would equate with Marlet. What did you say to her?" Hawk asked with a smile as he sat down.

"I let her think she was being let in on the case without revealing anything she didn't already know. I also let her know that it was because of her that we will be able to catch a serial killer and that we would keep her updated."

"My thanks for getting that woman calmed down."

They both laughed.

CHAPTER THIRTY-TWO

"HEY! JOE. YOU BACK THERE?"

"Is that you, Ted?"

"Yeah. You ready for another call? I have your whiskey and money. But I'd like to make the call up at Silver Heels Bar and Grill again. You with me?"

"Ain't that the one we were at the last time?

"Yeah. That a problem?"

"Guess not. You got the bike... Nah, I see it's the pick-up. You promised me a ride on the bike."

"Hop in! We'll do the bike next time. This is too long a ride for the bike."

"How come so late this time?"

"Want to shake her up. Let her know I mean business."

"Yeah, that oughta do it. Three or four in New York?"

"About three-thirty when you get the call made."

"How much ya got me?"

"Fifty, as usual."

"Not gonna do; the price has gone up. It's a grand now."

"Don't try to stiff me, bud. You think I need you? I can drop you off anywhere and get another homeless wino for half the price."

"Don't be so sure. You see the paper today?"

"What's that got to do with you trying to stiff me?"

Joe fished the newspaper from his pants pocket as Ted pulled over. "Here. Read it."

Ted read the headline, **Deputy Killer Still Out There**, and smiled. But reading about an MO, and possible phone tapping, caused a frown. Ted needed to think. Pretending to read more gave just enough time to formulate a plan.

"Okay. I see your point, Joe. Let's get to Silver Heels, have a few drinks, make the call, and then go get the rest of your money. But you need to do one more thing. Write a note that we can leave at the place in case the cops come checking."

"That'll cost you the fifty you brought tonight, and then the grand. We got a deal?"

Ted knew to be careful; this joker could squeal loud and clear.

"Joe, we make a good team. So, yeah. We got a deal."

CHAPTER THIRTY-THREE

THE RING of his cell phone was echoing in the fog, and he couldn't reach it. Touched by a slight breeze from fluttering eyelids, Hawk opened his eyes. Groggy, he listened. Nothing. A handful of sand sat behind his eyelids as they tried to close once more. A spill of moonlight tried to penetrate the fog when he heard another ring, much further away. Fingers of fear enveloped him. Before he could move out of their grip, his cell phone rang again.

Hawk managed to sit up. In the distance was a digital clock blinking four in the morning. He rubbed his eyes and wondered where he was. The incessant ringing of his cell brought him to his feet. Looking down, he saw he was garbed in pajamas. Rubbing his eyes once more, he walked out of his dream and entered the early morning hours of reality. The phone was still ringing when he grabbed it from the dresser. Caller ID let him know that it was Anna Marlet.

"Why are you calling at..." Hawk didn't get to finish his sentence.

"It's Ted... he's after me...you have to do something," Anna demanded hysterically.

"Calm down and tell me what happened."

"I can't calm down; he's after me, I tell you. After me... do you hear?"

"How do you know he's after you?"

"He called a little while ago. He's coming," she screamed.

"If you want my help, you will have to calm down. Tell me what he said." Hawk heard Anna gulp and take a deep breath.

"He said he had given me enough time to produce the bear and that he was coming after it. He said he knows where I live. Tell me what to do," she began to cry.

"Okay. Listen to me carefully. Pack what you need for a week or two, then come to my office. I'll get Jamie to put you up. Meanwhile, was there a number or name on caller ID when Ted called?"

"Just a number, with the same area code as the last call. But no name."

"Give it to me. I'll call it." By now Hawk was in his office. He laughed to himself at the sight it must provoke, a detective working in his pajamas. But this was no laughing matter.

"Okay, got it. Stay on the line while I call."

"Silver Heels Bar and Grill," a male voice answered.

"A friend of mine told me to meet him there. What's the address?" Hawk could only hope the guy didn't notice the out of state area code. He wrote down the address, thanked the man, and returned to his cell.

"The place Ted called from is in Silver Creek, Arizona," he told Anna, "so if he intends to come here, either by plane or car, it will be several hours or days. I still want you out of that apartment. But only after you get to a toy store, or wherever you can find a purple teddy bear. Then, call work and give them an excuse that you need to be gone for a month. Just be sure that the excuse won't put Ted on your trail. Call your parents, too. I don't care what you tell them either, except that you won't be in touch and *don't* tell them where you are going. Only go back to the apartment to put the bear on Miss Evans' bed. After the bear is in place, get out. Drop your cell phone and laptop off with Officer Williams, so Ted can't trace you. Then come directly here. Think you can do that?"

"Y... yes, I guess so. I'm so afraid. What if he shows up before I get out of here or bring the bear back?"

"That's not going to happen." Or, so Hawk hoped it wouldn't. "Does Ted know what you or your car look like?" Finding out that she wasn't sure, an idea formed in Hawk's mind.

"Don't wear any makeup, put your hair in a ponytail, and wear some old clothes, jeans preferably. Stay in touch. Any problems, call me immediately. And tell no one."

———

KNOWING he wouldn't be getting back to bed, Hawk was dressed and had his cup of tea at his desk while he called Wade. This was not the way he planned to start the weekend, as he heard a groggy Wade answer the phone.

"Time to wake up, sleepyhead," Hawk joked.

"Very funny, Hawk. I only got to bed two hours ago. Remember the time difference? This better be good."

Hawk went on to explain the wakeup call he received from Anna Marlet and his instructions to her.

"Sounds like a good idea with the bear. You say Ted's call came from Silver Heels Bar and Grill in Silver Creek?" Hawk mumbled a yes.

"I know where it is. North of where Parker's body was discovered," Wade continued. "I see duty calls—two o'clock on a Saturday morning —kinda like old times. I'll get Johnson and Price on this with me. Be back with you as soon as we get something."

Wade hung up, and Hawk wondered what he could do for the next few hours when he heard the back door in the kitchen being unlocked.

"What's going on? Everything all right?" asked Nick as he met Hawk coming out to the kitchen. "Something woke me up, and I noticed the lights on; thought I'd better check." Nick looked surprised. "You're dressed. What's up?"

"I started out as you, but I won't be getting back to bed anytime soon, so I dressed. My weekend workday has begun. Reminds me of when I was back at the department, getting a call at all kinds of hours. Let's sit in my office unless you want to return to bed or get dressed. And what's with the rod? Are you licensed to carry that?"

Nick pulled his automatic from his shoulder holster and laughed.

"I got this on, but not my clothes," he laughed. "But I'm ready for whatever it is. How can I help? I'll get dressed after you fill me in."

Nick re-holstered, and as he sat on the sofa, Hawk sat behind his desk and told Nick what happened—from Anna's phone call to the call he had made to Wade.

"Now I'm waiting for Wade to call me once he and two of his men investigate."

CHAPTER THIRTY-FOUR

PULLING up to Silver Heels Bar and Grill, Wade saw Johnson and Price standing near the entrance. They were dressed in jeans, each holding a beer, Price dangling a cigarette from his mouth. Wade also wore jeans, hoping to blend in. Approaching the men, he asked, "Either of you check for Ted on the inside?"

"Yep, and nothing," said Johnson. "Without an exact description, it could be anybody. And the people in there don't pay any attention to names. We did locate the phone cable box at the back of the building."

"Then, let's get to it. Got your kit?"

"Right here," Price said, as he picked up the forensic case.

"Okay, lead the way. Price, check for prints on the box, while Johnson and I search the area," Wade instructed.

Price aimed his flashlight on the back of the building. Wade noticed he had stopped short after a few feet. Near a dumpster lay what looked like a man's body. Wade hoped it was some guy passed out from a little too much to drink.

Price turned his light toward the figure on the ground and continued walking. Wade moved past the body; as he looked at it, he knew he didn't need to check for life.

"We have us a homicide. Same MO, including the mutilation." Wade said.

By then, Johnson had joined them.

"Cover him, and call the locals."

If Wade was any judge, sirens would bring the bar crowd out. He didn't need a nosy bunch of people milling around and messing up clues.

"Price. I want this guy printed now."

Wade and Johnson were in the middle of searching the body when the local police arrived. "Is this connected to the Parker case?" asked one the officers, as he jumped from his cruiser.

"That's what we hope to find out," Wade answered.

"Sir? Excuse me. I found this newspaper under the body and..."

"Bag it," Wade interrupted Johnson. He turned back to the officer. "You and your men can be the biggest help by roping off the area and keep it secured while we wait for the ME."

"Suppose this could be Ted?" Price asked.

"Not with this note pinned to his cuff," Wade remarked as he looked at the dead man. "Get the note bagged, then tackle the cable box."

HAWK HAD CALLED Jamie to come in for about an hour and promised her overtime for her effort. He and Nick filled her in on the morning's happenings, but she wasn't happy about the idea of Anna staying with her.

"Let her have your guest room, Boss," she barked.

"You know that's not possible, Jamie," replied Hawk.

"Then tell her to go to a motel."

"And take a chance that Ted would find her? Don't you think he'd check motels, hotels, or B and B's for any recent check-ins? He may still do that if he comes this way."

"That's another thing; he might not even leave Arizona. And if he does, it will be to the city." Jamie was actually pouting, and Hawk found that amusing. He laughed.

"What's so funny?

"You. You're pouting."

"You know how I feel about that Marlet woman. No way I want her staying with me. I like my privacy too much. Nick, help me out. You did so well with her on Thursday."

"You *have* gone quiet, Nick," Hawk said. "I can almost hear the machinery grinding in that head of yours."

"I guess it is," said Nick thoughtfully. "Jamie's mention of your guest room got me to thinking that maybe we could offer Miss Marlet my place. I could stay in your guest room, if you don't object."

"Oh, Boss, please?" Jamie begged.

"Are you sure, Nick?"

"I don't have anything to hide if she gets nosy. Yeah. I'm sure."

"Okay, it's settled. Jamie, you're off the hook. Nick, you go get whatever you need for a couple of weeks."

———

HAWK WAS BACK UPSTAIRS, hoping to get a little shut-eye before the next round, but Nick was already to move in.

"I don't need much. I put some food in the kitchen downstairs; she can at least buy her own groceries." Nick smiled as he hung his clothes in the expansive closet of Hawk's second bedroom. "This is real nice. I like what you've had done to make it your own. It's what I'd expect of you."

"Thanks, Nick. Make yourself at home. If you need to catch up on sleep, the bed is made up. I'm going to lie down before Wade calls back."

No sooner had he spoken, then his cell rang. "Hawk here."

"I'm here. Now how do I get to your secretary's place?" Anna asked.

"There's been a change in plans. I'll be right down."

Hawk had Anna drive around to the garage and park in the third bay.

"Grab your things. You'll be staying here in the apartment above the first bay. It's Mr. Valetti's place; he feels you'll be safer here, and so do I."

At the worried look on Marlet's face, Hawk added, "Don't worry; he'll be bunking with me. Also, you won't be using your car. If you need anything, one of us will get it. You will need to eat, so make a grocery list. I'll send Jamie."

"Okay. I'll do whatever it takes to feel safe... Ooh, this is nice and comfy," Anna remarked as she stepped into Nick's place. "Thank Nick for letting me stay here."

"You can thank him after you get our bill," Hawk chuckled.

———

BACK IN HIS OFFICE, Wade grabbed a cup of black coffee. It had taken two hours on the scene before the body was removed. He stared at the preliminary report. Male, five foot five, gray hair, hazel eyes, approximate time of death: midnight. His clothes looked like he slept in them, no identification, so possibly a vagrant. His prints were on the telephone cable box; some were smudged, but one set was clear. The alligator clips used to tap into the phone line were left at the scene; but no prints, except the dead man's, were found.

This case was becoming more complicated with each incident. Except for the fact that a man was murdered, the MO was the same as Gloria Parker's and the three cold cases. As Wade waited for the autopsy report, he debated about calling Hawk with what he had so far.

———

NICK WAS in the office kitchen, making a pot of coffee when Hawk returned. "How did she take the change?"

"Told me to thank you and she seemed quite pleased with the place."

"So, what's next?"

"We wait for Wade's call and keep an ear to the informant grapevine, in case Ted really does show up."

"The waiting always was the hardest part. Is there anything you need me to do right now?"

"Hmm," Hawk was thoughtful, stroking his chin, "now that you brought it up, there is one thing. I want to grow the agency, and I could use a man with your instincts and investigative background. I'd like you in the office full-time."

"I can't be a full-time paper pusher. I need to do a little gumshoe work, too. I guess you know I turned down the NYPD's offer to stay on at a desk for that very reason. I need to have my, as one famous detective often said, 'little gray cells' working."

Hawk laughed. "Not a problem, Nick; that's exactly what I want from you. There will be times out on cases. Some are humdrum, some not. Besides that, you have a way of keeping the peace. I also need that. Sometimes I just thunder about and make a mess, and I could use someone to keep my feet firmly planted on the ground."

"You know who does that Hawk, and it's not me." Nick sent up a short silent prayer for Hawk. "And yes, I'd be interested, but what about the job I was originally hired for? Who will take care of that?"

"I can hire a service. What do you say?"

"I say... okay." Nick extended his hand, which Hawk firmly grasped. It felt good to have a gentleman's agreement rather than a contract, but he knew the paperwork would come into the picture with tax and salary issues.

————

NICK FELT like a fresh breeze had just blown through on a beautiful spring day. God was good.

Thank you, Lord, for answered prayer. I pray that I may work in this *new position for Your glory and emulate the love of Jesus each day. Be with Hawk; help him find his way back to You. And if You can use me to guide him, I am here—*he prayed silently.

Nick heard Hawk's phone ring.

"Hawk here."

He watched Hawk's facial expressions change as he listened. Probably Wade. He hoped the news was good. Maybe they found their man without anyone getting hurt. Hawk closed his cell with a snap.

"Another murder. Seems like Ted is shaken up. We can only hope he begins to slip up also," Hawk said.

"That's good, isn't it?" Nick inquired.

"Not at the expense of another life, though."

"Sounds as though he's off his MO It was supposed to be a suicide, not murder. Was it another showgirl?"

"Not in the entertainment business at all. And it wasn't a female— some homeless guy. But killed in the same manner. This time there was a note attached to the man's clothing, that read, "Back off cops, or there will be much more." It's signed "Ted." It's in the hands of the analyst right now."

"Interesting. Let me know as soon as you get the results."

"Will do. Ted also left the alligator clip where he had tapped into the phone line. It will probably be the last call from him to Anna Marlet. I can't imagine him not coming after her now. Only we don't need to let her know that."

CHAPTER THIRTY-FIVE

HAWK WASN'T sure why he let Nick talk him into attending church. After his last visit he wasn't sure he'd ever be ready to return. But here he was. He could only hope Jamie would keep a good watch on their *house guest,* and that he could concentrate on the service. Nick chose the third pew from the back, and that made Hawk happy: easier to leave. He felt uneasy as he sat down. There were so many unanswered questions in this case, and it was getting more complicated each day. Hawk wondered if he had lost his touch, or was it the fact that it was a long-distance investigation and he couldn't get into the thick of it?

The praise and worship music began, but Hawk didn't feel as though he could get all *joyed* up. Yet he stood with the rest of the congregation. Rather than sing, he listened.

The music made him think of the Sundays he and Ellie would harmonize on some of the wonderful hymns; she with her beautiful soprano voice and he with his deep baritone. Oh God, I miss her so. Please tell her I still love her. He hoped God didn't consider that a selfish prayer. Maybe it wasn't a prayer, but just a longing.

The singing was over, and everyone was seated when Pastor

Hennings walked to the pulpit. "Our text comes from John 14:27 today."

When Nick opened his Bible, it only served to remind Hawk that he had left his at home. In fact, he hadn't even thought of it. A man, sitting to his right, handed him a pew Bible. "Thanks," Hawk murmured. Now he hoped he could find the Scripture as easily as he used to. As Pastor Hennings continued, Hawk tried to pay attention.

"Jesus is telling you *not* to let your heart be troubled. There is no reason. Not when you have Him to turn to. Didn't He tell us to come to Him, that His burden is light? We, humans, have a tendency to focus on our problems: difficult circumstances, illnesses that linger. We stress out over money. We don't want to forgive people who have caused us harm."

That's it. I can't handle this, Lord. I can't forgive. Hawk began to stir and realized that he would have to get past Nick, who was sitting on his left, at the aisle end of the pew. It was at that moment that Nick chose to look at Hawk. It was a look that told him to grab hold of that peace that Jesus offered and listen to the sermon. Hawk looked back at Pastor Hennings again. Unable to concentrate on the message, his thoughts began to wind down a darkened path. Where was the light he so desperately needed? Nick and Wade would say it was right in his lap. Hawk stared at the Bible and tried to promise himself that he would dust off his own, soon.

"So how do you get past the problems that seem to have you down for the count?" The question from the pastor broke through Hawk's thoughts, bringing him back to the morning message.

"How do you pull yourself up out of the deepest pit you've ever been in and get some peace?" the pastor continued. "You don't. Only Jesus can. Focus on Him instead of the distress that has you crippled. Trust Him to see you through it. Read the Scriptures and see what His word has to say. Then believe, and do as He says. Your heart will always be troubled if you don't. You can never have His peace without obedience to His Word. Go to the Lord in prayer, not just with your troubles, but also with thanksgiving. Trust Him that whatever has happened, He has a purpose. No matter how unfathomable it may seem. If you practice that kind of faith, it will bring His peace."

Hawk stood for the closing prayer. Feeling heavy, his heart questioned how Ellie's death could have any purpose.

———

ANNA HAD WATCHED a church service on television. Not her choice, but both Nick and Hawk thought it would be best if she didn't venture out. After they told her of the death of the homeless man, she had to agree. If she had only kept her mouth shut and never hired Hawk, she wouldn't be hiding out like this. She heard Hawk's car pull into the garage below and wondered if Nick would come up for something he may have forgotten. Right about now she would enjoy some company, anyone's company. She wished she could call a friend, but that was out of the question. After the demands she made on Hawk and Jamie, she wondered if they would ever visit. Cabin fever was beginning to set in after only twenty-four hours. It seemed more like twenty-four days.

———

"WELL, DID OUR GAL STAY PUT?" asked Hawk as he walked into the office kitchen. Jamie was drinking a cup of coffee.

"Not a stir."

"Everything else okay?"

"Not really," Jamie said. "Just before you returned, someone tried the front door but was gone by the time I got there. I ran to the back and still didn't see anyone. I went out and walked around to the front. I noticed that part of the hedge was, like, well, bashed in, as though someone ran something into it. I looked closer and in the dirt; there was a single track like it was from a motorcycle. The hedges certainly weren't that way when I came in this morning. But the weird thing is, I didn't hear any vehicle."

Hawk was out the front door in a flash. He saw where the hedge was "bashed in" as Jamie had put it and found the track. He would have Nick make a cast and get it to Williams at the NYPD.

———

AS ANNA GAZED out the window, Monday morning didn't look any better than the day before. The sun's rays were held captive by a blanket of early morning fog. It lay over the snow-laden treetops of the woods beyond. The quietness was almost more than she could handle. At any other time, it would be a beautiful sight, instead of one that made her feel so all alone.

Dressed in navy sweats, no make-up, and her hair in a ponytail, Anna felt strange. Comfortable. But strange. Things were not going as she had planned. She wanted the man responsible for Jill's death hunted down, and now she was the hunted. She didn't like it, and she was frightened: frightened by a symphony of mystery that had her wondering if Ted would, or could, be found before he got to her.

When Anna realized that she was no longer seeing the scene before her, and was only staring at nothing, she pulled away from the window. Making herself another cup of coffee, she hoped that today someone would up come to see her. About to settle in what she supposed to be Nick's favorite chair, a knock sounded on the front door. She jolted, spilling some of the coffee on herself. She set the coffee on the table and went to the door.

Anna remembered Hawk's admonition not to answer the door until she checked the peephole to see who was there. That seemed foolish, but, nonetheless, she did as she was told. She gasped when she saw a strange man standing on the other side. She prayed he hadn't heard her. Quietly she retreated to the bedroom, picked up the phone, and called Hawk's office.

———

JAMIE BURST through Hawk's door. "Miss Marlet on phone, a strange man..."

"Calm down, Jamie," Hawk said as he picked up line one.

"What's going on?" he asked.

"There's a strange man knocking on the front door up here, and I'm scared! What do I do?" Anna whispered.

That's all Hawk needed: two hysterical women on his hands. He almost laughed but realized this was no laughing matter. Ted would certainly have had time to get to New York, but how he would have found Marlet Hawk couldn't quite puzzle out.

"Where are you in the apartment?" When she told him that she was in the bedroom, he added, "Stay right there and keep quiet, no matter what you hear. I'll be... no. Both Nick and I will be right there."

"And you. You calm down," he said to Jamie.

Hawk headed for Nick's office. "Grab your gun, no time for mine, strange guy at your apartment door."

———

NICK TOOK the stairs closet to his front door while Hawk mounted the ones at the other end of the garages. Nick made good time even with his limp; he stood, back against the sidewall, and peered around the corner. He waited till he saw Hawk appear, then aimed his gun at the guy.

"Hold it right there! Take the stance; against the wall."

"What's a stance?" the young man asked.

"Hands against the wall above your head and feet spread apart! Now!" he bellowed.

Nick thought about the many times he had heard this game of innocence in the past. He had managed to have the foresight to grab his cuffs as he left the office and had the guy in them by the time Hawk reached them both.

"Fast work," Hawk remarked. "Turn him around and let's see who we have here."

"It's me, Mr. Hawkins. Jerry. Preston's friend."

———————

BACK IN NICK'S OFFICE, Hawk began. "So, what are you doing here, and back there over my garage?" Nick sat silently, and for that, Hawk was glad. Nothing had been said to the young man to alert him to the fact that it was Preston's father who had cuffed him. He also didn't want Jerry to know about Anna Marlet's stay in the apartment. He still couldn't be sure who anybody was, and he was taking no chances.

"I was looking for Preston's Dad. I was told he lived over the first garage on the left side."

"And," Hawk prompted as Jerry hesitated.

"I haven't heard from Preston, and I thought his father might be able to tell me why. Or tell me exactly where he is. All I know is, he went to Chicago. I called Jamie last week, but she didn't know either."

At that moment, Jamie knocked and entered.

"Hey! Jerry. What are you doing here?"

"Looking for Preston's father," answered Jerry.

"Hey, you don't have to look..."

"We have this under control, Jamie, and I'll fill you in later," Hawk interrupted, as he grabbed Jamie's arm and ushered her out the door.

"Preston's father is..." Jamie tried to say more, but Hawk quieted her with a gentle squeeze to her arm and a finger to his lips.

———————

"JERRY," Hawk said as he stepped back into Nick's office, "I'll let Preston's father know of your visit, and I'll leave it up to him to contact you. Leave your number with me."

"I don't understand. Why the handcuffs?"

"My partner and I weren't sure who you were at first, especially out back. Most of our visitors come through the front office door.

And we would appreciate it if that's the way you would do so in the future."

"I did, yesterday when I saw Jamie's car here. I tried the office door. It was locked, so I figured she might have had car trouble and left it parked here."

"Why would you think the office was opened on a Sunday?" asked Hawk.

"Ah, some people work every day of the week. Thought I'd see if anyone was here."

"And why would that be?'

"Well, if you must know, I went to Jamie's place, but she wasn't home, so I thought I'd see if she was working. I wanted some company."

Hawk noticed that Nick was still quiet, closely observing Jerry. So, he continued to question Jerry.

"You own a motorcycle?"

"Nah. But sometimes I borrow my friend's bike. I did yesterday if that's what you're getting at. I was hoping Jamie would ride with me."

"Okay. Now jot your phone number down for me."

Jerry wrote his number on a piece of paper Nick had handed him. Hawk watched Jerry leave the office, mumbling under his breath something about crazy people. When Hawk turned around, he saw Nick bagging the pen and the paper with Jerry's number on it.

"Prints might tell us something," Nick spoke the first words since he had cuffed the kid.

"I agree. This kid is hiding something. Meanwhile, I'll get this and the tire cast to Williams, while you handle Marlet and Jamie."

———

"HEY! Hawk. How's the investigation going?" Williams asked.

"Slow, Pete. There's been another murder, and Ted has threatened to come after Marlet. Just this morning we had a guy knocking on Nick's door, supposedly looking for him. I do know the kid had been acquainted with Nick's son, but that's all I know. We caught him and questioned him in the office. I had him jot his number on this piece of paper so you can run it and the pen he used, for prints. Check the phone number, too.

"So, you thinking he might be Ted?"

"It's possible. That's what we want to find out. He also made a visit yesterday morning on a friend's motorcycle; at least, according to him. I had Nick make this cast, and I need it run also." Hawk sat on the corner of Williams' desk.

"Why would he try the office on a Sunday?" asked Williams.

"He said it was to find Jamie, but I think there's more to it than that."

"Sounds like it. I can't promise, but I'll see if we can get this scheduled for today, and give you a call later. Hate to chase you off, Hawk, but I have a one o'clock court hearing, so let me get to you later."

"Sure thing. I appreciate the help." Hawk stood, shook Williams hand, and was out the door.

———

HAWK DROVE UP COLUMBUS AVENUE, nearing his and Ellie's condo. Perhaps he should stop at Teri Brown Realty and see if his home was showing. But, instead, he pulled into the parking garage and noticed Teri's car in his stall. He parked in the space that was reserved for Ellie. Funny how this still felt like coming home and Ellie waiting upstairs to greet him. Could he do this? Yes. He was getting stronger each day.

As he stepped off the elevator, he noticed signs that gave directions to a *Business Lunch Open House* in his condo. When he entered what he still felt was "home," he noticed people eating and touring the place. He looked for Teri and saw her in deep conversation with a young couple. Not wanting to spoil a possible sale, he joined others at the buffet.

There were salads of all kinds—potato, pasta, bean, crab, lobster, and Caesar—plus a few he wasn't sure about; an assortment of cold cuts, cheeses, and several antipasti were included. He took a paper plate and helped himself. He grabbed a bottle of water from the cooler and went to the kitchen table. So what if he sat there; after all, it was still his place, he thought.

"There you are," Teri said as she entered the kitchen. She sat across from him, sipping a cola.

A petite brunette with laughing eyes, she looked like a college kid dressed up for a job interview. Red stilettos matched a two-piece red suit. The jacket was opened showing a soft white blouse, patterned with dainty red flowers. She adorned the outfit with a few gold chains that matched her hoop earrings. Other than bright red lips, her make-up was natural.

"Food brings them in every time. Glad you could dine with us," Teri laughed.

Hawk only smiled. He felt as if his and Ellie's home had been violated by this invasion of people out for a free lunch. And he felt guilty for noticing the beautiful woman that sat across the table.

"This time it's good news," Teri continued. "I have an offer, and since I noticed you walk in, I asked them to get some lunch and wait. Is this a good time for you to look it over?"

Hawk felt his timing couldn't have been better. Yet he found himself hesitating. This would mean the end. As long as the condo was still on the market, he knew in the back of his mind that he could come *home* whenever he liked. But this would be like saying goodbye all over again. *Can I honestly do it? Maybe that was what the pastor was talking about in his sermon yesterday,* he thought. *Yes, I have to. I need to get on with my life. Ellie would want it that way.*

"Okay. Let me see their offer," he finally said.

Teri walked him through the paperwork, and he saw that it was a generous offer. Better than the one on his Island place. This would make up the difference.

"Yes, I can accept this. Where do I sign?"

When Hawk had finished his part of the paperwork, Teri excused herself to seek out the couple interested in buying. Hawk got up, suddenly not very hungry. He walked to the nursery Ellie had been working on. He sat on the toy box and stared at the frilly pink curtains. He had hoped that reminiscing about the dreams they had for their little girl would soothe his grieving soul. Instead, the pain started afresh. That was where Teri found him a few minutes later.

"Hawk. Are you okay? Perhaps you need to get out of here. I can call you about the closing."

He agreed, left the room, and walked past the people still in the middle of eating. He left the condo as fast as he could. Once he was in the parking garage, he drew in a deep breath and climbed into his silver Jaguar. With a heavy foot on the gas, he burned rubber pulling out of the parking garage. Knowing that he had one more thing to do, he headed back to Groveland Hills and his future.

CHAPTER THIRTY-SIX

WADE WAS at his wit's end. The more the evidence piled up, the more confusing the case became. It was time to call Hawk once more.

"Hawk Detective Agency," Jamie answered.

"Jamie, it's Wade. Is the boss man around?"

"He just got in from the city and asked not to be disturbed, but… for you, I think it'll be okay."

It took only a couple of minutes and Hawk was on the line. "Hey! Wade. What do you have for me?"

"A big, fat, zero. You were right. There were a lot of smudges on the cable box. We identified prints belonging to the dead man. The other set of prints belong to a Gerald Malone, who has a record of petty theft. Can't tell how old the Malone print is as yet. But it appears to be at least a week old, so we can't pinpoint him at Silver Heels Bar on the night of the murder. I sent a uniform to his last known address. He's been gone about five months from there. All the landlord knew was that Malone said he was going east."

"Did he sport a nickname by any chance?"

"The landlord called him Jerry."

Hawk relayed the story of Jerry's two visits, and the fact that he rode a motorcycle that belonged to a friend.

"Williams has all the info and is checking on Malone's story," Hawk added.

"So, when do you expect the results?"

"Hopefully, this afternoon."

"Call me as soon as you get them, no matter what the time. I'll leave word to put you straight through," Wade assured him.

"Will do." Hawk drew the two words out, then jumped out of his comfort zone. "I need to change the subject here, Wade. I have some big-time decision making to do, and I need your prayers."

"You're always in my prayers, but I'll make a special effort for this particular need. And when you're ready to talk about it, I'm here."

Hawk said thanks and hung up, leaving Wade holding the receiver, a bit bewildered. He hung up then and went straight to prayer for his friend.

———

HAWK FELT himself shaking as he hung up; he wondered why he could be so disturbed by a simple request for prayer.

A light tap on his door and Nick walked in. "Jamie mentioned that Wade called. Anything new?"

"Just that our boy, Jerry, was at the last murder scene, but not necessarily at the same time."

"Not what I like to hear. Does the iron gate out front work? It might be time to close it at night. And what about Jamie? Jerry knows where she lives since he helped Preston with her move. Think she'd go for staying up with Miss Marlet?"

"Hmm. You may have something. Call her in, would you?"

———

"YOU GOTTA BE KIDDING," Jamie remarked. "He and Preston are friends. And he's been really nice to me since Preston's been gone."

"Do you know where he lives?" asked Nick.

"I don't know exactly; somewhere in the Bronx."

"How often, and where, do you see him?" this from Hawk.

"Mostly, when I see Rebecca. He hangs around her shop, and I think they're a little sweet on one another. You know," she said thoughtfully, "he could be living with her."

"After this morning's fiasco, we think he might try to see you, especially if he is connected to this case in any way. If the prints we gave to Williams match the prints at the murder scene, it could get messy for you."

"Oh, Boss. No. What can we do? And what about Rebecca?"

"First, we are going to check out the gates to this place and get them closed after hours. Second, we would like you to stay here, up with Marlet." Jamie began to open her mouth, but Nick gently laid a hand on her shoulder as Hawk continued.

"I know you're not too fond of our *guest*, but you may not have a choice. It is possible Jerry could even be Ted, or at least working with him. I don't want any new people around the property for the time being. The less your friend, Rebecca, knows, the safer she is."

"Couldn't I sleep in here on your sofa? Or get a roll away for the third office?"

"No, Jamie. Not this time. It might prove safer having the two of you together. Please go home. Pack enough for two weeks, and bring any food that might spoil."

Jamie hesitated, but Nick gently escorted her out of Hawk's office.

———

"WHAT'S NEXT, Hawk? Want me to see to the gate now, in case we need to call someone in on it?" Nick asked when he returned to Hawk's office.

"I think you better change and get back into your *janitor* clothes."

195

Hawk gave a half-hearted chuckle. "Move the truck out, so Jamie can park her car in that bay, then check the gate. Meanwhile, I'm calling Williams."

———

JAMIE WASN'T THRILLED about having to bunk with Anna Marlet, but she was even less thrilled about being a possible target for Ted. If a policewoman could be taken in, what chance did she have? *This is one of those times I need to woman up,* she thought. After parking her car in the last bay, as Nick directed, she followed him up to the apartment.

———

ANNA HAD BEEN BRIEFED on the situation and was more than happy to have Jamie stay with her. She could only hope they could get along; perhaps sit and talk. Anna was beyond cabin fever. Then, she heard the door unlock, open, and noticed Jamie hesitate.

"Hi! Jamie," Anna ventured. "Scary, isn't it? I'm going stir crazy, especially not knowing what's happening." Anna knew she was rambling, but she wanted desperately to have Jamie as an ally.

"Yeah. A real bummer," Jamie said as she stepped in the room, with Nick behind. "I'm not real jazzed up about this setup, either."

"Let me show you where you will sleep," Nick said as he picked up her bag.

"I think we can figure it out, Nick," Anna offered. "You needn't stay.

"Uh, yeah. Okay. Then I'll see you downstairs after you get settled, Jamie." Nick locked the door behind him.

"At least it's a cozy place. First time I've been up here. So, you're stir crazy, huh?"

"Yes, and I only have myself to blame. If I hadn't hired Hawk..." Anna let her voice trail off.

"Hey! Don't blame yourself."

"I miss working and feel positively naked without my makeup and clothes."

"You know, you look... um. You look more comfortable, and more approachable."

"Oh?" Anna asked, a little surprised by Jamie's remark.

"Yep. It was as though you thought yourself above us petty peons."

"Oh, my. Is that the impression I gave?"

"It sure was, but not now. Ya know, this might not be too bad after all."

———

IT WAS late Tuesday afternoon when Jamie ran into Hawk's office with two envelopes. "It's here; the report on Jerry and the motorcycle."

Hawk scanned it quickly.

"Ask Nick to come here."

Then he looked over the results from forensic on the tire track. The bike was a Harley and registered to one Trevante Phillips of Groveland Hills. A background check showed the guy was clean.

"Is it the same guy?" asked Nick as he came in and sat across from Hawk.

"Yes, but now we have the owner of the bike to consider. Although his background is clean, I'd like you to question him. He's local."

Hawk handed the report to Nick.

"Another curious thing is the address listed for Malone. It's the same tenement building at Hunt's Point, where they caught Jamie's attacker. That building hasn't been lived in for a few years, so listing that address keeps him on the suspect list."

"Maybe he does *live* there. You said a lot of the low life does. I wonder how Preston got hooked up with him? And does he know anything about this guy's background? I think it's time I call my son."

Nick left, and Hawk stroked his chin as he picked up the phone to call Wade.

———

HAWK DIDN'T GIVE Wade a chance to properly answer the phone.

"It's the same guy," he blurted out. "Gerald Malone, also known as Gerald Maclay and as Jerry Malley: six feet: one hundred ninety-five pounds: brown hair, brown eyes, a scar about two inches long from the left elbow down toward his wrist: last seen in the vicinity over four weeks ago. Word was he was headed west. His purpose for a trip out there is a big question, especially if he went to Silver Heels Bar and Grill. He then returned to the Bronx and somehow became friends with Preston. We're not sure he has a permanent address. A lot of questions are popping up," Hawk sounded frustrated. "Meanwhile, the motorcycle track has created a new player. I'll have Jamie email over the reports. Is there anything new happening on that end?"

"Nothing. It's as though Ted dug a hole and buried himself. No recent suicides in the state and no murders since our vagrant. I think you may be right, Hawk. Ted is either on his way or is already there. It's sounding like Jerry may be our man. Just get him before he gets anyone else."

CHAPTER THIRTY-SEVEN

HAWK WAS ALREADY at his desk when Nick stuck his head around the door. "You have time to talk?"

"Sure. What's on your mind?"

"My cop instinct tells me something's not right. "

"And, what might that something be?" asked Hawk, as he readied papers for Jamie to file.

"I'm not sure. I'm thinking; maybe we should get the key to Miss Marlet's apartment. Ask Williams to get forensic on it. See if anything turns up, like Ted or Jerry's prints."

"Not a bad idea. We might even check with Williams and see if any messages have come through on her cell or laptop. I'll call him to set it up."

Disappointed that Williams could not promise anything until after Christmas, and maybe not even then, Hawk guessed it was time he and Nick took matters into their own hands. This couldn't wait. Ted —or Jerry—needed to be off the street. Now.

"I KNOW it was my idea, but I feel uneasy," Hawk said, as he unlocked the apartment door.

"Marlet gave us the key and said she'd swear she asked us to pick up her makeup case when we went to the city. Now, don't let me lose confidence in you," Nick chuckled.

When he stepped through the door, Hawk gave out a long, low whistle. Nick joined him.

"Guess Williams will have to give this some priority now," said Hawk. "This place has been torn to shreds by a mad man or a wild beast."

"Ted, or someone, has done some serious damage. I'm calling Williams now," Nick said, as he pulled out his cell phone.

Waiting in the hall for Williams and his team, Hawk looked back at the apartment and wondered what kind of anger Ted carried around that made him mutilate anyone, or anything, that got in his way.

———

HAWK AND NICK talked with Williams in the hall, while forensic did their job.

"You touched nothing?" Williams asked.

"Nothing. Nick called you within two minutes of opening the door. Before you ask—Marlet wanted her makeup case; that's why we are here."

"I know. It's your story, and you're sticking to it."

Hawk chose to ignore Williams' barb. "It looks like one angry person went through the rooms with a knife, and I'm thinking Ted. He and Jerry may be one and the same. I tried the number Malone gave us, but it's no longer in service. Jamie says he's been hanging around Rebecca at her shop, Becky's Florist on..."

"Yes, I know where it is. I got my wife's birthday roses there," Williams cut in. "We'll check it out. Anything else I need to know?"

"It looks like he may be connected with the murders in Arizona since his prints were found at the scene of the last one, and he lived out there," Nick spoke up.

"Okay. I'll be in touch the minute we have some results."

———

"NO, NO, NO," Anna Marlet shrieked. Jamie put her arms around her, and Nick held her hand, as she began to sob. Hawk walked to the window, his usual stance and stroking his chin. It hadn't been easy telling Marlet, and now he had to face Jamie with another scenario.

"I'm sorry," he said as he turned to face the trio hunched together on his office sofa. "I dislike having to say this, but I think it might be a good idea to check out your apartment also," Hawk told Jamie. "I better have the key. And, Nick, I don't want these two left alone, so I'd like you to stay with them."

"Boss, do you really think Jerry is Ted? That he might have tried to trash my place, too?" Jamie asked as she handed him her key.

"I don't know what to think, except we need to check all possibilities. Has he tried to call you?" Jamie shook her head. "Good. I think. Perhaps you better turn off your cell. Also, we may need to keep the gate closed both day and night until Ted is found."

———

AFTER SEVERAL HOURS away from the office, Hawk returned to find Jamie at her desk. "Your place is fine. Where is Nick and Marlet?"

"Thanks, Boss. Anna went back to the apartment. I think she needed to lie down for a while. Nick's in his office."

"Jamie, you continue to work in the office, but either Nick or I will escort you to and from the apartment, even if it is over the garage. Nick has already taken to patrolling the grounds."

Hawk entered Nick's office and plopped on a chair.

"After all those years of investigation work, it must be frustrating to leave it to someone else," Nick said.

"Guess I could say the same for you, Nick. Except for questioning the bike owner, you're left out of this one, too."

"Yes, but it may have its advantages. We don't have to hold with department procedure. Instead, we can look at this case in an entirely different light."

"I think you may be right, Nick."

"So. What's next?"

"The waiting game: see what Williams reports. Hopefully, it will include nabbing Jerry."

CHAPTER THIRTY-EIGHT

THE NEXT MORNING, Hawk came downstairs lugging a big box that was labeled "Christmas tree!"

"Is that what I think it is, boss?"

"Yes. Nick is bringing down the ornaments. It's a job for you and Marlet today. You can put it anywhere and decorate however you both want. You two may not be able to get out, but at least you can have Christmas."

As Nick carried the other large box down, Hawk heard the familiar ping of a new email from his laptop. He hoped it was Williams' report, and he was not disappointed.

He was studying the email on his computer when he noticed Nick standing in his office doorway.

"It's the report on Marlet's apartment. Take a seat." Hawk gestured toward the couch.

"They found Jerry with Rebecca at her shop," he said. "They're holding him for questioning on breaking and entering Marlet's apartment."

"Wait a sec, Hawk. I don't think it was a B and E. When we entered with the key, I didn't notice anything that would indicate the door had been jimmied." Nick said.

"You're right. Let me see what else... hmm," Hawk thought for a moment. "It seems forensic went over that apartment with the proverbial fine-toothed comb and, except for our shoe prints, came up empty. This is one time I'm glad I'm not officially involved."

"No prints? Nothing for DNA?"

"Nothing out of the ordinary. Prints from Marlet, the Evans girl, both parents, some friends, but not Jerry or any other odd prints. Williams' conclusion is someone used gloves, picked the lock, and was covered from head to toe so that nothing could be inadvertently left at the scene. We have us a crafty killer."

"Wouldn't someone, fully covered, be noticed entering the building? So, is Ted another alias for Jerry?"

"Good questions. What did you find out when you called Preston? Any leads there?"

"Nothing there either. Jerry walked into Georgios one day looking for a job. That's when Preston first met Malone. My son saw him as a guy down on his luck and tried to help him out. He really didn't know anything about him. He just took Jerry at his word. I thought I taught him better than that. What else does the report say?"

"It goes on to say they interviewed a few neighbors, but most were at work. The few that were home didn't hear or see anything. This case is getting curiouser and curiouser."

"Hawk," Nick hesitated, "I don't know how you worked when you were with the department, but I do know you're a believer..."

"I have been having a rough time coming to grips with that fact since Ellie was killed. And I wonder if I'm ever going to get through it," Hawk interrupted.

"You know you will, but not alone. Listen, Hawk; this isn't what I intended to talk about when I mentioned that I knew you were a believer. But evidently, God has His agenda at work here. So, I'd like to continue."

"Sure, Nick."

"I can't imagine how you feel. I only know what I felt when Preston's mother walked out on us. I don't know how I would have made it, except through God's grace. I was bitter and angry, but I had to forgive her before I could find peace and move on."

"You don't need to say it, Nick; I know I'm supposed to forgive Doogan for killing... for killing my Ellie, but I can't." Hawk didn't want this conversation. He wanted Nick to leave his office, return to his own, but he couldn't bring himself to dismiss the man.

"She wasn't *your* Ellie, Hawk. She was, and is, God's. We all have an appointment with Him. We just don't know the time or means He will use, or allow to be used. Not forgiving will eat at you, and unless you trust God instead of blaming Him, bitterness will consume you, and you'll never find the peace that only God can give."

"Easier said than done." The intercom buzzed and before Hawk could answer it, Nick had leaned over the desk and told Jamie they were not to be disturbed until further notice.

———

HAWK HAD WALKED to the window while Nick was on the intercom. He stood, looking out at nothing but a fog of thought-provoking memories, stranded somewhere between anger and forgiveness.

"I don't even know where to begin," he mumbled.

"Begin with prayer, Hawk. Ask God to forgive you. Then go and do as the Holy Spirit directs. I'm praying for you, and I'm here if you need me." Nick got up to leave when Hawk turned around.

"Nick, wait... perhaps we could have that prayer now."

Nick turned back, pulled a chair next to the sofa and motioned for Hawk to join him.

"I'm here for support, Hawk, but you're the one who needs to talk with God."

Hawk was uncomfortable. How long had he gone without real

communication with God? He knew he needed his soul mended. So, he began.

"I am angry, God: angry at the man who killed Ellie. Why did You allow it to happen? If You have a purpose, I sure don't see it."

Tasting bile, Hawk struggled to end the prayer, but could not. He heard Nick briefly end it by asking God to bless him and give him peace and the strength to forgive. Hawk also heard the door close behind Nick.

———

HAWK'S PRAYER was from the heart. It was a deep-down cleansing prayer, one that made Nick feel drained when he returned to his office. But he continued to pray silently that God would also give Hawk the strength to make the trip to Sing-Sing. Nick had offered to go with him when he had admitted that he knew God was pressing him to face Doogan and to forgive him.

Nick's intercom buzzed.

"Yes, Jamie."

"It's Chief Fields, Groveland Hills PD, on line one."

"Shouldn't this call go to Hawk?"

"I tried, but he said you could handle it, that he was tied up right now."

———

"CHIEF FIELDS WANTS A MEETING. How 'bout it, Hawk?" Nick asked as he stood at Hawk's desk.

"You go, Nick. You know as much about this case as anyone."

"It's not about the Marlet case. It's about possibly retaining our office for homicide cases. He wanted to meet with you before going to the mayor."

"You still go. I trust your judgment, and you're in a better frame of mind than I am. I've decided to call the Big House and find out if Doogan will see me."

"He'll see you," Nick said with confidence. "If for no other reason than to spit in your face."

"Then, I will take you up on your offer to go with me."

CHAPTER THIRTY-NINE

"OKAY, Malone, you know why you were picked up. Now, let's hear your story," Williams said as he practically went nose to nose with the suspect.

"Hey, I told my story already, and besides I haven't done anything. Just because I have a record, you guys think you can pick me up for anything."

Williams was used to hearing suspects whine about innocence while trying to hide their guilt behind injustice. Malone didn't seem any different.

"It's not because of your record, but because your prints were found at a murder scene in Arizona. Now, tell your story to me."

The door opened, and a large man with spiked hair the color of straw strode in. He was dressed in a blue business suit, white shirt, and a multi-colored tie.

"Not without my presence," he said as his black patent leather shoes squeaked in cadence with his steps.

"Who are you, and who let you enter this interview room?" Williams was ready to call one of his officers on the carpet.

"Robert Talon of Talon and Talon Law Firm," he answered as he placed his brown leather briefcase on the table. He handed Williams his card and took the chair next to Jerry. "And Mr. Malone is my client."

"Fine; sit in on the questioning if you want."

Williams wasn't exactly happy with the unexpected arrival of an attorney. He thought he might have a little time before Malone would think of calling one. For that matter, when did the suspect call one?

"Sorry to burst your bubble, detective, but I need some time with my client before you proceed. And I think you can pretty well dispose of any previous Q and A's since I was not present."

"Fine. I'll question my other suspect while you use this room." Williams kept his cool although Talon was getting on his wrong side.

"I think you'll find my associate, Richard Talon, with Miss Holland," the attorney smirked.

———

"REBECCA HOLLAND LOOKED like she had been crying when Williams stepped into the next interview room. And, sure enough, there was Talon's associate. Or was it? It was as though Talon himself had walked through the walls and emerged to play lawyer in this room also. Richard and Robert Talon were twins. The same build, the same spiked, straw-colored hair. He had a rugged looking face, as though he spent every free moment outdoors doing something physical. Only this Talon wore a brown business suit with a cream-colored shirt and a solid brown tie. He sported brown loafers with tan socks. His black briefcase lay opened with various sheets of paper spilling out, and Miss Holland was quite intent on what Talon was saying. Williams gave a slight cough to announce his arrival, and both heads turned toward him.

"Mr. Talon, I'm officer Williams, and I'm here to question Miss Holland. Are you ready yet?" Williams didn't want the same encounter with this Talon as he had with his brother.

"Quite ready, Officer," Talon said.

"Okay, Miss Holland, I'd like you tell me how you know, and what you know, about one Mr. Gerald Malone? And how you fit into all this?"

Williams thought she was going to burst into tears as she looked down at her hands that were fidgeting in her lap. The little bit of mascara she wore, mingled with tears, looked as though someone had tried to finger paint on her face. Her short brown hair also had the spiked look. *What is it with the spiked hair today?* he wondered.

———

ROBERT TALON UNLOCKED A RATHER exquisite looking briefcase and took out a handful of papers. "Alright, Mr. Malone, shall we get down to business? I have some papers for you to sign, and then we can begin to unravel this mess." His smile looked as though it was pasted on just for Jerry's benefit.

"Sign them yourself," Jerry said as he shoved the papers back at the lawyer. "Who asked for you anyway?"

"Since my associate was called in for Miss Holland, we thought it was best to have me along to represent you."

"Well, you thought wrong. I don't need a lawyer... I have friends. I don't need you, so why don't you just pack it up and get outta here. Besides... I'm innocent."

"But Mr. Malone..."

Jerry stood and called for the officer outside the door. "Get this guy outta here. I don't need no lawyer. Especially him."

———

HAWK WAS ready to call it a day. He went over all the reports and evidence, trying to find anything that might have been missed. He was exhausted. Since he wasn't officially involved, he needed to leave it in the hands of those who were. He didn't need a repeat of Hunts Point.

Nor did he need to burn bridges with Williams. He just might need him in the future.

Hawk also needed to leave what happened to Ellie in the hands of God. He appreciated that no one interrupted him for the rest of the day. Although he was curious about Nick's meeting with Chief Fields, he knew it could wait.

Hawk had called Sing-Sing and was informed that Doogan would see him, and the sooner, the better. Whatever that meant. He set it up for the next day. As much as Hawk didn't want to leave the women on their own, he wanted Nick with him. He knew he needed a prayer warrior along. Maybe the GHPD Chief could spare a uniform to be here in their absence. It would be worth paying the man.

Hawk closed the door behind him and was greeted with the sight of Ellie's Christmas tree and all her ornaments. He felt a stab of pain and wondered when his heart would quit sinking to his stomach, every time he saw something that Ellie had touched. The reception room was beautiful. Jamie and Marlet had done a great job at giving the office some Christmas spirit, and he let them know.

"So, Boss. Ya want some hot apple cider?"

"Where did you get the makings?"

"Nick did our shopping for us; we just gave him a list," offered Anna.

"Did I hear my name mentioned?" asked Nick as he came out of his office. "I'd say it was time to call it a day. You gals have done a great job. It looks like Christmas!"

———

SUPPER CONSISTED of TV dinners for Hawk and Nick. They discussed the case and how Hawk needed to leave it with the NYPD and Wade. Yet, he needed to be ready to assist whenever needed.

"I'm glad you agreed to have me tag along when you see Doogan," Nick said. "I'll stay in the waiting room, praying while you meet with Doogan."

Nick had called the GHPD and hired an off-duty family man to stay at the office for a few hours in the morning. All in all, things seemed to be shaping up. *Then why am I waiting for the other shoe to drop?* Hawk asked himself.

———

AS HAWK LEFT Nick in the waiting room and followed the guard, he bowed his head and said a silent prayer. *Father God, please search my heart for the unforgiveness I am harboring against Ellie's killer, and take it away. Please forgive me and help me to forgive without any more anger, judgment, or thoughts of revenge. In Jesus' name, amen.*

The guard pointed Hawk to a chair and left the room. As he surveyed the room, Hawk noticed that there were only two visitors, each sitting in front of a window. There were small, circled holes at the bottom, like a bank teller's cage, for conversation to take place. Then a door opened beyond the barrier, and there stood Tank Doogan with that cocky grin of his, in leg irons and cuffs.

Lord, help me here, I want to grab him, and kill him. Please forgive me. Hawk's heart cried his prayer. This was not where he wanted to be. It took all his strength just to stay in his seat.

"Well, well, if it isn't the high and mighty detective himself. Not enough you put me here; now ya want to gloat too? Too bad I didn't have Link kill you, too, then I wouldn't have to look at your ugly kisser. So whaddaya want?" Doogan asked as he sat down.

Hawk's throat felt dry as he tried to speak. He cleared his throat and then said, "Forgiveness. Forgiveness for harboring anger, bitterness, and the desire to kill you." There. Hawk finally voiced the sin that was eating him alive. "God has forgiven me; now, I ask your forgiveness."

"Ha. So ya want forgiveness from me, just to soothe your conscience? Well, ya came to the wrong place." Doogan continued his tirade with a string of obscenities.

Hawk wasn't ready for the barrage of profanity lashed out by

Doogan. It made him anxious, and he wished he could leave, but he had to see this through. He had hoped that he could have said something that would have touched Doogan's heart with God's love. But evidently, it wasn't to be.

"Hey! guard," Doogan bellowed as his stare bore a cold shiver right through Hawk. "Get me outta here." Then to Hawk, "You may believe all that holy stuff, but me, ha, I'll take my chances with the devil."

Doogan spat at the plexiglass that separated the two men. Standing, he let the guard lead him away. Hawk stared at the chair Doogan just vacated, then held his face in his hands and wondered how he could feel so drained.

CHAPTER FORTY

HAWK WASN'T SURPRISED to hear his cell ringing at seven Monday morning, but he was surprised when caller ID showed it to be Wade. "Early hour for you. Have we got a break?"

"No. Couldn't sleep, so I decided to call, hoping that something is breaking there. We're not quitting because of Christmas, but it has been dragging. I hope that Williams' investigation is going better. And what did you find out on brainwashing from that professor friend?"

"I hope to hear from Williams today, and I'll be calling Professor Hoffmann later. He's on holiday break from NYU. He might be able to come here so both Nick and I can pick his brain. Meanwhile, I hope you're sitting down; I have something I want to share." Hawk let Wade know about his prayer of confession, his visit with Doogan, and Nick's moral support.

"Praise God! I've been praying for this, Hawk; and God sent Nick. I look forward to meeting that man one day."

"All you need to do is come home. Not only will you meet Nick, but you will have a job and an office waiting for you."

"That's a tempting offer, but we have to get this case solved first. Then we can talk."

Hawk realized that he needed to let the subject drop for now. He also knew it would be no easy decision for Wade to make.

"What are you doing for Christmas?" asked Hawk.

"Church. Then sit at home. I'll make a few calls to the kids and such. How about you?"

"Believe it or not, I let the girls decorate the office. I even brought down the Christmas tree and ornaments—quite a difference from last year. Guess I'm beginning the healing process, although it still hurts. Hey, pal, I need to ring off and get downstairs to begin my workday. I'll call you as soon as I hear from Williams. And I'll make that call to the professor a priority."

———

IN HIS OFFICE, hand perched on the phone, Hawk sat like a wooden soldier. He wondered if Professor Benjamin Hoffmann would think that the idea of suicide by subliminal messages would sound as foolish as it was beginning to sound to him.

"I'm seeing Hawk Detective Agency on my caller ID. Could this be my old friend the Hawk?"

"Hello, Ben. It's good to hear your voice again."

"So, tell me: what can I do for you?"

"To be honest with you, I'd like to hire you for a case I'm working on."

"Hire me? Whatever for? I do you favor without money. I owe you, friend."

Hawk related his thoughts on the possibility of someone brainwashing another to commit suicide. "It sounds foolish now that I've had time to think about it, but I had to call anyway."

"Intriguing. I come to your office. We explore together, ja? I leave now." And with that, the professor ended the call.

Hawk thought about his friend's offer to help without pay.

It was nearly ten years, but the memory remained. In the precinct,

Hawk had been at his desk when he had heard a big commotion at the booking desk.

"What's going on?" he asked Detective Donavan.

"Ah, just some old coot blabbering that his teenage daughter was kidnapped. He's a professor at NYU and is known to be a little eccentric. We're trying to get rid of him. Have a go if you'd like."

Hawk walked over to the man and heard his unheeded pleas. He noticed tears in the man's eyes and decided that he needed to be heard. Hawk escorted him into his office and listened as Professor Hoffmann told him about an angry student who was upset because the professor had given the young man a failing grade. The professor received a note stating that unless the student received a passing mark, the professor's daughter would come to harm.

"May I see the note, Professor?"

Reading the note, Hawk realized that it *was* police business. But to get Donavan to realize that would be something else. Again, he would have to go behind his back to work this case. But work it he did. He not only found the young man, but also the professor's daughter before any harm could come to her. After that incident, Hawk and the professor became fast friends.

————

JAMIE WAS ENJOYING a second cup of coffee before going over to the office when Anna walked in the kitchen. "Umm, coffee smells good," she said as she poured a cup. "Are you planning to be late?"

"I'm thinking about it. There's not a whole lot to do since Christmas is in a few days."

"Yes, I'm really upset about that. I don't see why we have to stay cooped up here now. After all, they have Ted, Jerry, or whatever his name is, behind bars. I want to be with my parents, where I spend every Christmas. Don't you want to get out of here, too?"

"Yeah, but I also don't want to be a target. They may have Jerry in jail, but they're still not sure if he's Ted. I wouldn't want to chance it."

"It's okay for you; at least you can work. I can't."

"Well, from what I hear, it's not like you need the money."

"Hey, money or not, my career is important to me, as I would hope your job is to you. This lying around has me climbing the walls. It's not for me."

"Well, why don't you tell Hawk how you feel?"

"I might just do that."

———

THE INTERCOM BUZZED, and Jamie announced the arrival of Professor Hoffmann. Hawk had opened the gate earlier in anticipation of the professor's arrival.

"Show him in, Jamie, and ask Nick to join us."

Hawk stood to receive his old friend.

"Ben. It's good to see you again. Come on in and have a seat."

The professor sat as Nick walked in.

"Professor, my partner, Nick Valetti," Hawk said. He then gave the professor a synopsis of the case to date.

"So, you can see the dilemma we're in."

"Only dilemma I see is the person you call Ted is not operating according to norm. Maybe we have to consider the importance of his mental state, and this thing commonly called brainwashing."

"What do you mean, Professor?" asked Nick.

"You say you have email and other messages from this person? And you say this Ted—he was in model's apartment and made a mess, maybe looking for a purple teddy bear? So, we read the emails, the messages, and if I may be allowed, see the mess he made in the apartment. Sometimes the person will tell things about themselves in the words they use and in their actions."

Hawk picked up the file of emails and photos of Marlet's apartment.

"I'll have Jamie make copies so you can take them with you."

"Nein, nein. I stay here and read. I am not in your way, ja?"

"You are not in the way," Nick spoke up, "and you can use my office. I have other work that needs my attention. So, I will be out of the office for a few hours. Plus, coffee is on the house."

"That sounds good, Nick; coffee sounds good." The professor chuckled, took the file from Hawk and followed Nick to his office.

———

ANNA FINALLY CAME over to the office and smiled as she approached Jamie. "What are the chances of seeing your boss?"

"Now?"

"I'm not going to make an appointment. I'm already here."

Jamie walked around her desk and asked Anna to follow. She opened Hawk's door and almost pushed Anna inside. As usual, at least as far as Anna figured, Hawk was standing at the window stroking his chin.

"Got a minute? Jamie said it would be okay."

Slowly, he turned, and it appeared he was staring right through her. It gave Anna the chills.

"Sit down, Miss Marlet. Tell me what's on your mind."

"I'm tired of being here. I've decided to go out to my parents for Christmas, as usual. But first I need to stop at my place and pick up some more clothes and such."

Hawk tried to interject, but Anna figured she didn't need to let him start giving her a hard time. She'd made up her mind, and that was it.

"Besides, you got the killer behind bars." There. She let him know she knew.

"I wish we knew that for sure, Anna."

He called me Anna. Where did that come from? She thought.

"The only thing we do know is this Gerald Malone, who calls himself Jerry, lived in Arizona and his prints were found there: nothing more. No prints of his were found in your apartment. And that's another thing: your place is considered a crime scene, so no one is allowed to enter. The NYPD have been running tests, investigating, and checking out Malone. Since they don't have anything to hold him any longer, he's being released today. But we still can't rule him out of the equation."

"So, he's being released. So what? I could be at my parents before that happens. And if I can't go to my apartment, my mother and I can shop for new clothes. Besides, I want to attend church with my parents. Tell me: what is Christmas without attending church? Or don't you think that's important?"

"I do think it's important, but not at the risk of your life. I tell you what. Groveland Hills Community Church is having a Christmas Eve service, and I think that you and Jamie could attend that with Nick and myself as escorts. Will that help?"

"I suppose it would. But I still don't see the danger."

"Anna..."

"Hey! That's the second time you've called me by my first name. You never did before."

"I guess it's my cop's background that I use last names. You're not supposed to get personal with anyone involved in a case since you don't know where they stand. Donavan showed you that when he thought you might be capable of murder. But I feel responsible for you and Jamie, and I guess "Miss Marlet" just didn't sound right anymore."

"Oh," was all Anna said.

"As I began to tell you," Hawk continued, "we're still not sure if Ted is in the city looking for you. We think he may be. And whether Jerry *is* Ted is still a question. This isn't over yet. So, keeping you safe is still a priority."

———

LUNCH DIDN'T SETTLE WELL with Hawk, and now his head felt like someone was banging a hammer from the inside out. Jamie walked in without any fanfare and quietly placed a cup of tea on Hawk's desk.

"Thank you, Jamie. How did you know?"

"You've been too quiet. You haven't buzzed me once and haven't been out of your office except to the kitchen for a sandwich. I figured you might like your tea."

"Thanks again. Has the professor made a stir yet?"

"Not really. I stuck my head in the door and asked if he wanted some lunch. He didn't."

"Since there's nothing pressing here at the office, Jamie, I would rather you kept Anna company. I think she might try to leave otherwise."

"Yeah, she thinks you've caught Ted already. But I don't feel that way. Sure, Boss. I'll head back to the apartment."

After Jamie left, Hawk went to the kitchen for some aspirin. He wished Nick was back from his investigation. He was curious as to what he would find... if anything.

———

BACK AT HIS DESK, Hawk swallowed the tablets and washed them down with his tea. He was getting edgy, and he never liked it when he felt that way.

"Excuse, please, you ready to talk?" It was the professor and Hawk had not even heard him walk in the room.

"Yes. Come in."

Hawk was more than anxious to find out if the professor would validate any of his own thoughts about subliminal messaging. He stood to allow the professor to sit at his desk.

"Very, very interesting, this Internet romance."

A slight knock drew Professor Hoffmann and Hawk's attention to the door.

"Am I on time?" Nick asked.

"That you are. We were just getting started."

"Ja, ja. Come, Nick. Interesting relationship, this Ted and Jill. Come, we put our heads together."

Sitting down, Professor Hoffman spread out the paperwork he had been poring over.

"What I don't understand," Nick said, "is how could Jill Evans be in love, really in love, with a man she never met?"

"The Internet has spawned an online media parlor game." Hawk stood to pour the coffee and tea that Jamie had placed on the credenza, then continued. "Pretending to be someone else isn't something new, but it's been made easier online."

"Yes," said Nick, "but that doesn't explain how she could fall in love, especially online."

"Ja, Nick, it's true. When you do not see, face-to-face, you can become the ideal version of yourself. A person can form a closeness that feels safe. It feels good, and grows, especially by rereading emails or the conversations of the instant message. Then the feeling of love begins. Usually, messages are loving, as Ted wrote. And for Jill, he was perfect. He gave her what she wanted, and needed."

"People like Ted are called romance scammers," Hawk sat down again, "and are out for the money. But Ted was out for their deaths."

"Ja. Either way, they are addicted. They love the game. It's all a part of brainwashing: using repetition on another person to get whatever results they want. In this relationship, I see a repetition of overwhelming affection. Yet something seems to be missing," the professor said as he pawed over the papers on the table.

"I thought that also. But that was all that was on Miss Evans' computer. We can't find her cell phone or the purple teddy bear. We even had the laptops of the friends examined by forensic, here and out west. We also included the computers of the women that were murdered and those who committed suicide within the last year. We have the transcribed interviews from everyone we know that was involved with Ted. We sent the computers to the NYPD forensic department; still—nothing more," added Hawk.

"Ja, ja; very thorough as far as it goes. You are dealing with an intelligent, very clever, but sick minded person. I see the serial killer here, Hawk. You are right about the modus operandi. It is the work of a single person. This Jill—she was the one who committed suicide that her friend hired you?"

Hawk shook his head, wishing the professor wasn't so slow and deliberate in his conclusion.

"This Jill, she was having emotional problems. I think her childhood was troubled. It would not take very much persuasion from this Ted to commit suicide. She believed she was in love with him, and his messages enforced that belief. I think she was in love with the idea of being in love and the mystery surrounding the idea, too. Yes, she was definitely in love. In love enough that this Ted's words, promises, and his unfaithfulness with other women would make her think all was lost. Yet something else sent her over the edge." The professor stopped speaking.

"Something else? Like what?" asked Nick.

"A suicide pact perhaps."

"Whoa. A suicide pact?" This was a thought that never crossed Hawk's mind. Re-questioning of all the people involved wasn't what Hawk looked forward to. He could only hope that Jerry proved to be Ted.

"Ja, usually that is what happens. But in this case, this Ted is still alive to kill more. As I said, he is clever. So now we look at him. He mostly said the same words to each of the women. He met some and killed them. Others committed suicide. He was after the same type of woman each time. So, he had a hate-love complex, perhaps with his mother. My confusion comes with the murder of the homeless man. It does not follow this Ted's modus operandi."

"We think he may have been using the man to make the phone calls for him and perhaps more," Hawk said.

"Ja, ja. It sounds right. He no longer needs him, so he kills. This Ted will find another to work for him when he is ready to kill again."

"Or he may change his MO to mess us up, as he did with the homeless man," Nick said.

"Nein, nein. He will not change his MO on purpose. He will only change if he is flustered, ready to be found, or ready to end his own life."

"End his own life. Hmmm," Hawk walked to the window. "Where do we start?"

"You say they have arrested a man that may be this Ted, so wait to find out. If this man is not Ted, then start with the suicides. See if there was any pact. See if the way of suicide was the same, like this, Jill."

"Malone is being released today. Not enough evidence to hold him," Hawk said.

"Ja, this is good. You follow him?

"I'll check with Detective Williams about a tail."

Hawk turned, but stayed at the window, stroking his chin. "Professor, I must say it's an interesting conclusion you have reached."

"Hawk, I have appointment at four," the professor said. "I can be available tomorrow if you need." He then left abruptly, and Nick followed.

Hawk stared at the door that closed behind them, thinking that the case was becoming more confusing with each day.

———

AFTER CLOSING the gate electronically from the entrance hallway, Nick returned to find Hawk resting on the sofa. "You look done in, Hawk. You okay?"

"I am tired, plus a headache. I hope the aspirin kicks in soon." Hawk sat up. "What were your other jobs?"

"Where's Jamie? I'd rather she didn't know I'd been checking Preston's old digs."

"I sent her up to keep Anna company. I'm concerned that Anna will try to leave. She thinks we've caught Ted and wants to be at her parents for Christmas. After what the professor had to say, I have my doubts that Jerry and Ted are the same person."

"I think so too, Hawk. I don't see how they can be the same person.

I don't imagine Williams is going to find much more on Malone either." Nick paused. "Preston gave me the key to his apartment. His lease isn't up till the end of the month, so I checked it out, and everything's okay there. Then I went to Georgios and questioned a few of the people I knew that had contact with Jerry. They haven't seen him since Preston left. So, he's not bothering with Groveland Hills. His being here may have been legit. And maybe he was also looking to hit me up for a few bucks."

"You may be right. I'll just be glad when we hear something. But if Jerry isn't Ted, then it's back to the board. You heard the professor's ideas."

"Yes, and it's given me an idea. Maybe you should let Anna go to her parents for Christmas. Return her laptop and cell."

Hawk jumped off the sofa, but Nick set him back down.

"No, hear me out first. If it was actually Ted in her apartment, then maybe we can lure him. We can put a few undercovers on Marlet without her knowledge, or... with her knowledge. One could be her *boyfriend*."

"One thing wrong with that. Anna says Ted has never seen her or her car."

"I think he has. I remember looking at Jill's site on FriendsPage, and in her photo album, there was a picture of Anna. If she dressed in the same clothes, maybe Ted would take the bait."

"Too risky. Look what happened when Wade sent his undercover out to meet Ted. I won't take that kind of chance."

CHAPTER FORTY-ONE

"HAWK DETECTIVE AGENCY," Hawk answered the early morning call.

"Answering your own phone, son? What happened to your secretary?"

"And good morning to you, too, Dad. If you must know, my secretary is off for Christmas."

Hawk wasn't about to let his father know that Jamie was actually babysitting his client. The last two days were wearing on everyone and hiding out wasn't something Hawk was used to doing. He didn't like it; he never ran scared. He always faced trouble head-on. But then he never had two lives he was responsible for. No, this was not any of his father's concern.

"I see you sold the Manhattan place too. Where are you living?"

Great. That's all I need; but the truth must be told, Hawk thought.

"At my office. I had the place renovated and turned the upstairs into living quarters for myself."

"I see," his father hesitated. "We need to talk, son. I have some apologizing to do. I'd like to come out."

"If it's about your visit here with Nick, he told me. Plus, I'm in the middle of a case."

"It's a little more than that. Your mother and I would like to come out. She misses you, Alistair."

His mother. Now how could he refuse that? Maybe he could work something with Nick and the gals so he could see his parents without too many questions. Nick may be right about his father needing time to come to grips with everything, but this sure was lousy timing.

"Dad, when did you want to come out?"

"Now if we could. We're in town. We could be there in five minutes."

Quick! Hawk. Think! "Give me fifteen minutes. I have some paperwork I need to finish. Then I'll have some free time."

As soon as Hawk finished the call with his father, he was in Nick's office telling him about his parents' pending visit.

"Take it easy, Hawk. I'll open the gate, talk to the girls, and be in my office if you need me." Hawk hoped he was ready for their visit.

———

ALISTAIR HAWKINS the Second was on time as usual. Hawk greeted his parents at the outer office door, and his mother threw all protocol out the window and gave him the biggest hug her petite build could muster. She still wore the same perfume he had first given her for Christmas when he was ten. The lady at the counter had told him that his mother would love it.

Then Hawk extended his hand toward his father. But instead of shaking hands, his father pulled him into a bear hug, surprising Hawk.

As they passed Nick's office, he paused to let him know they were going upstairs. "Take care of anything, Nick," he said.

Mr. Hawkins led the way upstairs, with Miriam on his arm. Hawk looked at his parents and did not notice any hardness to their demeanor. Perhaps this would be a good visit. Once on the landing, Hawk opened the door for his parents to enter.

"Oh, Alistair. This is beautiful," his mother gushed.

"Yes, son, this is fine, very fine," his father agreed. "I need to say how sorry I am about how I have treated and spoken to you since you and Ellie returned from your honeymoon. That day, in the bank, where I caused Nick's partner to be killed, put me in a deep abyss. All I could think of was that it could have been you that was killed. Then when Ellie *was* killed, it only sunk me lower, while heightening my fear. I was not trusting God."

Hawk noticed his father's eyes were glistening, and knew what it had taken for the man to open himself to his son.

"Alistair," his mother's sweet voice began, "we've come to the realization that your career is in law enforcement and that it isn't going to change. I know these incidents have been eating at your father for years now and that he's been concerned for you, just as I have. But we have forgotten to leave it with God. As parents, it is so easy to think we know best. We forget that God is the ultimate Parent. We asked and received God's forgiveness. Now, we are asking for yours."

Hawk hugged his parents as he gave them both a resounding "yes." The rest of their visit was pleasant, with a tour of his home and a cup of tea. The hour his parents stayed went by quickly, but he was glad when they were gone. The chance of them asking to see to see the rest of the grounds was too risky.

———

"ANOTHER CUP OF COFFEE?" Anna asked. Even with Jamie to keep her company, she was ready to climb the walls once more.

"This seems to be all we do: drink coffee and sit around," she complained as she handed Jamie her coffee mug.

"It could be worse. We could be in the morgue like the others."

Although Anna was dressed in lined jeans and a green plaid flannel shirt, she shivered at the thought. She had to agree that alive was better than dead, but she was tiring of lying around. Anna missed wearing her dressy clothes, heels, and make-up. Jamie didn't seem to mind at all and was, perhaps, enjoying the change.

"How can you stand it?"

"It's all up here," Jamie said, tapping her head. "I have a good self-talk about how I prefer to stay alive. And if this is what it takes to stay that way, I'm for it. You need to learn to chill."

"But for how long? Surely Jerry is Ted. Who else could it be?"

"They don't know for sure, yet. We need to wait."

"Wait, wait, wait. That's all we do and then wait some more. I'm fed up with waiting; I want out of here."

Anna was reaching the end of her tether. Her last nerve was being exposed for anyone to step on. She carried her coffee mug to the kitchen for a refill, and as she did, counted to ten.

THE DAY WAS DRAGGING, and Hawk was getting impatient; he hadn't heard from Williams since Friday, and here it was Wednesday. Nick walked in, sat on the sofa, putting his feet upon a newly acquired ottoman.

"You needn't say it, Hawk. Frustration is written all over your face. Waiting for some word from Williams is not what you want to be doing right now. Maybe you ought to get out for a while. I can take a call as well as you."

"How do you do it, Nick?"

"You have to remember: you've been through a lot recently, especially Saturday. Facing Tank Doogan wasn't an easy task. Take a break, and quit being so hard on yourself."

Nick leaned back looking very comfortable. Hawk only wished he could do the same. Then the phone rang, and they both jumped.

"Hawk Detective Agency," Hawk answered. "Yes, Chief, he did... I've been so wrapped up in this case I haven't been very diligent in getting back to you... No, I like the idea, and after I get the report from the NYPD on the suspect they have in custody, I'll give you a call so we can get together... Give me a week, sooner if I can... sure... thanks." A faint click on the other end assured Hawk the call was over.

He walked to the window, stroking his chin, and Nick sat back.

"Well, that wasn't the call we were waiting for. The ringing of the phone even made me edgy," Nick chuckled.

Again, the phone rang, and again, both men were startled. Hawk motioned for Nick to pick it up. His nerves were doing a little dance in his stomach and another headache was floating around his cranium looking for a place to settle.

"Hawk Detec... Yes... hold on a sec," Nick said, then to Hawk, "It's Williams."

Hawk almost tore the phone from Nick's hand, plopped down on his chair, and grabbed a pen. "Is he Ted?"

"Sorry to disappoint you, Hawk, but he isn't. I'm having a complete report, including the interviews with Malone and Miss Holland, emailed to you as we speak. I've sent the lab people back to Marlet's apartment for another look around. We must be missing something."

"Thanks, Pete. I wouldn't mind looking myself."

"If nothing else is found at Marlet's, I may just let you have a go at it; unofficially, of course. Read the report, and let me know what conclusions you come up with." Hawk hung up, and Nick joined Hawk at his computer to look over the report.

———

AN HOUR LATER, Hawk let out a huge sigh.

"What is being missed, Nick? I usually have it figured out by now. Here we are a few days away from Christmas. Anna hired me in mid-September, a few weeks after Jill Evans' suicide. That's three months. Too long."

"I'll repeat myself, Hawk. Quit being so hard on yourself. If it wasn't for Anna coming to you in the first place, Ted Ashby would still be an unknown, and the cold cases just that. Now we have a face, so to speak, for the crimes."

"I've read through this entire report, so have you, and nothing jumps out. I thought there might be a tie in with Jamie's friend,

Rebecca Holland. When she was questioned, all she knew was that Jerry was a friend of Preston, and he helped Jamie move. She thought he seemed like a real nice guy. She knew he was out of work and didn't have a place to stay, so she offered him her spare room. Williams got a warrant for her place from the assistant DA and forensic went over her place while she was being questioned. Nothing there."

"When I read that she made a call from the station to her father and filled him in, he got Talon and Talon on the case immediately. I thought she might be involved. If she's innocent, why the rush for a lawyer?" asked Nick.

"Williams said she was scared to death, and that her father figured a lawyer would help. So, Richard Talon was for her. His brother, Robert, from what I hear, is an ambulance chaser and decided to tag along to claim Malone for a client. Only Malone didn't want a lawyer and had the guy chucked out. I know you've read this, but let me read it again. This is where Williams questioned Malone.

Williams: *How do you explain your prints at the last murder scene?*

Malone: *Yes... I was there, but not that night. It was a couple of nights before.*

Williams: *Tell me about it.*

Malone: *I was having a couple of beers when I got a call from... uh... a friend wanting to meet me out back of the bar.*

Williams: *Why out back?*

Malone: *Uh... he... uh... he had a uh... he didn't want to be seen.*

Williams: *Sounds like some shady business.*

Malone: *Hey, the guy could ask me outside... nothing wrong with that.*

Williams: *What is his name?*

Malone: *I don't remember.*

Williams: *Thought you said he was a friend.*

Malone: *Uh... you know how it is, you meet someone a couple of times, and you catch a nickname or something... uh... maybe Sam. Then you have a few beers, and you don't remember. Anyway, what's he got to do with it all?*

Williams: *Maybe he could back up your story.*

Malone: *Well, he can't. He left town, and I don't know where he went.*

Williams: *Okay, then. What happened after he called?*

Malone: *I finished my beer and headed out back so I'd be waiting for him to show. That's when I saw these two guys kneeling on the ground near the far side of the back of the bar. I heard one of 'em talking about a phone call. I couldn't hear what the other one said, 'cause he mumbled.*

Williams: *Can you describe them?*

Malone: *The talking one looked like a bum. He wore ratty looking clothes and an old hat that looked like it was from the garbage dump. The other one had on jeans and a thick black leather jacket, boots, and a biker's helmet. I didn't see their faces. Whatever they were doing, they seemed to be done. They got up and left.*

Williams: *Did you hear any names mentioned?*

Malone: *Uh... I think the bum called the helmet guy Ted.*

Williams: *Did you see a vehicle, get a tag number?*

Malone: *Nah. I stayed in the shadows, didn't want to get messed up with nothing and wind up being used as a punching bag or worse. I waited till I heard an engine start up and pull out.*

Williams: *Could it have been a motorcycle?*

Malone: *Didn't sound like it to me. More like an old pickup.*

Williams: *Okay. What happened next?*

Malone: *I got curious like, so I looked where they had been. All I could see was a box for telephone wires. I tried, but it wouldn't come loose. It was screwed on tight. Maybe that's why my prints were there. Probably got 'em on the building, too, cause, I leaned my hand against it to stand up. Then my friend showed up.*

Williams: *What was the date?*

Malone: *How do you expect me to remember that? I don't keep track of every time I go for a few beers. It's not like I'm some CEO or something.*

Williams: *Yet, you remembered that the bum called the other guy Ted.*

Malone: *Well, maybe. Maybe it wasn't Ted.*

Williams: *So, which is it, Ted, or you don't know?*

Malone: *I don't know. I was too far away to hear what they were saying. I figured if I said Ted, you'd get off my back.*

Williams: *Lying will only make it worse for you.*

Malone: *Yeah. Okay. No more with the lies. I got it.*

Williams: *Okay, so where does Miss Holland fit into all this?*

Malone: *She don't! I just met her when I helped Preston move his girl into her new digs. Becky doesn't know nothing. She was just helping me out, giving me a place to sleep and some grub till I got on my feet. I helped a little in her flower shop. Keep her out of this; she's a nice girl.*

Williams: *Okay. Is there anything else you can think of?*

Hawk looked up. "The report goes on to say that Williams was called out to take a call from Wade. Seems as though Malone was telling the truth. Latent finds that his prints are older than the ones forensic collected the night Wade found the body of the vagrant man. It would appear to coincide with the first time Ted made a call from the Silver Heels Bar."

"I'm hoping Malone is still our man," Nick said thoughtfully.

Hawk looked over at Nick. "What was it that Williams told you concerning Jerry and Preston's friendship?"

"It was superficial, as with Miss Holland. A brief mention in the report." Nick let out a sigh and stretched his legs toward the ottoman. "Not good news. I was hoping to get my apartment back. But since Jerry's not Ted, we need to leave the girls there and change our focus. So where does this leave us, Hawk?"

"With a lot more questions."

CHAPTER FORTY-TWO

SITTING AT THE TABLE, Anna was on her third cup of coffee when Jamie walked into the kitchen of Nick's apartment.

"Wow! You look like you've been on an all-night bender," Jamie exclaimed.

"You would too if you didn't get a good night's sleep."

Jamie poured a cup of coffee for herself and sat down across from Anna. "Yeah, I guess the walls are closing in for you. But for me, it's like an adventure. Now I'm thinking that maybe Jerry isn't Ted, so, maybe I'll get to go home."

"Did Hawk tell you that?"

"Nah. But I caught a few snatches of the boss and Nick talking. It sure will be nice to sleep in my own bed again."

Jamie seemed too bouncy and happy to suit Anna; plus, she was not looking forward to staying here alone.

"Do you really have to leave? I mean… it's almost Christmas, and I can't go home or contact friends, not even my parents. It would be nice to share Christmas with someone."

"Hey, Hawk and Nick will be taking you to a Christmas eve church thingy. That ought to help."

"You're going too, right?"

"Not if I don't have to. As soon as the boss says I can go home, I'm gonna try and get out of town for the holidays."

A knock on the door brought both women up out of their chairs.

"Be careful; take a peek, first," whispered Anna.

Jamie looked through the peephole.

"Hey, it's okay. It's Hawk and Nick," she said as she opened the door.

"It looks like you girls have been taking care of the place," Nick said, as he walked in first. "Even the coffee smells good."

"Good morning," Hawk announced.

An announcement was all it sounded like to Anna. She sat in the recliner, bracing herself for more bad news.

"Help yourself to the coffee, Nick. So, what brings the two of you up here so early?" she inquired of Hawk.

"I think you better have a seat, Jamie." Hawk grabbed a straight-backed chair, swung it around, and saddle sat.

"I sure don't like that serious tone to your voice," Anna quipped.

Nick brought his cup of coffee and sat on the edge of the sofa. Then Hawk related the report on Jerry.

"So, I get to go back to my apartment, right?" asked Jamie.

Anna sat stunned by the news that Ted was still out there somewhere, and was near tears when Jamie asked about returning to her apartment. As opposite as the two women were, Anna really didn't want Jamie to leave.

"I'm not too sure," Hawk answered, "at least not right away. We know someone—presumably Ted—has broken into Anna's place and we're not sure if he's still in town. If he gets wind of what's going on and connects you... well, it's still too risky."

"I never knew Anna before, so how could Ted find out about me?"

"He's very clever, Jamie," Nick chose to answer.

"What are you going to do next?" Anna inquired of Hawk.

"Search your apartment."

"Again? The NYPD already did that."

"Yes, but I'm looking for something that's out of the ordinary. Something that wouldn't be the norm for forensics."

———

THE POLICE TAPE was still across the door, and a chair was positioned on the left, where a studious looking uniformed officer sat. "One of those hotshot newbies," Nick chuckled.

The young man stood. "Detective Hawkins?"

"Sounds like Williams got the word to you that Detective Valetti and myself would be here this morning." Hawk flashed his ID in unison with Nick.

The young man removed the tape and unlocked the door. "Sir? Before you go in, I thought I'd better mention, there was a guy here earlier, dressed in jeans, a thick black leather jacket, and boots. He got off the elevator, looked down this way, hesitated, then got back on the elevator. He had a biker's helmet, and the strange thing was, instead of carrying it, he was wearing it."

"Did you call that info into Williams?" Hawk asked.

"No, sir, not yet."

"Do it. Now!" Hawk's words were sharp.

———

"DRESSED as he was keeps us from putting a face with the guy," Nick remarked, once they were in Anna's apartment. "So where do we start and exactly what are we looking for that wasn't seen by forensic?"

"Some clue from Ted that tells us he was here. I'm not really sure what that will be, but we need to look. It seems he has been messing up, leaving bits of information recently. You remember what Professor Hoffmann said: he may be looking to get caught."

"The professor also said that he could want to end his own life. Maybe clues will only lead to his body, Hawk."

"Perhaps. But either way, we need to find anything that will lead us to him. So, let's get started."

Hawk walked through the living room, not believing how really trashed the place was. He knew that Anna could not come back to this. He had to keep her away until it was cleared and cleaned. Opening the door on the right, the sight jolted him.

"Nick," he called, "you need to see this."

"What the... I can't believe it." Nick said when he joined Hawk. "Nothing's been touched. Is this Miss Evans' room?"

"Must be. Marlet said it was the one on the right, beyond the living room." Hawk went in with Nick on his heels. He looked in dresser drawers, the closet and under the bed.

"Okay Hawk: you gonna clue me in? What are you looking for?"

"The bear. The one I asked Anna to buy and place on Miss Evans' bed. It's missing."

"Maybe we should try Marlet's room," Nick suggested.

There it was. The purple teddy bear was lying in the middle of Anna Marlet's bed. It was torn, and the stuffing was strewn all over the room. "Is that it?" asked Nick.

"It's the purple bear, or at least what's left of it. Evidently, Ted didn't want the bear but wanted what was or is in the original bear. If we could find it, I'm sure we would find Ted."

BACK IN HIS OFFICE, Hawk placed a call to Williams, letting him know that he and Nick had concluded their search of Marlet's place.

Nick walked in as Hawk finished his call.

"So, what did Williams have to say?"

"That he's having the *mess* at Anna's picked up and dumped at the lab. He can't believe there's no prints or DNA."

"And meanwhile?"

"Meanwhile, I need to question Anna about the original purple bear."

"How about, meanwhile, you give it a rest, Hawk? Tomorrow is Christmas Eve, and there's no sense upsetting the girls any more than they are now. I think they need a break. We could all use a break."

THE CHURCH WAS CROWDED Friday evening, but Nick found a pew where all four of them could sit together. It was decided that Jamie and Anna would sit between Hawk and Nick for safety. This whole scenario seemed a bit bizarre, but they were dealing with a crazed man who could be anyone and be anywhere. Although both he and Nick were armed, Hawk was wondering if coming out for the service was the best idea. The Christmas drama had begun, but Hawk couldn't keep focused. It felt almost sacrilegious to be packing a gun in church. If the situation called for it, could he even use it?

Hawk scanned the congregation, on the lookout for anything or anyone out of place. *Right. I'm at a disadvantage since I really don't know the church or the people here, yet...* his thoughts drifted. He looked at Jamie sitting to his right, who looked bored with the whole idea of being in church. She looked at him and then whispered, "Isn't this just for kids?" Hawk shook his head. Then he glanced to Anna who seemed to be enraptured. Nick was paying attention somewhat but also appeared to be scanning the pews.

When the drama was over, Pastor Hennings read the Christmas story from Luke. When he finished the reading, he spoke to the congregation.

"It's a wonderful gift we have been given. Better than any we will receive tomorrow morning. Since this gift from God was only wrapped in swaddling clothes, and not bright shiny paper with beautiful bows, we might miss it. Don't let that happen to you. Look in your heart. If it seems empty, and you can't find God's gift, ask Jesus to come into your heart this very night. What better Christmas gift could you receive then the gift of salvation?" The Pastor closed with a prayer and invited everyone to refreshments in the fellowship hall.

"Hey! Boss, can we go?"

"I think it would be better to leave. We can have some refreshments back at the office. Seems Nick has done more shopping."

CHAPTER FORTY-THREE

ALTHOUGH HAWK HAD DECIDED to keep the office closed for the week between Christmas and the new year, he still went down to his office Monday morning. With a cup of tea in hand, he stood at the window, gazing at the garden that was covered with a fluffy white blanket of freshly fallen snow. God's beauty was evident even in the midst of this baffling case. He thought about how Nick had taken into account the emotions of Jamie and Anna, neither woman wanting to be cooped up here, especially at this time of the year. But with refreshments back at the office after the Christmas Eve service, and a few gifts Nick had purchased, wrapped, and put under the tree, everyone seemed to be more at ease. Jamie had even remarked that this Christmas was one of the best she had ever had.

Hawk wished he could have agreed with letting the two women spend Christmas elsewhere. But without Ted behind bars, he didn't feel it was safe for them to be anywhere else.

Where is Ted? Who is Ted? Where is the purple bear? I'm sure it would lead us to Ted if only we could find... Hawk's thoughts were left hanging when the phone rang. Caller ID showed Williams' precinct.

"Hawk here," he answered without bothering with the formalities of identifying the office.

"We found a note from Ted," Williams began. "It was lying on the bed in Miss Evans' room. So, we know he went back after you and Nick looked around."

Perhaps Ted had been hiding very near while he and Nick did their searching, Hawk thought. It was as though Ted was everywhere and nowhere. He already felt better about his decision to keep Jamie and Anna secluded. But now he was concerned that Ted might know where.

"What did he write?"

"Okay Cops, you can quit trying to mess with me. Produce the real purple bear, or you'll find more bodies," Williams read.

"Prints, DNA, anything?

"Yes. But it led to yet another homeless man. We found him in Central Park. Seems Ted gave him a bottle and a ten spot to write the note."

"And Ted was dressed in jeans, boots, a thick black leather jacket, and wearing, not carrying, a biker's helmet?"

"Yes, plus gloves. The same description Malone and my officer gave. The old guy also said Ted had a raspy voice, almost a whisper. The guy was pretty tipsy when we got hold of him. He didn't notice anything else, except the bottle Ted had for him. Not a whole lot of help there. But I thought you should know. You better keep the Marlet woman up there. With Ted still at large, we don't need her to be his next victim."

"Have you checked her cell phone? Maybe Ted has tried to contact her. We'll check her email and FriendsPage page from here. Get back to me as soon as you do."

———

HAWK DIRECTED Anna to the chair facing his desk. "Please have a seat, Miss Marlet."

"You're scaring me; this sounds too official. What's happened? When can I go home?"

"It *is* scary, and it *is* official." Hawk related that Williams found a note from Ted.

"So, it looks like you'll be staying for a while longer. Williams is checking your cell phone. I want you to check your email and FriendsPage page, using the computer at Jamie's desk."

———

NICK CAME in as Anna scanned her emails.

"Ah, a new receptionist. Not sure Jamie would approve," Nick chuckled as he passed to his office.

Anna just smiled and continued scanning her emails. There were ninety-five: some from a couple of guys she dated off and on, several from her parents, her father, to be more precise. Her mother never did get the hang of using the computer and didn't seem interested either. There were some advertisements and free offers from a few of the companies she had purchased from online. The last few were from a couple of other models: one from Stella herself, and a few from her other close friend, Dolly.

Oh, how Anna wanted to open and answer each one of these, but she knew she had to play it safe. She continued to look down the list of emails: none were from Ted. She wondered if this was good or bad? The office phone rang, and she knew Hawk or Nick would be answering. It was probably Officer Williams. Anna was anxious to know if he found anything on her cell, so she reluctantly shut down the computer.

———

"HAWK HERE."

"You had a good hunch, Hawk," Williams said. "There was one text to Anna from Ted; I'm emailing the copy as we speak. Meanwhile, I traced the phone. It was a prepaid cell in Arizona, only activated yesterday at a small store in Sun Point. There were only two phones purchased that day: one was a male teen, who checked out okay and the other was who the salesperson described as a bum. Fake ID was used, so no luck, unless we have Wade do a roundup of homeless men. We also checked all the airlines, bus stations, and railways. Came up with a big fat zero. Ted must have left immediately and drove straight through."

"I'll read the email, then contact Wade, and get back to you. Thanks, Pete." Out of the corner of his eye, Hawk noticed Anna standing in his doorway. "Come on in, Anna. I guess you're wondering what Williams found on your cell."

"More than wondering," Anna said as she sat on the sofa.

"I got the email. *And* it's quite interesting," Nick interrupted.

"Have a seat, Nick," Hawk said as he looked over the email from Williams. He decided to read it aloud. Nick sat next to Anna, and Hawk presumed it was to steady her if necessary.

Where's things from bear? Jill promised. I'll call in new year. Better have or else. Ted

"I don't understand. What things?" asked Anna. "Jill's note only said he was to have the bear; it didn't say anything about things."

"That's what we need to find out. Tell me what you know about that stuffed purple teddy bear, and what made it so important to your friend."

"I don't know, except that it was one that she had since she started school. When she was a little girl, she didn't want to attend her first day of school because all her toys might be gone when she came home. So, her mother took her shopping to find a stuffed bear to protect her toys while she was at school. She always liked the color purple, and when she saw the purple teddy bear, she had to have it. She always kept the bear on her bed, for as long as I can remember." Anna stood and began pacing around the room.

"Okay, Anna," Nick said. "I think you better spill the rest."

Anna stopped her pacing and looked from Nick to Hawk, then back to Nick.

"Just what do you mean?" Anna was shaking. She sat back down. Only this time it was in the chair near Hawk's desk.

"Yes, Nick. What are you getting at?" Hawk wanted to know.

"Been a cop too long not to know when some things are being held back: that faraway look in the eyes. It's usually a good sign that a person may not be sure if they should tell all they know." Nick turned to Anna.

"If you really want to see Ted caught and put this case to bed, I suggest you tell us *all* that you know. This is not the time to be true to your friend's memory if that's what you're trying to do."

Anna looked as though she was holding back tears.

"This is something no one knows. Not Jill's parents and, perhaps, Jill didn't even know that I knew." Anna hesitated. "Please. Can you promise me that you can keep it quiet?"

"I can't promise anything," Hawk said, "especially since we don't even know what it is. So spill."

"Jill was under a doctor's care for anorexia."

CHAPTER FORTY-FOUR

NICK HAD RETURNED to his apartment, and Hawk sat in his office, alone with his thoughts. With New Year's Eve on the following day, there was nothing else to do. Knowing Ted had returned to Arizona, Hawk felt it was safe for Jamie to return to her place. With Nick's encouragement, he had been able to convince Jamie to invite Anna to stay with her. Perhaps being at Jamie's place and getting out about town would keep Anna from climbing the walls, as she had put it.

Hawk leaned back in his chair and closed his eyes. The stillness of being alone gripped him as his thoughts drifted toward Ellie and the little girl he would never know. He disliked the approaching night. It was always worse when darkness fell. A cloud of loss worked its way into Hawk's thoughts. Like a valiant warrior, he fought down the feeling and chose to reflect back to the vile reality of the case and the last couple of days.

———

JILL EVANS' doctor planned to close on Wednesday for a skiing holiday, so Hawk's visit on Tuesday was a last-minute fit into a busy day for the physician. The doctor wasn't able to shed any light on the situation and agreed with Anna that announcing that Miss Evans was being treated for anorexia would serve no purpose. It wasn't as severe as some cases he had seen. Miss Evans' only symptoms were fear of gaining weight; this led to some weight loss, due to dieting, sleep problems, and more exercise than usual. He felt he had caught it in time. He put her on 2.0 milligrams of alprazolam for anxiety and 500 milligrams of chloral hydrate, a sleep aid.

What the doctor didn't plan on was the trouble he may have caused for himself. His diagnosis of anorexia and his prescription for the tablets that caused Miss Evans' death might lead Williams' to call the doctor in for questioning and delay the man's skiing holiday.

This was definitely the wrong week for unofficial investigations. Miss Evans' parents were out of town visiting other relatives, as they didn't think they could handle the first Christmas at home without Jill. Talking with them would be just one more thing to add to the waiting game.

Hawk's cell rang, and he was happy to see it was Wade. "Glad to hear from you. Anything new on the case out your way?"

"We got word from Williams that Ted was back out here. We've beefed up patrol at the places he has been. But he's still quite elusive."

"It's been that way here also." Hawk proceeded to tell Wade of the new information Anna shared and how he was now just waiting for Miss Evans' parents to return from Florida so he could question them in hope of inadvertently finding a clue.

"I gotta say that this waiting is not for me. What's eerie is, there haven't been any more murders with Ted's MO, or any suicides that have been connected to him."

Hawk heard Wade's other line ring and guessed he would hang up, but instead, Wade asked him to hold as he took the call. Returning to Hawk's line a few minutes later, he said, "That was Johnson. I think Ted may be getting nervous: at least, I hope so. The last cell he used has been found. Along with a message to back off the patrols or next week, there will be another body... maybe two."

———

THE NEW YEAR came in without a bang for Jamie and Anna. On TV, they watched the ball drop in Times Square.

"Last year I was there, with Jill and the gang from the studio. I sure do miss it. It's the only way to celebrate the New Year." Anna sighed and took another sip of coffee. "I'm so tired of this past week and a half. It's been like living in a prison."

Jamie ignored Anna's laments about not being able to enjoy New Year's Eve and living like a prisoner. She continued her dinner and kept her thoughts to herself. *I'm beginning to wonder if I want to keep working for Hawk. This business with Ted has hit too close to home, and I don't like it. I feel like a prisoner, too. And I don't like being asked to attend church every Sunday.*

———

JAMIE HAD REFUSED to go with Nick and Hawk when they showed up for Anna. Church wasn't her thing. Oh, she believed there was a God, but she was a good person, and she could pray anywhere, whenever she felt the need. She sure didn't need church, and if her job depended on her going, then she figured she didn't need it either.

It was time to get on with life beyond the office and habits of other people. Time to touch base with her own friends, especially Rebecca. Now that she could use her cell again, she hoped Rebecca would be up. While the others were at church, she could talk privately with her best friend.

"Hello," a sleepy voice said after the fourth ring.

"How's my best friend doing?"

"Jamie? Why haven't you returned my calls? Has that boss of yours got you on his side?"

"What? What are you talking about?"

"You know what I'm talking about: what he did to Jerry and me. We were brought in for questioning, and they practically accused

Jerry of being some sadistic killer just because he has a record. And that's all it is: a record. He's gone straight!"

"Hey! I don't know what my boss does. But I understood it to be about some Manhattan break-in. It was the NYPD, not my boss, who arrested Jerry for suspicion. But I didn't know about you."

"Oh, come on, Jamie. You had to know; you're not that stupid. I think you coulda called and let me know. I coulda helped Jerry."

"Don't tell me you're still gonna see him knowing he has a record?"

"Jamie, I happen to be in love with him, and he loves me. He's trying to make a go of it, and I'm willing to give him a chance, which is more than I can say for some people I know."

"Hey. I was just asking." Jamie was really snapping her gum. "Ya know it hasn't been easy on this end, being cooped up with..." Jamie hesitated, realizing she was about to give away Anna's hiding place.

"Let's just say I've been cooped up all because of the threats from that crazed killer you're talking about. Do what you want about Jerry. He seemed nice when I met him, and he was very helpful to Preston when he moved me. So, when do you want to get together? It's been a while."

"Uh... I'm not really sure, Jamie. I mean... Jerry's living with me now. He's also helping me in the shop and making deliveries while he's looking for work. I mean... now's not a good time. We gotta get things figured out, me and Jerry. You know how it is."

"But... I thought we were best friends, and didn't we make a pact about guys not coming between our friendship, at least not unless the right guy came along? And Jerry sure isn't that!"

"Yeah? Well, a lot, you know. Jerry is the right guy for me. So maybe it's time to break up the friendship. If your guy hadn't taken a powder, we coulda... well, you know, been friends or something."

"I can't believe you'd say that. He didn't take a powder. He went to work at a Chicago law firm. Nick tells me about how he's doing." Jamie wasn't about to admit that Rebecca might be right, especially since Preston hadn't been in touch.

"Yeah, Nick tells you. But I bet you haven't heard from that so-called good boy at all. At least Jerry's real, not a fake, like Preston. He didn't even stay in touch with Jerry like he said he would. He puts himself above everyone else just because he goes to church. I'm surprised they haven't got you going to church, too. That's a bummer of a job, worst one you've ever had. You've changed, Jamie, and I'm not sure I want to be friends with this new snooty girl. You live in a different world. I mean you even moved to Groveland Hills. How uppity is that? Let's just call it a great memory and end the friendship now."

Jamie heard the sound of a click in her ear that sounded so loud and final it brought on a wave of tears.

————

AFTER CHURCH, Hawk and Nick dropped Anna off at Jamie's place. She had convinced, or rather, Nick had managed to convince Hawk a few days before, that she needed her car. There would be times she just might want to take a ride around town or go to the park on the bluff. With Jamie back at work, Anna figured she'd be sitting around with nothing to do. In exchange for her car sitting in the guest parking area of Jamie's apartment complex, Anna agreed to leave her cell phone and laptop with Williams at the station.

When she walked into the apartment, she noticed the quietness. Perhaps Jamie was still sleeping; nothing else to do in this little burg of a town. Anna looked in Jamie's room, but she wasn't there. Strange, she thought. Out in the kitchen, she poured herself a cup of coffee, then noticed a note.

Hey, Anna, I need to clear my head, so I'm taking a ride over to Jersey. I'll be back in a couple of hours, and we can go over to Georgios to get a pizza or something.

"Perfect," Anna said aloud. Leaving her cup of coffee on the kitchen counter, she went to the guest room. Not usually a spontaneous person, Anna decided today was the day to start. She packed her suitcase and left for her Manhattan apartment.

———

NICK LOOKED concerned when Jamie arrived Monday for work. She wondered if he and Hawk knew Anna was gone when he called her into his office.

"Yeah. What's up?" she asked.

"Everything okay between you and Anna?"

"Yeah. Why do you ask?"

"You don't seem to be your happy, bubbly self today."

Whew. So that's all it is, she thought.

"Well, if you must know, my best friend ended our friendship." She told Nick what happened. "And Rebecca is blaming me."

Everything seemed so mixed up, and Jamie wasn't sure if now was the time she should bring up the fact that Anna had packed her things and left. Maybe something happened, and they decided to hide Anna somewhere else, and it was some kind of secret. Instead of asking Nick that question, she asked if he needed anything else.

"No. But Hawk has work for you," Nick smiled. "He put some files on your desk and said you'd know what to do with them. If not, ask him."

Jamie sat at her desk after putting her coat in the hall closet. She felt she was in some kind of a weird dream. Nothing of the life she knew was here. So why was she? Did she even care where Anna was? No; just curious, she thought. Yet she knew she had to find out. She didn't want to be responsible if Anna was in trouble.

Jamie finally got the courage to walk into Hawk's office and relate the fact that she hadn't seen Anna since she left for church with them.

"She never came back?"

"Well, she must have. Probably when I went to the store." She wasn't about to tell him she had been riding around and in Jersey at that.

"It was enough time for her to pack her stuff and leave. But where she went, I don't know."

———

HAWK PRACTICALLY KNOCKED Jamie over getting out of his office and storming into Nick's. "She's gone! I knew we shouldn't have let her have her car." Hawk was steaming and pacing.

"Whoa! Slow down. I assume you mean Anna's gone. Well, what did you expect? With your paranoia you were practically keeping her a prisoner here—her and Jamie both. And because of that Anna is gone and Jamie has lost the friendship of her best friend. Enough, Hawk."

At Nick's words, Hawk stood ramrod straight, stared right past Nick, and appeared to be in very deep thought. Nick felt concern for his boss. He walked around the desk and guided Hawk to the big overstuffed chair. Looking out at the snow that still covered the hedge and ground, Nick wished the turmoil of this case could become as serene as the outdoor scene.

"Come on, Hawk. Have a seat. You can't protect everyone. And the case is out of your hands. You need to let it go. You've done all you could and more. Quit trying to do God's job."

As Hawk sat gazing out the window, Nick buzzed Jamie.

"Bring you and me some coffee and a cup of tea for Hawk. We all need a break."

———

NICK SAT at the office kitchen table with a ham on rye and a glass of milk, trying to make sense of the morning. He managed to calm both Hawk and Jamie and got them to go to their respective homes, and had assured Hawk that he would handle anything and everything. He almost had to promise Jamie the same, which might include Preston. The heartbreaking question of "what's wrong with me?" coupled with "why did Preston break up with me?" from Jamie didn't set well with Nick.

After Jamie left and Hawk went upstairs, Nick got busy on the phone. The first call was to Wade to whom he related all that had been going on. He asked Wade to keep his best friend in his prayers. Nick also wanted to be informed as soon as anything broke.

The next call was to Williams to inform him of Anna taking off. "She was here, Nick. Yesterday afternoon. She wanted access to her apartment so she could get all her belongings out. At least anything that wasn't destroyed. I sent a man to escort her in and out and to stay with her while she packed."

"Did she let on what her intentions were, where she might be going?"

"She said she didn't really know what she was going to do. She realized she couldn't go back to work, but she did plan to get in touch with her parents and let them know what was happening. Could be she went there to stay."

Nick decided to let Hawk handle speaking to Anna's parents. The phone rang just as he took the last bite of his sandwich. He dashed to Jamie's desk and hoped he didn't sound like he had a mouth full of cotton candy.

"Hawk Detective Agency, Detective Valetti speaking." Best to keep it professional was Nick's policy.

"Hi, Nick." It was Anna. "I'm sorry for running out on you guys. Can I speak to Hawk?"

"Hawk took the rest of the day off. Unless it's an emergency, I'm not to disturb him. How about telling me where you are and what's up. If it's important enough, I'll ring Hawk."

"No, let him be. I'm at my parent's home in East Hampton, and I plan to stay here until Ted is caught and this nightmare is over. I got a new laptop and cell phone, so they can destroy the others if they want. I couldn't take it any longer. I felt like I was going batty. My parents have good security here, and I'll keep my car garaged. The paperboy will deliver at the gate, and we'll keep that closed, too."

"Okay. But what about your job, and the travel time to and from? How secure is that?"

"I asked for six months off. Anyway, I felt bad and thought Hawk should know. And by the way, this *was not* Jamie's fault."

"I'll pass this on to Hawk, and please, stay put. He'll be in touch when needed." Nick said his goodbyes and hung up.

———

HAWK MANAGED to sleep an hour after coming upstairs. Then, with a cup of tea and cheese and crackers, he felt some fortification. He knew he was being overly protective. He also knew he couldn't afford to become tyrannical. He was also certain Nick was aware of what was happening. He had to thank God for sending Nick his way, for the man certainly knew how to calm the storm that was raging within him. The case was out of his hands, and he didn't like the feeling of not being in control of things. If only he could find Miss Evans' purple bear... perhaps he could crack the case. He walked to the window, stroking his chin. His cell rang.

"What is it, Nick?"

"Hawk, Jill Evans' parents are here, and I put them in your office. They want to speak to you most urgently, they say."

"I'll be down in ten minutes." Hawk snapped his cell closed and went to freshen up. Surprised by their visit, he hoped they were not going to ask him to back off.

———

"MR. AND MRS. EVANS," Hawk began. "First my condolences for the loss of your daughter and secondly, how can I help you?"

Mr. Evans had stood when Hawk walked in. He was tall and lanky, dressed in a black business suit and striped tie. His hair, gray at the temples, and a pencil-thin mustache, gave him a rather distinguished look. When Hawk sat behind his desk, Mr. Evans sat back on the sofa next to a petite and demure looking woman. Her hair showed signs of once being a brunette. Her eyes looked quite sad, and her face was void of make-up other than a touch of light red lip color. She wore a simple black dress, unadorned except for a short strand of pearls and earrings to match. Mr. Evans embraced his wife as if trying to shield her from additional hurt while giving her comfort. He then looked straight at Hawk.

"Detective Hawkins, we have heard about Jill's teddy bear and wondered if you could tell us why you think finding it would be so important to the case."

Hawk buzzed for Nick to join them.

"I hope you don't mind, but I'd like my partner to join us."

Nick sat on the chair near the sofa, moved the ottoman aside, and gave a nod to Hawk.

"Your daughter's teddy bear might very well carry all the clues we need to find and capture the man behind the suicide of not only your daughter but several other women. Plus, the murder of several more, including an undercover female deputy, and a vagrant."

Hawk didn't like having to rehash what had to be a very disturbing subject for Mr. and Mrs. Evans, especially when he looked at Mrs. Evans, who seemed to be shrinking under the weight of his words.

"I still don't see how the bear would carry any clues." Mr. Evans held his wife closer. "The thing has been banged around ever since she was a little girl. So, what can you hope to gain by it?"

"Your daughter's cell phone is missing, and so is the picture of Ted that she alluded to in her emails. Because she spoke of the bear so much in her emails to the man, and the fact that she put his picture on the bear's lap using it as a frame, we think she may have put these items inside the bear the night she, um... passed away."

"Oh," was all Mr. Evans could manage. There was a pause as he looked lovingly at his wife. There were tears in her eyes, and she dabbed at them with her handkerchief.

"Beth, I think we have to, dear." Hawk heard Mr. Evans speak.

"I... I... can't," Mrs. Evans whispered, and then her tears began.

"Beth... it's no longer a question of feelings. We must. We must do whatever we can to keep this monster from harming anyone else. We don't want to be the reason another mother and father would have to go through what we've endured. If we can do anything, then I think that is what God expects of us. Remember dear; Jill is not in that grave, but with her Heavenly Father."

"Are you... if this is the only way. Oh, Ralph... I imagine it has to be. You are right. God will see us through this also."

Hawk had allowed the two a modicum of privacy by not interrupting the couple. He was intrigued by the conversation, and his gut told him that here sat the link that was needed to put a serial killer away. Of this, he was certain.

Ralph Evans, still holding his wife close, looked up at Hawk. "The bear is buried with Jill."

CHAPTER FORTY-FIVE

RIPPING open a grave just to retrieve a teddy bear not only seemed ugly, or sounded ugly—it was ugly. Hawk, Williams, and the local police chief stood ten feet away as the backhoe did its job. Hawk noticed that Anna had arrived with Ralph Evans, and they stood near a thicket of oaks approximately fifty feet the other side of Miss Evans' grave. Hawk was glad to see that Evans had taken his advice to leave his wife home, but Anna's appearance surprised him. He hoped she was there to support Miss Evans' father.

Hawk could only imagine what was going through the man's mind and what he was feeling. Hawk's own emotions had a jolt when he realized it was the same cemetery that was home to Ellie's body. He glanced to his right where, about a hundred yards away, there was another thicket of oaks that bordered the road through Oak Grove Cemetery. It was just across that road where Ellie, with little unborn Emily, was laid to rest.

The scraping of the vault being opened brought Hawk's attention back to the reason he was here. The concrete lid had been lifted, and now the crane was bringing up the coffin. Two men guided the coffin to a resting spot left of the headstone. The local chief and Williams stepped forward when the coffin lid was raised. Snapping on gloves, Williams reached under the silk covering on the right side of the body. He pulled out the bear and bagged it. He nodded to the men to replace the coffin.

———

HAWK HAD DISLIKED TELLING Anna and Mr. Evans that the teddy bear was in the hands of forensic and that their presence at the opening of the grave was allowed only as a courtesy. Hawk understood their emotions and questions.

He also wondered what would be found inside the bear. As he stood alongside Williams in the lab, a scalpel guided gently by gloved hands, cut into the bear.

"I'm surprised the shoddy stitching wasn't noticed at the time of investigation, before the mother took it," the voice belonging to the gloved hands remarked. Then the hands pulled out what looked to be a letter. Next came the cell phone, a torn picture, a ring, and a wadded piece of paper.

"Anything else?" Hawk asked.

When the Head of Forensics assured him that was all, he followed Williams to his office.

"How long?" he asked after he took the chair Williams offered.

"It has priority, Hawk. After each piece is tested, it will be brought here. Coffee? No, I forgot, you're a tea drinker. I think we have some tea bags around here and we have a hot water spigot on the cooler."

As much as Hawk would enjoy a cup of tea, Williams' idea sounded barbaric. He evidently had no idea how to brew a proper cup of tea. Hawk expressed his thanks, but no thanks. Then he pulled out his cell phone and called Wade.

———

HAWK INFORMED Wade that the purple teddy bear had been retrieved, and listed the items that were found inside.

"As soon as the report is finished, I'll get it sent to you."

"Or," said Wade, "you can put the report with the evidence in a sealed package. I'll send one of my men to pick it up. Give me fifteen minutes, and I'll call you back with the particulars."

―――――

"HE'LL ARRIVE at JFK 3:31 Eastern tomorrow afternoon," Wade began his call. "Officer Carson will have the necessary papers with him. Have Williams get the release ready, and you or he can meet the plane. I'd like Carson to make the return flight that departs at 6:40 Eastern, also tomorrow. The sooner we get that package here, the sooner we can nab this sicko."

―――――

THE ITEMS of evidence began to filter into Williams' office. The most interesting so far was the wadded piece of paper, dated May eighth, and written by Ted.

Hello, My Love,

I hope this letter finds you getting better, my darling. When Ginger emailed me that you were sick, I decided to write you and send the enclosed promise ring. Wear it with my love, and think of your teddy bear each time you look at it.

I'm sorry that I had to say no about you coming out here just yet, but things are still so unsettled for me. It's only ten more months, my love. I'm also sorry that your so-called friends and others have chosen to give you bad advice. I hope the ring will convince you and them of my love and promises.

I want so much to hold you in my arms and be with you forever. Perhaps we can be found in one another's arms even in death. If anything, or anyone, were to keep us apart, then death would be better, don't you agree my love? If you change your mind, then I choose to no longer exist. I hope you feel the same. Ours is a deep love that no one can take away, especially in death.

I wish I could be with you now! But I know that day will come and I can't wait until I can hold you, my darling. I will wait to hear from you, either on email or text.

Take care, my darling. I love you. Your Teddy Bear

"Not as steamy as some I've read, but..."

"This letter doesn't exactly fit the MO we have for this guy," Williams interrupted.

"Not as far as we know. We're not sure of all that's involved in the suicides as opposed to the murders. The writing is very mixed. Emotions seem to be jumping from one to another, as though he isn't sure how he feels. There's also a lot of reference to death, or more precisely, suicide. Do you suppose this was the convincing persuasion for Miss Evans' suicide? Or, as strange as this may sound, had Ted actually fallen for her?"

The office door opened, and the last of the evidence, including the bear, was placed on Williams' desk. Picking up the note written by the dead woman, Hawk began to read.

Oh, Teddy Bear, why couldn't you tell me about the cancer? Why did you lie? When I read the letter that came with the ring, I was so happy. I believe you love me. But I would have come to you, no matter what. I'm confused, but I do believe no one can separate us, especially in death. That is where we are sure to be together with you holding me in your arms. Your last text convinced me of that. I tore your picture so no one else can have it and I wadded your letter, so it isn't as pure as when I got it. Please wear the ring on a chain around your neck. Knowing I wore it on my hand may give you some

262

comfort until the end. I will always love you, even in death, and I'll be
waiting for you. Come to me soon. Your Jillybean.

"What the...?" Hawk picked up the now charged cell phone labeled,
"Jill Evans." As he handed the note over to Williams to read, he waited
for him to finish. Then he punched in saved texts. "Let's begin with
the last one, the one mentioned in her note. It's dated September 2nd,"
Hawk said as he began to read with Williams looking over his
left arm.

Muah. Cancer taking its toll. Not 2 long.
May end sooner. Meet u other side. Luv TB

Hawk then checked the previous texts where Ted wrote about his
cancer.

"The rat may cheat the hangman, so to speak." Williams pounded
his fist on the desk.

"If it's true."

"You doubt it, Hawk?"

"He was here, looking for the bear that contained evidence that
could possibly put him away. Or execute him. Why would he risk that
or make the trip if he was already dying? Remember, we're dealing
with a cold and calculating serial killer who kills by his own hands...
or by persuasion."

———

FRIDAY EVENING and the office was closed. Jamie had gone home,
and Nick was in his apartment. Hawk stood at his kitchen window
stroking his chin, trying to keep the anxious feeling that was building
in his gut tamped down. After the kettle boiled, he prepared a cup of
tea and padded into the living room. Hawk was disconcerted and had
been, ever since he had met Carson to hand over the evidence. At least
Williams allowed him that official act. Hawk wasn't used to handing a

case over to someone else. He had always seen his cases through to the arrest. This one was different... and unnerving. It was out of his control, and he felt lost.

Hawk had Nick working the other cases in the office. They were too mundane for him to think about or to receive his full attention. Nick seemed happy to be working on them. A few involved finishing up paperwork; one came from a woman wanting her husband tailed. He wished he could get involved, but until Ted was caught, Hawk guessed he would stay antsy, waiting to hear from Wade.

———

WADE DIDN'T CARE to be in his office late at night, yet eleven wasn't as late as some nights. The plane was on time when he had met Carson earlier. Now it was time to get to work. He opened the evidence package while Carson, Johnson, and Price looked on.

"Well, Carson," Wade smiled, "your initiation is about to begin. Read over these letters and make some notes. I want a fresh take on them. Johnson! Run a trace on the phone that the text messages came from. Price! Read over the forensic report from the NYPD; see where we stand."

Wade picked up the promise ring and the torn picture of Ted. Grabbing the tape dispenser, he taped it together. "We need to get this out," he said to no one in particular. Wade continued to stare at the picture: a man between twenty-five and thirty years of age, brown hair, brown eyes, short beard, and a thin mustache. The man had a small diamond stud in one earlobe. In the background was a silver motorcycle and a dark blue pick-up truck, both parked near a house with mountains behind it.

Johnson had returned. "I put a rush on the trace. I told them we need the address ASAP. What else we got?"

"This picture. Let's check the mug shots in our database." Wade handed Ted's picture to Johnson. Examining the ring, he said to Price,

"See if we can find the jeweler that sold this; I'm assuming back in August or September." Wade didn't expect any sleep for this night.

Carson was kept busy making pot after pot of coffee, and Wade's office was beginning to look like the whole of the detective Division had shown up.

"We have Ted's address," this from Johnson. "He lives in Silver Creek. We have a surveillance team on their way: Mitchell and Harrison. Price and I are going to join them."

"Anything on the photo yet?"

"Nothing yet. Tillby is working on it. She'll let you know as soon as she has something."

———

MITCHELL AND HARRISON were parked a block from the given address when Johnson, with Price, came on the scene. Johnson drove past Mitchell's car and parked across from Ted's house. Dressed in black, and about to exit the car, Johnson stopped when he heard a motorcycle. He saw it, with its rider, turn into the drive of the house. The man parked the bike, dismounted and headed for the front door, still wearing his helmet. Johnson closed the car door and radioed Wade.

"He's inside, so it should be an easy take. Mitchell and Harrison can cover the rear," said Johnson.

"This guy is a clever serial killer," said Wade. "No telling what is in the house. Get Mitchell and Harrison to the rear: you and Price out front. And wait. I'm on my way with backup."

———

WHEN WADE ARRIVED, his adrenaline was pumping. This was exactly why Linda had divorced him. He thrived on danger. He motioned the two-man backup team toward the rear and waved Johnson and Price to close in on the front.

The house was dark. Wade had several questions that begged answers. *Was Ted aware that there were officers surrounding his house at this very moment? Was he setting a trap for Wade and his men? Would he give up peacefully or put up a fight?* When everyone was finally positioned, Wade drew his automatic and stealthily walked to the door.

Bam, bam, bam!

"Sheriff! Open up!"

The usual remark sounded corny in Wade's ear, as though he was playing a part on a police show. It was still quiet. Once more, Wade banged on the door and made his announcement. This time he heard a stir within. He plastered himself against the stone slabs of the house, aside from the door. Any other time it would be a sight worth looking at: agave plants, cacti, and boulders surrounding the house. The mountain range stood black against the approaching dawn.

The bullet came whizzing through the door. Wade dropped, gun trained on the entrance to the house. Another shot. Then another. A rustling sound from within, and two more shots toward the rear. Then the front door slowly opened. Wade felt his heart beating out of his shirt. He was sure Ted would discover that he lay in wait on the ground. He wanted Ted alive. There were too many unanswered questions.

The man stepped out; Wade noticed he was hit in his left arm. Ted had a rifle, and he kept it lifted. He was ready to let off another shot when Wade stood, his gun beaded on Ted.

"Drop it! Now!"

Ted turned, dropped the rifle, and grabbed a pistol from his jacket pocket. He took off on a run toward his bike and let off a shot that ricocheted off the stone wall. Wade returned a warning shot in the air and ran after him—Johnson close on his heels. Ted had his bike started and was out of the driveway before any of the officers could stop him. Wade and Johnson commandeered the nearest vehicle and began the chase.

At the sound of gunfire and engines roaring to life, the other officers came running and met with the sight of taillights. Jumping into one of the other cars, they joined the pursuit.

Johnson radioed their position as Wade maneuvered the turn from West Old Silver Road onto North Desert Road.

The bike was still in sight, but Wade knew that Ted could hit the dirt anytime and lose them. He asked Johnson to try shooting the bike tire. He didn't want Ted dead, but he also didn't want him free to kill again.

Gun out the window, Johnson let off a shot. It missed. He tried again just as Ted made the turn onto North New River Road. They heard the tire blow and saw the bike flip. Wade slowed to make the turn and saw Ted get up and run toward a stance of trees on the west side of the road. Wade braked, was out, and running after the guy. Johnson followed, radioing their position as he ran. The other officers arrived within minutes; the manhunt was underway.

———

WADE FELT the sting of a bullet tear into his flesh. It had been a long time since he had been on the receiving end of one, and his body didn't like it. He stopped and let his gun fall as pain ran through his right shoulder. He dropped to the ground and began to apply pressure with the palm of his left hand. He wondered if he was getting too old for this kind of stuff. Ted was still going, even after being shot in the arm and flipping off his bike. And here he was, giving into a shoulder wound.

Johnson caught up with him, ready to help.

"No, go. Get him. I'll be alright," Wade urged. Then he noticed blood seeping through his shirt and wondered if he'd been hit anywhere else. It seemed to be too much blood from just one bullet.

Price, Mitchell, Harrison, and the backup team were close on Johnson's heels, but Price stopped to help Wade.

"They'll get him," Price said. "We need to get you to the ER and patched up."

The sound of gunfire kept Wade riveted to the spot.

"No. I'm not leaving till I see them bring Ted out."

———

JOHNSON COULD SEE the automatic aimed right at his forehead. Mitchell was on Ted just as he pulled the trigger. The bullet missed its intended target.

Harrison and two backup officers arrived as the two men struggled for the gun. Johnson motioned the men down. Then the gun fired, and Mitchell reeled, clutching his chest. Pulling free, and with energy that belied a wounded man, Ted was off, running deeper into the woods.

Harrison ran to his partner's side, all thoughts of obeying his senior officer gone from his mind.

"How is he?" Johnson called, as he rose to his feet.

Harrison looked up and uttered one word.

"Dead."

Johnson hesitated only a moment.

"Call it in and stay with him. Bishop, Sanchez: follow me."

As the officers took up the chase once again, Johnson mumbled to himself.

"We'll get him—alive or dead."

CHAPTER FORTY-SIX

THE GUNSHOTS ENDED; a sudden silence pervaded the woods. Wade rose from the ground, his arm now in a sling, thanks to Price.

"Easy does it, sir," Price remarked. "You're still a little wobbly."

Gun in hand, Wade took a few faltering steps forward, when a faint snap sounded. He spun around, but Price was right where he left him. They were both watching the approaching officers and medical examiner.

"When did you get called? And why?" asked Wade.

"I'm surprised as you, sir."

The ME stepped up to Wade with a solemn look on his face.

"Where's the body, Detective?"

"Body? Price, you know anything about a body. Did they kill Ted?"

"No, I don't..."

"It's Mitchell," the ME interrupted.

Wade wasn't sure where the energy came from, but he was off on a run. Two officers down on his watch; he felt the anger burning in his chest. First, Gloria Parker. Now, Frank Mitchell. His heart was pounding as he ran faster and faster. When he came to Mitchell's body, he paused only long enough to ask Harrison which direction Johnson and the other men were headed.

"North, sir. And don't spare the rat's life."

Wade picked up the pace; he could hear Harrison spouting obscenities that weren't fit for a dog to hear.

———

JUST BEFORE SUNRISE, when the moon had not completely disappeared, Johnson heard, crack-creak, crack-creak. The rhythm of running feet sounded close ahead. They were gaining on Ted. Then silence. Johnson motioned the men to stop. In that one moment, the woods cracked with a flourish of rifle fire. The men hit the ground as one.

———

WADE NOTICED A SHANTY OF SORTS, about fifty yards ahead, that couldn't have been more than six-foot square. Sudden movement, at the side of the hut, caught his eye, and he darted behind one of the larger trees. As he peered around, he saw it was a man... with a rifle... with a helmet on his head. Ted.

Where did he get the rifle? Wade wondered.

Then he heard the rifle fire. It was random shooting. Ted was getting rattled.

"No," he silently screamed as he took aim.

———

BY THE TIME he got to the shanty, Johnson, Bishop, and Sanchez were approaching from the opposite direction. Wade grabbed the rifle and pushed the butt into the man's chest. Ted was bleeding. His jeans and jacket were torn; one boot was missing. His helmet, however, had managed to stay on his head. As he struggled to free himself, with more strength than one would have thought, Wade applied greater pressure.

"You're lucky I didn't kill you. Don't give me a reason to now."

"You got him!" Johnson said as he reached the scene.

"Sanchez, cover him. Bishop, take a look in the hut," Wade commanded. "Johnson, time for the unveiling."

Johnson holstered his gun, knelt down, and removed Ted's helmet.

"No," Wade said in disbelief. "It can't be."

CHAPTER FORTY-SEVEN

THE RINGING of his cell phone brought Hawk out of a fitful sleep. The LED read 5AM. He hoped it was only Wade calling at this hour.

"Hawk. Speak," he said groggily.

"Johnson here, Detective Hawkins. Wade asked me to call to let you know that it's over, but not before Ted took out Mitchell. Wade got it pretty bad in the shoulder, and Price took him to the emergency room. I'm guessing he'll be there awhile. Said he wanted to be the one to give you the details and will call later."

"You can let me know," Hawk began. Then realized he was talking to dead air. Johnson had terminated the call.

Wide awake now, Hawk dressed and headed to the kitchen for a pot of tea. While it steeped, he picked up his phone to call Nick and Jamie. Thinking better of it, he decided to let them sleep. He would tell them when they arrived for work. Instead, he took his tea and went down to his office. He decided to look through the Marlet file one more time.

He spread the contents of the file on his desk and began to re-read everything as he drank his tea. At least he could feel as though he were involved, even though it was vicariously at this point.

About an hour into the task he had assigned himself, Hawk heard the back door to the office open. Nick. At the same time, Hawk's computer pinged, indicating a new incoming email. Hawk looked up to see Nick standing in his doorway.

"You're up early. Must mean you've heard something about Ted." Nick seemed as anxious as Hawk to know what was happening.

"Wade's partner, Johnson, called about an hour ago to tell me they got him. Wade took a bullet in his left shoulder. One of his men, Mitchell, was killed." The email address of the incoming email caught Hawk's attention.

"Looks as though we're getting some more info coming in." Hawk gestured his head towards his computer.

"Anything interesting?" Nick asked, taking a seat.

"Very. It's from Johnson, letting me know that Wade wanted the pertinent info in my hands as soon as possible. Wade's doing okay but will be relegated to playing desk jockey. Seems the bullet tore some ligaments, muscle, and nicked the bone causing fragments to lodge in the tissue. Darvon will be on his menu for a few days at least."

"And Ted? Did they get him in a cell peacefully? What's his story?"

"As of now, all I know is, that after they patched him up, they took him to the psych ward of Mountain Side Hospital. He was going bonkers in the car. When they arrived at the hospital, they were ready with a straight jacket. They called in a psychiatrist; what follows is this preliminary report." Hawk turned his computer to face Nick when he finished.

PRELIMINARY REPORT *of Patient T. Ashby*
Dr. Jeremiah Prill, Mountain Side Hospital

The patient appears to have a need to rid the world of females who expose their bodies to make a living, e.g., models, stripteasers, exotic dancers, and prostitutes. The patient's mother earned her living in a brothel in Nevada, where she raised the patient. She also modeled in the nude. The mother committed suicide when the patient was ten years of age. The patient continued living at the brothel under the care of the other women until the age of eighteen.

At first exam, it appears the patient was abused in the brothel, leaving the patient with the desire to destroy all women in any profession that was similar to that of the mother. The patient apparently developed a love-hate relationship with, not only the mother but also the women at the brothel. It also appears that the patient used the Internet to look for these types of women. Using subliminal messages appears to have been the patient's method of promoting suicide for the victims.

My recommendation is to move the patient to the Forensic Hospital facility for the criminally insane for further evaluation. Dr. J. Prill, PhD

"I didn't see that one coming," Nick said, as he turned the computer back to Hawk. "Anything else?"

"Only the forensic report of Ted's house. Not much there except a shrine to Jill Evans: pictures of her, candles. It appears as though he might have really loved her. It says here that they will have a medical doctor give the suspect an examination to see if the cancer story is real, or if it was just a ploy. Guess we'll just have to wait for the time-consuming investigations and to hear from Wade."

"At least they caught him." Nick stood. "Think I'll have my coffee. Call me if you need me. Otherwise, I'm enjoying a weekend relaxing."

"Um, wait a minute. There's something else here. It seems Ted had a small shed in the woods that he used as an arsenal. They have forensic on that also. Report pending."

"Interesting. It seems he was one messed up guy. Wonder if he'll talk? And, if he does, will he make any sense?" Nick asked as he stepped out the door.

After Nick left, Hawk read through the report once more. Some questions weren't answered, and this fact would keep him anxious until the investigations were completed. If only he could be there.

———

THE WEEKEND DIDN'T GO by fast enough for Hawk, but finally, Monday arrived. He came down to his office earlier than usual. He had hoped to hear from Wade before now. Hawk checked his email: nothing. No messages on voice mail, either; at least, none that he was interested in. Nick was coming in the back door as Jamie was entering the front.

"I see you two have perfect timing." Hawk tried making a joke.

"I gather you haven't heard from Wade yet," Nick said.

"So, what are we waiting for?" asked Jamie.

"They caught Ted." Nick helped Jamie with her coat.

"Wow! Boss, tell me all about it. Have ya called Anna yet?"

"No and no," Hawk answered. "All anyone needs to know, for the moment, is that he's been caught. Nick, you call Anna and let her know. I'll be in my office."

Hawk entered his office, closing the door behind him. His thoughts were all over the place, from Johnson's call early Saturday morning announcing the capture of Ted, to yesterday's church service. He was thankful he was able to concentrate on the Pastor's sermon and actually take some much-needed time with the Lord in prayer. It felt good to be rid of the hate and revenge that had taken up residence in his heart after Ellie was killed. He continued to thank God for being patient with him and still loving him. And he thought he'd better pray for some much-needed patience right now.

———

NICK CAME out of his office as Jamie was closing up for the day. A light snow had begun to fall, and he knew she didn't like to drive in snow, light or heavy, even for a short distance.

"Is Hawk still in his office?"

"Yeah, he's been shut up in there all day. Would you tell him I'm leaving?"

"Sure, Jamie. Drive safe." Nick smiled and went to Hawk's door. A light tap, he entered, and found Hawk in his usual spot, at the window, when he wanted to do some deep thinking.

"Since you haven't heard from Wade yet, I'll tell you of my conversation with Anna Marlet."

Hawk turned, and Nick waited for him to sit behind the desk. Nick took a seat on the sofa. "Before I catch you up about Marlet, let me bring you up to date on the cases I've been on. I finished with the Walker case and gave all the evidence to her attorney. They have a court date for February ninth. We haven't received a summons, so I may not have to be in court, but I'm holding that date open. Mindy Bennett, the night dispatcher from the GHPD, called about a guy named Curt Jackson needing a PI. Seems Bennett is very aware of your reputation, and she suggested our office. Jackson had been arrested for a heist, which he claims was a frame. So, I visited him at the station, and I think it's a case worth going after. Jackson has his own business and is not a slouch with his money. I took it on and would like to follow it myself. And get out of the office, too."

"Sounds good, Nick. Now, what about Anna? How did she take the whole thing?"

"She was glad he was caught and hopes he gets the chair. I had to explain to her that he may not. That piece of news didn't make her happy. I went on to let her know that if it hadn't been for her, Ted would still be out there. That seemed to settle her down. I also let her know we would keep her informed as soon as we knew anything."

"Good; hopefully that will keep her from breathing down our necks every few days, until she gets our bill," Hawk gave Nick a quirky grin. "Now if I could just get myself off the anxious train."

"Why not call Wade?" suggested Nick.

"I've been tempted, but I also know Wade. He'll call as soon as he can."

"Well, I'm gonna call it a day. Jamie has left. I guess you've noticed it's begun to snow."

"You go ahead. I'll give you a buzz if Wade calls before tomorrow morning. And yes, I did notice the snow. The garden ought to look crisp and clean soon."

Before Nick got to the door, the office phone rang. Hawk grabbed it quickly.

"Hawk here."

"The doctor kept me over the weekend." It was Wade. "Hawk, I hope you're sitting down. I didn't want the info I'm about to share in an email. I wanted to tell you myself."

"Well, get to it," Hawk interrupted.

"You *are not* going to believe this. Ted... is a female!"

"What?" Hawk almost screamed.

"What's happened?" Nick asked.

"Ted is a female!"

"What? No way!"

Hawk put the phone on speaker so Nick could get in on the conversation.

"Nick's here with me, so go ahead."

"It all makes sense now. The homeless guys used to make the phone calls: keeping the helmet on: only texting or emailing. But male or female, this person is a sick, serial killer. We finally got a judge to sign some papers today for commitment *and* for tests."

"So, is Ted, or whatever her name is, in the Forensic Hospital that Dr. Prill suggested?"

"Her name is Theodora Ashby. As a child growing up in a brothel, she was called Teddy."

"So, what about the online photo?" asked Nick.

"It seems that when she decided to *rid* the world of women like her mother and the other women in the brothel, she went online and used the name, Ted. The profile picture was of a guy she'd met and dated in the past. We ran a check on him, thinking he might be in on this with her, but found that he had died of cancer a couple of years back. And yes, she will be hospitalized in a couple of hours. That's why we wanted to get a judge to sign papers quickly."

"What's the chances of this going to trial?" Nick asked.

"We're not sure. But if it does, it will probably end with a decision of *guilty, by monomania.*"

"That's a new one on me, Wade," Hawk said. "What exactly does it mean?"

"Someone with monomania has an excessive, insane fixation on just one thing: an idea, urge, object, or a person, but to the point of mental and physical destruction. It's kind of a partial insanity. Otherwise, they are as sane as you, and I are. The psych doctor thinks Teddy shows signs of being a monomaniac. Because she had a shrine to Jill Evans, he thinks she also shows signs of erotomania; that is, being in love with the person you want dead. There may have been a lot more going on in that brothel than we could even guess. It's crazy, but... well, let's just say, it's crazy."

Hawk and Nick sat in stunned silence as they listened to Wade's explanation. Finally, Hawk spoke. "Crazy isn't the word for it, Wade."

He thought for a moment, then asked, "What about the cancer: real or a ploy?"

"Evidently the cancer was just a ploy, for Jill Evans."

"So, will Ashby be kept in the hospital for the criminally insane?" Nick interjected.

"Looks that way. From what I understand, they will be running tests to see if she is sane enough to stand trial. Don't know what after that. Our part is over... unless we receive a subpoena."

"I suppose then, for Hawk's Detective Agency, the case is also closed."

"It looks that way, my friend."

———

HAWK STOOD at the window and stroked his chin. As he watched the snow blanket the garden fountain, the thought of putting past cases to bed and the closure he would feel, crossed his mind. But this time it wasn't the same. Hawk expressed his feelings of disappointment to Nick.

"Why don't you make a trip out there? Maybe it would help."

Hawk turned from the window and sat back at his desk, thinking over Nick's suggestion.

"That's an idea, Nick. Maybe I will. Perhaps I'll find the closure I'm looking for," Hawk replied. "Anything else would be anti-climactic."

"Before you leave, there is one thing you need to put your mind to," Nick said. "Chief Fields called. He's meeting with the mayor this week about hiring us to handle homicide for the police department."

"That's not the way a police department works, Nick. They won't hire outside. But if it ever happened..." Hawk let the sentence hang in the air. "I think we've spent enough time in the office for one day. I'm ready to head upstairs, and you might want to get up to your place before you need snowshoes," he laughed.

CHAPTER FORTY-EIGHT

"HANG THE BUDGET!"

Chief Elliot Fields was frustrated, pacing the floor in front of the mayor's desk. This was not the first time in the past six months that he had found himself in the same place for the same reason. But this time he hoped the proverbial squeaky wheel would get oiled.

"Of course, we need a detective. We've always needed a detective. We had a detective. But what did our town officials decide at their last meeting?" Elliot was sure his face was beet red by now.

"Better have a seat and settle yourself, Elliot," Mayor Jim Conklin remarked, as he buzzed for his secretary to bring them each a cup of coffee.

The Chief realized he needed to heed the mayor's advice or his blood pressure would be out of range before the day was over. He already felt the sweat through his uniform. Elliot knew that wetness didn't look good on tan. That was another thing he was never happy about. Instead of a nice navy-blue uniform like his officers wore, someone decided that the GHPD chief would wear tan. Supposedly, people would automatically know that he was the Chief of Police because of the uniform's color.

"Okay, okay."

Trying to compose his thoughts, Elliot took the straight back chair next to the mayor's scarred oak desk. He supposed Mayor Conklin kept the chair there so appointments would not run overtime. The old Grove home was on the National Register of Historic Places, and in 1945 it was converted into offices for Groveland Hills City Hall. The mayor's office was on the first floor and quite spacious. Bookcases lined two of the walls, all of them filled with books of the city's history, various protocols, and the Grove Family Bible. A fireplace, surrounded by walnut paneling, almost covered a third wall. The fourth was all windows, floor to ceiling, overlooking the city park. Elliot wondered if Mayor Conklin would miss any of it when he retired at the end of May.

The idea of firing a competent detective hadn't sat well with Elliot when it happened, and it didn't sit well now. He was still on a tirade about firing Detective Maxwell Sellars.

The mayor's secretary entered, almost on tip-toe, placed the two coffee mugs on the desk and left as quickly and quietly as she had entered.

"We've had this conversation numerous times, Elliot. What is it going to take to convince you?" The mayor seemed upset that his day was being interrupted. Possibly he had a golf game, and Elliot was making him late for his tee time.

"What's it gonna take to convince you?" Elliot fired back.

"Okay, let's get this over with. Tell me your new idea that's not going to break the budget."

"Hawk Detective Agency."

"There is no way we..."

"Just hear me out," Elliot interrupted.

———

"TAKE A LOAD OFF, Hawk. Relax. I'm going to grab a cup of coffee for

myself and brew your favorite tea. English Blend, right?" asked Wade
as he headed to his kitchen.

"Yes," Hawk answered in a sleepy voice. He sat in the recliner and
instantly felt relaxed. He thought about the fact that only six hours
ago he had boarded a plane at JFK and now he was sitting in Wade's
living room. He remembered it had taken him less than a week to put
Nick in charge, have Jamie secure his Thursday evening flight to
Phoenix, pack, and be on his way. He liked the idea of gaining two
hours. When he arrived at nine-thirty, Wade was waiting at the gate.
Being in law enforcement sometimes had its perks.

Wade returned with tea and coffee. "You look comfortable. Good.
Tired from your flight?"

"Not the flight as much as being weary over this case taking so
long. I'd like to hear more about it," Hawk yawned as he drank his tea.
"But I think you better show me where I sleep. Tomorrow will be
soon enough for the rest of the story."

———

NICK FOUND himself once more talking with the GHPD chief of
police but in his own office this time. Jamie had made the
appointment for the afternoon. Things had slowed, and Hawk had left
the night before to see Wade.

"Glad to see you again, Chief," Nick said as he extended his hand.
"Have a seat. Would you care for some coffee or tea?"

"No, thanks. I was hoping Hawk would be here."

"Sorry. But Hawk is out of town for the week."

Nick didn't like being seen as second choice. After all, he had a
brain and could make decisions as well as anyone. But here he sat,
playing second best. Nick secretly wondered if that would also be the
case when Wade finally moved back to take the job Hawk had offered;
perhaps he'd be regulated to third choice then.

"So, what can the agency do for you today, Chief?"

"First, call me Elliot. Secondly, I'm here as spokesperson for the

City Council. The city of Groveland Hills has finally come to the realization that the department needs help. It was at the last City Council meeting," Elliot continued, "that it was decided. Instead of putting another detective on the payroll, or call the County or State on a homicide case, they agreed I could hire from the private sector. I suggested we officially hire Hawk, uh... Hawk's agency that is."

The Chief's careless slip was not lost on Nick—another blow to his ego. The gunshot wound had made him feel as though he was only fit for desk work. But when Hawk hired him, he felt sure he was gaining the respect he'd had back on the force. Now he wondered if the only reason he had this position *was* pity.

"A little unorthodox, isn't it?"

"It may seem that way. But we're not ruled by County or State laws, and since there has only been one murder in the last five years, the city feels it can't justify hiring another full-time detective. I have a contract here with all the figures spelled out. Of course, it would be on a case to case basis and, only homicides."

Nick took the papers the Chief handed him and scanned the contract. Everything seemed well in order; he was sure Hawk would approve.

"It looks good, Chief. I mean... Elliot."

———

A FEW NIGHTS LATER, Nick was, once again, dragged from blissful sleep by the sound of sirens. Would tonight be the night Hawk's Detective Agency got the call?

ABOUT THE AUTHOR

A native Floridian, AnneGale has been a writer for most of her life, beginning with poetry as a little girl of six. She enjoyed all types of writing, but one genre stood out: Mystery and suspense, *and* the detective who would solve the cases.

Now a widow, AnneGale still lives in the south with family, where she enjoys the sunshine and retired life—not to mention the mystery.

Made in the
USA
Columbia, SC